THE
SCOPE
OF
PERMISSIBILITY

THE

SCOPE

OF

PERMISSIBILITY

ZEYNAB GAMIELDIEN

ultimo
press

Published in 2023 by Ultimo Press,
an imprint of Hardie Grant Publishing

Ultimo Press	Ultimo Press (London)
Gadigal Country	5th & 6th Floors
7, 45 Jones Street	52–54 Southwark Street
Ultimo, NSW 2007	London SE1 1UN
ultimopress.com.au	

   ultimopress

 A catalogue record for this book is available from the National Library of Australia

The Scope of Permissibility
ISBN 978 1 76115 217 7 (paperback)

Cover design Mika Tabata
Cover images Silhouettes by Melianus Usmany Getty Images; pattern by Aksana Shum / Shutterstock
Text design Simon Paterson, Bookhouse
Typesetting Bookhouse, Sydney | 13/18.5 pt Garamond Premiere Pro
Copyeditor Deonie Fiford
Proofreader Nilufer Kurtuldu
Additional editorial support Hamza Jahanzeb

10 9 8 7 6 5 4 3 2 1

Printed in Australia by Griffin Press, an Accredited ISO AS/NZS 14001 Environmental Management System printer.

 The paper this book is printed on is certified against the Forest Stewardship Council® Standards. Griffin Press holds chain of custody certification SCS-COC-001185. FSC® promotes environmentally responsible, socially beneficial and economically viable management of the world's forests.

Ultimo Press acknowledges the Traditional Owners of the Country on which we work, the Gadigal People of the Eora Nation and the Wurundjeri People of the Kulin Nation, and recognises their continuing connection to the land, waters and culture. We pay our respects to their Elders past and present.

1

Sara

She would not look at Naeem, she simply would not. Sara had made the same resolution before, but today it would stick. She sat in a chair alongside the other girls and placed her hands in her lap. Around the room, she heard the low rumble of voices, smelled the sharp chemical whiff of deodorant that signalled the arrival of the boys. She kept her head lowered. Naeem would have arrived by now, would be seated on the other side of the table where the boys maintained an appropriate distance from the girls. But she had to focus. It was the first Muslim Students' Association meeting of the university semester and there was so much to discuss.

A sheet of paper was passed around the table. When it was placed in front of her, Sara scanned the names on the list before adding her own next to Ahlam Dib. Naeem's name was already on the adjoining side of the page below

1

Wahid Faridi and Ziad Allouche. Naeem Kazi. For Sara, names held weight. She knew that Ahlam, for instance, would be forever marked by the inability of Australian English to cater for the deep-throated 'h' sound, which would have skimmed over the tongue in Arabic. Ahlam would have learned from her early years to spot the furrowed brow of the teacher as they arrived at her name on the classroom roll, trained her ears to recognise the approximation of her name they conjured into being. Naeem would not have experienced this difficulty, his name being phonetic and orderly, while her own name could not be of interest to anyone except to wonder how it was that Sara Andrews was born to two Muslim parents.

Sara passed the paper on to Abida, the last person to mark their name. Three boys, three girls, a tiny subset of the much larger MSA cohort on campus. There were the hundreds who came to pray at the musallah but who were uninvolved in the MSA, the dozens who drifted in and out of their events, and then there were the dedicated few who made events happen. More recently Sara had found herself in the latter category. She noted the liberal application of pink blush across Ahlam's high cheekbones, the nascent wisps of hair on Abida's chin jutting out from under her hijab. There was no one else to look at now, not unless she chanced a glance across the empty space demarcating male from female. Instead, she examined the thin carpeted floorings of the musallah, a former science classroom the university had allocated to its Muslim students for prayer. It was shabby, hidden down an obscure corridor at the edge of campus, but it was theirs. Sara leaned over to Abida, intending to whisper something about going to the cafeteria for a meal afterwards, but just as she did Ziad rapped his knuckles against the table and began to speak.

'Assalamu alaykum, all, and thanks for coming to the first meeting of the Muslim Students' Association for this year. We don't have a big turnout today and our president, Mustafa, sends his apologies, so it should be a quick one. Does anyone want to write on the board as we go through the agenda?'

Abida would volunteer, she was noisy and impassioned, but it was Naeem who reached for the marker and walked towards the whiteboard at the front of the room, standing alongside it with his arms folded. His beard did not sprout beyond his chin, indicating that he was still in that transitional phase approaching manhood, but his height and pressed dark denim jeans suggested to Sara that he was some way along. She twisted about in her seat, wondering if she could reposition her chair so that her view of him was unobstructed. Already, she was faltering. She was so seldom afforded a pretext to observe him.

'The first item on the agenda is Islamic Awareness Week. Although it's still a while away, there's so much to do that we really need to start planning the theme and events now. This is our biggest opportunity to really get the message of Islam out to all the students here on campus, so if anyone has an idea for a theme, let's hear it,' Ziad said.

'I was thinking it would be nice to do something about Islam and its contribution to arts and literature. Everyone loves Rumi poetry and apparently Leonardo DiCaprio is going to be playing him in a movie soon, so there's bound to be a lot of interest,' Ahlam said.

Someone clicked their tongue on the boys' side of the table. The sound was too immediate for it to have emanated from Naeem, and she did not think Ziad would have been so unkind. This eliminated everyone except Wahid, who now leaned forward in his chair.

'No offence, sis, but you're not going to get anyone coming if you make Islamic Awareness Week all about things like that,' he said. 'People come to our events for hard-hitting topical discussions on Islam and contemporary issues, not fluff.'

'I would hardly call Rumi fluff.' Ahlam addressed Wahid's vicinity without seeking to meet his eye. Sara had learned that this imprecision of manner was expected in the MSA when a boy spoke to a girl and vice versa. Elsewhere on campus, flirtation was obsolete, a relic from a pre-Tinder age, but she thought it touching that the spectre of it was still alive in here, colouring even the most innocuous of gestures.

Wahid shrugged and ran his hand through his backcombed hair. Afghan and burly, he was the most handsome boy Sara had encountered in the MSA, his shirt fitted to the precise contours of his upper arms. But she turned now to Naeem, who had written the words ISLAM AND CULTURE on the board in capitals. His fingers were long and slim with trimmed nails. As her gaze travelled up the planes of his neck and towards his eyes, Sara realised that he too was looking at her, and they both looked down at the floor.

'If people want a dose of controversy and Islam they can just pick up their phone any day of the week, not come to Islamic Awareness Week events,' Abida said, gesturing at Wahid with her index finger as she spoke. 'We need to show people the flaws in their understanding and make them think differently.'

Abida had been a prefect at the competitive selective school she and Sara had attended and was accustomed to leading, to shepherding people into agreement with her views. Unlike his deputy, Ziad, Mustafa possessed enough gravitas to manage the differing perspectives within the group. But Sara liked Ziad, liked his ungainliness. Many of the MSA boys possessed the mannerisms of much older men, assuming a form of stiff ceremoniousness she presumed they equated with piety. They wore hoodies and pinstriped shirts and chunky, expensive sneakers. The girls were far more varied, in anything from formless dresses like Abida's oversized mauve abayas to boyfriend jeans and spiky bejewelled necklaces placed atop their hijabs coiled like snakes.

'What would you suggest then, sis?' Ziad flicked his phone about in his palm, rotating it until it fell to the table.

'I was thinking we could explore a theme on the wreckage of the post-colonial Muslim world, looking at a range of countries people think they're experts on just because they've read a headline about how backwards and war-torn they are. And, of course, we can't forget the ongoing colonial invasion and genocide of the First Nations People of this very country,' Abida said, her hands moving about before her, the scalloped fringe of her hijab dusting Sara's shoulder.

Of late, Abida made frequent references to colonialism and feminism and neoliberalism and other isms Sara did not always recognise. She wrote lengthy online diatribes about it and reproached MSA boys who shared memes and videos she deemed misogynistic. She decried Jordan Peterson as a 'proto-fascist' and wore Black Lives Matter t-shirts over her abayas. Sara supposed she ought to care about these issues too, but she thought it was taxing to perceive the world as Abida did, as a series of vexations and slights to be redressed. She was resigned to the world's ills, to the surname and green eyes she had inherited from slave-masters and settlers of centuries ago.

'I think that's a good idea, actually,' Wahid said. 'It builds on our theme from last year, Extremely Moderate, on the pressure to be a so-called "moderate Muslim" and how it's always outsiders who get to define what that means.'

Naeem continued to write on the board as the others spoke. Sara noted, not for the first time, the slick of his black hair, the erect posture which denoted money and rigorous parenting and ironed shirts appearing with regularity on his bedside table.

'We'll leave it at that for now,' Ziad said, 'and we can have further discussions on the group chat, inshaAllah. Now on to the next agenda item, our upcoming charity bake sale to raise money for the crisis in Yemen.'

'I'm happy to take charge of this one, Ziad,' Ahlam said, quickly.

'Thanks, sis. Can I please get everyone to send through what they're making to sister Ahlam by the end of the week so we can coordinate the display? We really want to raise a thousand dollars at least, so let's put on our best baking hats. Or should I say baking hijabs, for the ladies?'

There was a collective groan, a splutter of muted laughter. Sara smiled, to show Ziad that she appreciated his attempts at injecting some levity into the situation. She noticed though that Naeem did not laugh or even smile, that his eyes remained watchful. He seemed a very solemn person. If he could not laugh at a sophomoric joke, she was glad that she had been able to suppress a giggle at the mention of Extremely Moderate, the earnestness with which MSA members peddled their beliefs to the student masses.

'Okay, let's move on to our mentoring scheme for the new MSA members starting at university this semester. We've already started matching the first years with some of our second and third year members –'

'Brothers are only being matched up with brothers, right? And sisters with sisters?' Wahid said.

'That goes without saying, bro.' Ziad glanced across the table to the girls, seeking an affirmation that did not come.

'Good,' Wahid said. 'We want to show the new students that, while the rest of the university gets on with all their toga parties and hook-ups, we in the MSA can maintain some standards.'

'But some MSA people hang out with the opposite sex too, surely?' Sara spoke without forethought. The steady thrum of her internal radio had somehow transmuted into audible speech; Naeem's presence had interfered with its transmission. When Naeem was in her vicinity, she found herself behaving in a manner she did not always recognise. Her voice seemed too brash for the setting now, and she was conscious of Abida pinching the soft fat of her upper thigh under the table, of the tightening of Naeem's fingers around the whiteboard marker.

'Some do, definitely,' Wahid said. 'And the ones who don't could be chatting on their phones, where no one can see what they're up to – I could be doing it right now – but we can at least try to ensure that we don't give them opportunities to do it.' He enunciated all the consonants in the word *opportunities*, his elbows raised from the table as he gesticulated. From the vagueness of his address, it was obvious that he had no idea who she was. Sara did not speak at meetings, did not offer observations on the frequent and lively group chat discussions. They discussed everything from climate change to the Taliban, Harry and Meghan to the permissibility of Botox injections. She was a silent observer throughout, embedded in their midst, devouring their content and discussions, but set apart by her own unwillingness to be noticed and pinned down on her stances.

'I guess so,' Sara said eventually. She had no desire to engage in arguments, theological or otherwise. In any case she held no opinion on the issue – 'freemixing', as she'd seen it referred to on group chats. She had spoken more out of curiosity than conviction. Her Capetonian parents had not prepared her for the correct way to interact with boys. They were careless about such things, kissing men and women alike on the cheek in greeting. In her time in the MSA Sara had attempted to learn it all through Abida and through covert observations of her own. She had seen some of the cool MSA boys and girls in the cafeteria together or walking to the train station in threes or fours. She, too, was friendly with boys from her engineering course, who she exchanged notes and trivialities with as they chomped on kebab boxes. But the MSA position seemed to be one of controlled exposure, requiring the boys and girls to interact in group chats, meetings and events while simultaneously demanding formality and distance. It was cruel, Sara thought, all this obsequious dangling of the forbidden carrot.

'Sara might have a point though. Most Muslims at our university aren't part of the MSA and don't attend any of our events, and you have to wonder why,' Naeem said.

Naeem's voice projected from where he was standing, a little bit posh and from north of the Harbour Bridge. He knew her name! Sara was both ecstatic and afraid. She wondered now if the others had discerned the glances they had exchanged, if Wahid categorised them as those who behaved with reserve in the day while sexting by night. Abida said that some of the Muslim boys on campus were disgusting hypocrites, that they planned to marry virginal little princesses Mummy picked out but were having sex with anyone they could get their hands on in the meantime. They went to nightclubs and parties; they swiped right on apps or very likely had sex with girls they sat across the MSA table from. Even so, Sara felt her mouth twitch with the beginnings of a smile.

'That's their prerogative, bro,' Wahid said, shrugging once again. 'If they think it's too tough, then there's plenty of other places where that kind of thing is acceptable. The entire campus in fact.'

A silence now pervaded the room, save for the smacking of Ahlam's chewing gum, filling the air with a strawberry tang that mingled with the musallah's ever-present odour of damp and feet. All mosques and musallahs Sara attended smelled of this same mix of sweet and rancid. The university had installed custom foot-washing stalls in its bathrooms after numerous complaints about the Muslim kids perching their feet in sinks before prayers, but she thought this had the unfortunate effect of scattering the water around the bathroom, the floors slushy with fetid water and paper towels.

'Okay, let's get all of these ideas typed up and sent around and we'll continue the discussion on the group chat,' Ziad said. 'Thanks for a productive first meeting everyone. Let's make this our biggest year yet, inshaAllah. We'll end the meeting with a recitation of the Quran from brother Naeem.'

Without preamble, Naeem commenced his recitation. Sara closed her eyes. Naeem's voice was now a rich, mellifluous warble emanating from the back of his throat. It did not seem to align with what Sara had just seen of him, nor did it align with the broader picture she had assembled to date: he was twenty years old, studying a medical degree and had been privately educated at an Islamic school in Sydney's inner western suburbs. He donned long-sleeved shirts and pants in all seasons and when he had a pimple, it would hover somewhere in the region of his right eyebrow and then disappear without leaving any sign of its presence.

When she opened her eyes, Sara saw that Naeem's were now closed as he continued to recite. Naeem had memorised all thirty chapters of the Quran; this was another fact she had acquired some time ago, when she had first noticed his presence at meetings and events. It lent him distinction among the other boys, and caused her to question whether she could hold any interest for him or whether she was nursing an inane crush, entirely one-sided in its dimensions.

When Naeem concluded no one clapped; she had learned that this was deemed unseemly. They murmured among themselves and began placing chairs back against the wall, preparing for the roller door separating the side of the musallah apportioned to the boys and the side apportioned to the girls to be fastened once again. Ahlam departed first, followed by Ziad and Wahid.

'You never say a word in MSA meetings, and then suddenly you want to debate gender mixing?' Abida said. 'Even I wouldn't go there, girl. Let's go eat and we can debrief.' She walked ahead of Sara without waiting for a reply, joining Wahid and Ziad where they stood in the corridor.

Sara reached for her backpack and followed. At the doorway, she paused. Naeem had lingered in the room and was wiping the board with his sleeve to erase its contents. Sara relied on Abida's pronouncements on most topics, including on the opposite sex, but Naeem did not look disgusting or like he had sex with anyone. His back was too rigid, his movements smooth and assured. He did not seem to be aware that he was being watched. She cleared her throat, jiggled her foot.

'No need to get your sleeve all messed up. The eraser is over there,' Sara said, pointing to the windowsill.

Naeem turned around in a single deft motion, his head dipped. From this angle, Sara could see only his eyelashes, far longer and thicker than her own.

'Thanks,' he said. He bent down and grasped the eraser in his outstretched hand. As he straightened, he looked at her face. Sara felt that she had not been mistaken in her initial appraisal, that Naeem was not the kind of boy who looked very much at girls, let alone had sex with them. He held her gaze for a moment. He stood as straight as a ruler. What would it require for such a boy to slacken, to whimper with pleasure or pain?

'No worries,' Sara said, adopting a briskness she did not feel before turning away. Her face burned, her fingers cold and clammy. She could not conjure any additional words to prolong their conversation. It was too precarious a situation, with several MSA members standing just outside in the corridor. But there were other ways. Sara had contemplated attempting it on previous occasions, but there had been an implicit challenge in Wahid's speech she now could not resist. As she joined Abida in the corridor and laced up her boots, Sara thought that he was right: it *would* be easy enough to chat on their phones, where no one else could see.

2

Abida

Marriage was a dull and inherently patriarchal insti-
tution, but Abida viewed it in the same way as she
viewed vaccinations or seatbelts: unpleasant, necessary
protections against greater evils. Sara had laughed at this
pronouncement and labelled her cynical, but it was true.
It was for this reason that she had resolved some time ago
to marry someone her parents had sanctioned. It would
have to be someone Muslim and Bangladeshi and educated
to university level. She anticipated it would be quick and
expeditious, avoiding much of the messiness that choosing
a partner based on finite feelings entailed. She prided
herself on her lack of sentimentality.

'Sometimes I think I'm never going to get married, you
know what I mean? It's just so hard to find a good guy.'
Ahlam spoke as she arranged leaflets around the table,
placing a stack on Islam and women's rights under its front

leg to stabilise where it wobbled. The wind blew their hijabs into their faces and blew the leaflets onto the lawn outside the library until they weighed them down with various objects: the wrapped chewy lollies they distributed to fellow students, Ahlam's car keys, a hefty pebble given to them by a sympathetic dreadlocked white boy who was passing by. They had endeavoured to give the stall a professional look, having unfurled the MSA banner stand and placed it adjacent to them, but it had toppled over twice already and knocked Abida's collarbone as it did. Abida stood in front of the table, took a photo and sent it to Sara with the caption, *Can't believe you chose mechanics of solids over this*, before turning back to Ahlam to reply.

'I honestly don't think about marriage that much. It'll happen when it happens, right? It's all naseeb, fate, all of that jazz.'

'It's different for you, though.' Ahlam smoothed the left flank of her hijab, which was propped up by a concave pearl brooch, smiling over at a lanky girl in overalls on a bicycle as she pedalled at speed through the crowd.

Abida did not ask Ahlam to elaborate. They both understood that there were those for whom marriage and parenthood were aspirations, and then there were those who would get married and have children because that was just what you did when you reached a certain age. Abida would probably get married and have a child or two, but she would not be defined by the enterprise. She had observed the alternative and thought it distasteful; having six children had subsumed the entirety of her parents' lives, much like a tumour. Whether it was malignant or benign, her parents seemed reconciled to it, content with whatever bounties Allah bestowed or withheld from them. They were weary and poor, but not angry. She had absorbed the rage they had long jettisoned.

A boy approached the table, oversized headphones over ears, neon blue singlet and shorts on despite the fierceness of the wind. Wahid had been rostered on for this shift at the da'wah stall, but he had not yet arrived. The MSA attempted to ensure that there was an even mix of boys and girls manning their fortnightly information stall. Instinctively, Abida knew why this was: the girls were there to field all the questions on hijabs and burqas and oppression, the boys to demonstrate that they were unthreatening and not a source of the girls' oppression. They were there to prove a point, or disprove one, chafing against impressions that had been long solidified. She leaned on the table as the boy in the singlet picked up a leaflet entitled 'Islam: spread by the sword?', turned it over and examined it.

'Do you want to ask us anything? We have heaps of leaflets on all sorts of topics,' Ahlam said, grinning with all of her teeth in what she deemed to be a welcoming manner. Abida hated her then, hated how she tried so hard to be liked. But the boy gave no indication of hearing them through his headphones, putting down the leaflet and walking off.

Ahlam turned back to her.

'Anyway, Abida, I've been meaning to ask your opinion on something relating to marriage. It's –'

'It's Ziad, isn't it?'

'Ummm . . . well, yes. I was thinking about it after the meeting last week and wanted to see what your thoughts were. Do you think we have potential as a couple?' Ahlam shuffled a pile of leaflets on Islam's stance on human rights and looked across to the lawn, where they watched a boy in a tricolour pullover remove a strand of grass from his female companion's hair, their backpacks and notes scattered in front of them.

'Sure, I don't see why not,' Abida said immediately.

'The thing is, I've seen him looking at me but he's so shy, he'd never say anything to me about it. He's just not that kind of guy. I think the only way something would happen is if someone else sets it up, but of course I wouldn't want him to know that I've noticed, he'd be so embarrassed. Whoever suggested it to him would have to make it seem like it was their idea.'

Abida was unconvinced by this annotated account of events, and she did not suppose Ahlam expected otherwise. The real conversation lay in what was being omitted and talked around, the harsh truths that decorum would not permit them to acknowledge. At the age of twenty-two and nearing the end of her primary teaching degree, Ahlam was astute enough to appreciate the paucity of suitable candidates and had assessed Ziad as an achievable target. Abida thought it plausible that Ahlam was in love with him, but love in their world did not so much erode common sense as shadow it. There were several points to recommend Ziad: their shared Lebanese heritage, his computer science degree and convivial disposition. That he was slow on the uptake was of little consequence. As it was, Abida approved of Ahlam's pragmatism. A girl could do far worse than a well-intentioned fool.

'I'm happy to talk to him for you. I could mention it to him sometime and see what he thinks.'

'Are you sure you'd be cool with that?'

Abida nodded and smiled. She was pleased at being entrusted with such confidences. It felt adult, weighty.

'Just leave it with me. But make sure to pray istikhara and see how you feel before jumping into anything. In the end, it's all with Allah, right?'

'Of course.' Ahlam nodded with fervour. She believed in the power of istikhara to steer a course of action, as they all had been instructed to. But Abida was sometimes unsure if she referenced Him with real feeling or because the situation seemed to necessitate it. She said inshaAllah when making any statement pertaining to a future event, mashaAllah whenever cooing at someone's baby or sharing a photo of a sunset online and alhamdulillah for any crisis averted, no matter how minute. This was what she believed in, but it was also what a girl in an abaya did. She had chosen to dress this way, and with this choice came expectations of behaviour. She could swear and laugh and rage, she could be inappropriate and wild, but to the world she would still be defined by this cloak, this fabric.

Wahid's arrival prevented any further tête-à-têtes. He wore a maroon t-shirt and black jeans, tiny droplets of water dripping from the gelled bouffant of his hair onto his forehead and down his neck.

'You're late, bro. And you're dripping water onto the table.' Abida spoke in what she hoped was a suitably austere manner. She refused to be counted among the many MSA girls who lusted after Wahid, their eyes downcast, their thoughts occupied with how best to induce interest without appearing immodest.

'Sorry, I had to go pray after class. I just made wudu and rushed off here.'

'You had hours to do that, bro. If we can manage to be on time, so can you.'

Wahid smiled and placed his hands in his front pockets, chunky thumbs protruding. Abida could not penetrate his reserve, the implacable distance he maintained from girls. She knew that many of the MSA boys were afraid of girls and women. It showed in their inability to conduct a conversation with any modicum of civility. A small handful, like their president, Mustafa, were able to convey both respect and commonplace cordiality. But Abida did not believe Wahid was fearful. She did not trust good-looking people who feigned disinterest in the opposite sex. How could they be, when members of the opposite sex were so obvious in their interest in them?

'Sisters, I may have some news. I have it on good authority that Mustafa is looking to step down as president in the not too distant future,' Wahid said.

'Why would he want to do that? He's such a great president, mashaAllah,' Ahlam said.

'He's been offered a full-time marketing job, so he's going to be dropping to part-time study soon, and the president needs to be around full-time,' Wahid replied.

'Is that an actual rule, or one you just made up?' Abida felt her acerbity in Ahlam's exaggerated performance of shuffling the leaflets on the table, Wahid's foot tapping against the cobble-stone ground. She did not know how other people negotiated the boundaries between warmth and reserve, between being assertive but not peculiar or offensive. She seemed to either bore people or piss them off; there was little in between.

'Being the MSA president is a big commitment, sis. We're the representatives of Islam on this campus, especially with Islamic Awareness Week coming up. Nothing less than one hundred per cent will do,' Wahid said.

'Well, let's wait to hear it from Mustafa, I guess,' Ahlam said. 'Ziad will probably step up for it if Mustafa goes.' She glanced at Abida, and Abida wondered at the competing impulses of people in love, noisily proclaiming the need for discretion when they exposed themselves at every turn.

'Have we finalised the schedule for Islamic Awareness week yet?' Abida steered the conversation away from the topic of the presidency as though it was of little significance. She did not wish Wahid to detect her interest just yet.

'Yeah, I think we have a first draft at least. Let me open it up and we can run through it now.' Wahid reached for his phone.

'So we have the talk on colonialism and the Muslim world on Monday, the pizza night and film screening of the First Nations Muslims documentary on Tuesday, the Islam and conquest debate on Wednesday.' Wahid was scrolling through his phone. 'Then there's a break from the theme with try-on-a-hijab Thursday –'

'I really don't think we should go ahead with that,' Abida cut in. 'I told Mustafa that when it first came up on the group chat. It's totally demeaning.'

'It's popular, and attracts crowds, and it's good da'wah. We can't always be crusading against everything all at once. Sometimes it has to be enough for us just to be here, you know?'

Abida shook her head, resolute. She saw the merit in Wahid's argument; people possessed a finite capacity to agitate. Back in Bangladesh, her father had fought in the Liberation War of 1971 against the marauding Pakistani forces. He had fought with his hands and on his belly in the lowlands where the mud melded clothing to skin, only to abandon the country he had bled for in search of the abstract notion of a better life. Now all that lingered was the fight to pay the rent on their modest fibro house in Sydney's far south-west, to prevent Hamina and Farah from pulling each other's hair out because there was insufficient space or attention for them all, and even those were tepid exertions. But Abida would not surrender to her parents' brand of fatalism, not yet.

'I'll get the girls together to discuss it. It's us who'd be running the thing, we should decide if it's going ahead,' she said.

Wahid was about to reply, just as a boy with cropped sandy hair accompanied by a taller boy in tatty khaki shorts walked towards the stall. The boy with the sandy hair crossed his arms across his chest and furrowed his brow, as though his body was tightening up at the very sight of them. Abida was certain that if she could have seen his toes inside his boots, they'd be crossed too.

'Hi, what can we help you with today?' Ahlam repositioned the bowl in which the lollies were placed, shaking it until they settled into a more attractive formation. The lollies were cast-offs from the corner shop Ahlam's father owned, their ingredients listed in Arabic and Polish but not in English.

'Yeah, can you guys help me? I'm in need of real help.' The sandy-haired boy raised his hands as if to plead with them, while the other boy sniggered.

'Is there anything in particular we can help you with?' Wahid tilted his chin, looking only at the boy who was speaking. Although she would not have admitted it, Abida was glad for Wahid's conspicuous muscles then, the bulkiness of his frame. She wished Sara was here too, so that they could look at each other – the two of them against the brutalities of the world, as it had always been.

'Well, the thing is, I need help understanding something. Why is it that a strapping lad like you walks around in a t-shirt yet you have these two all covered up from head to toe?'

The boy in the shorts sniggered again and reached for a lolly, unwrapping the layers of plastic with exaggerated zeal before placing it in the centre of his tongue.

'What a lot of people don't know is –'

'What a lot of people don't know is,' the boy mimicked Wahid. 'Why don't you let the ladies speak for themselves?'

'There are rules for men's clothing and there are rules for women's clothing,' Ahlam said. 'The rules are just different, that's all. Men and women aren't the same, and while both are equal in the eyes of God, He recognises that difference and has devised a system in which these differences are catered for and honoured.'

Ahlam's response was regurgitated from a training session the MSA had run in the previous semester entitled 'How to do da'wah in one minute or less', and while Abida had enjoyed the role-playing exercises in which common questions about Islam were posed and answered, Ahlam's answer now appeared to dance around the essential truth: that Wahid was allowed to style and display his hair and they were not. Abida would have preferred to tell everyone to suck it up, that not every religious dictate could be distilled into a palatable aphorism. She was not troubled by having to obscure all but her face and hands. Sonia Gupta at school had been upskirted in the stairwell and the boy who had done it stated that it was because her skirt was short, but he had tried to do it to Abida in her floor-length pleated skirt too, this time citing a thirst for a challenge. The world was one place for women and another for men, of this Abida was certain.

'Right. Okay then,' the sandy-haired boy said. 'You keep on believing that. Whatever floats your boat. You're not bad though, hit me up if you ever change your mind about this Islam thing. I think we could have some real fun together.'

The boy in the shorts, who had still not spoken, bit into his peach lolly and it exploded with a loud crunch, while the sandy-haired boy picked up a leaflet on the true meaning of jihad and winked at Ahlam before turning around and walking away. Abida exhaled. Her armpits were sweaty, she could smell the stink of it.

'I don't know how some people get into university,' Ahlam said, pursing her lips into a bow.

Abida leaned against the stone wall. Its warmth calmed her, a buffer against the crowd. The sandy-haired boy had echoed the axiom of people their age. They all proclaimed how much they did not care what anyone did, how everyone should just do what made them feel good and that no one could tell you what or who you were. It was as untrue as it was banal. In every discussion, in every debate she had seen on Islam and Muslims and hijab and niqab, people only supported your right to choose until that choice diverged from what they deemed explicable, and from that point on you were deemed brainwashed or stupid or both. She felt the familiar tug of anger at the injustice of it, the presumption that she was being crushed under the boot of some tyrannical male and required liberation.

'Who cares anyway?' Wahid said. 'We've had much worse. People threw rubbish and spat at our Prophet, so who are we to complain about a few harmless idiots? Just forget it.' He began scrolling through his social media feeds. Abida watched his phone screen as he clicked on the app which featured Quranic verses of the day. Today's verse related to breastfeeding, stipulating that mothers could do so up until their child's second year of life but not beyond it. Wahid scrolled away from it and onto TikTok instead.

Abida wanted to escape from them both and depart for the long journey home. She picked up her bag and began to tuck a stray hair back into her hijab, then decided against it, yanking the hair right out of its root, feeling her scalp smart.

'I've gotta go, guys. Catch you soon, inshaAllah.'

'Are you sure you have to go now? Text me later, inshaAllah. Salam!' Ahlam kissed Abida's cheek as she departed, leaving the sticky residue of gloss where her lips had been.

All MSA members knew they were not supposed to leave a boy and girl alone at the da'wah stall, even if it was in the middle of the university campus. Ahlam would not linger for much longer. She would mutter some excuse and Wahid would nod and wave, both relieved to be extricated from the awkwardness of the situation.

Abida pictured this scene as she walked through the curved sandstone archway beyond the library and onto the main walkway, where a boy swerved past her on a skateboard, the cord of his red headphones snaking from his head into the pocket of his low-slung jeans. A girl in a double denim combination of skirt and jacket was handing out flyers about veganism, her nose ring reminding Abida of the photos she had seen of her parents' wedding, her mother's heavy gold tikka and nose ring obscuring most of her unsmiling face in profile. Abida accepted the flyer and thanked the girl, thinking of how she had transformed into yet another face in the student crowd when minutes ago she too had been spearheading a cause.

It was essential to possess a cause. A life without some form of focal point was not a life, merely a series of fragmented, random events. If you did not steer your course towards your own target, you would be steered towards someone else's. There was so little time to leave a mark, so little time to affect change. She had said this to Sara when they were still at high school and envisaging all the things they would do when they started university. They had both concluded that once people finished university it was already too late: they would have solidified into the people they would always be. It was these years in between which would determine everything.

Abida reached into her bag, feeling the edge of her raggedy constitutional law textbook before she located the apple she had been seeking. She bit into it as she crossed the road towards the bus stop, almost colliding with a boy and girl who were holding hands and talking in Hindi going the opposite way. She understood a few fragments, something about the boy's assignment being overdue and his request for an extension. Adam Smith required no translation; Abida had learned about his theories in high school economics and had thought that the invisible hand was a load of shit designed to benefit the rich. She had been gratified to read on Wikipedia that Smith had expressed dissatisfaction in his achievements on his deathbed.

The electronic screen at the bus stop stated that the bus was due to arrive in three minutes. This gave Abida enough time to record a voice message to send to Sara. Her thoughts flowed better with an audience, they always had. Alone, her opinions on the world seemed ambiguous, shifting like quicksand; in front of others she assumed a certainty that silenced her doubts, even if just temporarily. And Sara was her favourite tried-and-tested audience. She took another large bite of her floury apple and began her recording, recounting the incident at the stall with the two boys and how insolent the second boy's chewing of the lolly had been. She mentioned how Wahid had been tardy once again and that she had left him with Ahlam, and finally, that the MSA could require a new president in the imminent future and that she wondered who among them could fulfil the role.

3

Naeem

The girl in Naeem's lounge room was fidgeting. She was dressed in a baby pink shalwar kameez embossed with diamanté swirls, her lips lined and painted in the same shade of pink. Combined, these things suggested a level of effort that made Naeem nervous. The other occupants of the room were absorbed in their respective tasks: her parents in being regaled by his, her younger sister accompanying Tasnia to her bedroom to do whatever it was that thirteen-year-old girls did when they were alone. The other guests had not yet arrived, the lamb pulao and basted chickens and mango and jujube chutneys were arranged across multiple tables in preparation. His mother, Meherin, was not the most proficient cook of the aunties, nor the most hospitable, but Naeem knew her crockery was the most expensive, their house set against a steep driveway in one of the leafiest streets in the north-western suburbs.

He could feel his mother's eyes upon him now, compelling him to attempt to entertain this girl with stories, engage in animated conversation. Meherin and his father, Professor Kazi, were anticipating that he would marry a girl like this in five or six years, after he graduated and completed his internship at a hospital. He was expected to practise his approach at regular social gatherings like these, take stock of what was available. Naeem knew nothing about this girl except that her parents were both doctors in a general practice out in Rooty Hill, where the houses were Sydney-cheap and humungous, and that she had repeated her final year at high school in order to have a second attempt at the medical school entrance examinations. She was pretty and most likely very impressive, but he just couldn't do it.

If Sadia were here, it would be easier. Sadia was his kindest, most gentle cousin, the least likely to judge him for his lack of savoir faire. Sadia would ask both him and this unknown girl questions and maintain the flow of conversation. But Sadia was not here. She was too obliging to say no to her parents and the meetings they arranged with potential suitors on most weekends, and so there was just Naeem and this girl, each wishing the other would speak first. The girl eventually tired of the game and began swiping at her phone. He had bored her before they had even spoken. Once he had said his salams to the latest round of guests, Naeem slipped out of the room and up the staircase towards his bedroom.

It had been several days now since Sara had sent him a message with the words, *hey, what's up*, followed by a link to an article about a new translation of the Quran which had just been released. The message contained nothing of consequence, but the very fact that it was so unnecessary had marked it as an overture, a tentative promise of further contact. For this reason, he had vacillated. Naeem knew his reaction was unusual. The boys and girls on his course seemed to possess permeable bodies, leaning on shoulders and arms as they traversed the campus, exchanging kisses and hugs. They had once or twice treated him in a similar manner, assuming he was like Zafar Qureshi, who had hooked up with Stephanie Evans at the Halloween Ball, or Ahmed Saleem, who was dating Carmen Leung and whose father was acquainted with Professor Kazi from a stint at the same hospital. But Naeem had somehow projected his discomfort with physical contact between the sexes, and they had withdrawn, swapping notes and study tips but nothing further. He had dodged invitations to the end of year dances, fancy-dress fundraisers and snooker nights at the pub, just as he dodged the MSA girls who were angling for husbands.

Naeem sat on his bed and picked up his phone, then placed it down again. He couldn't decide what to do. He liked Sara, had liked her for some months. He could not now discern if it had begun in response to her tiny displays of interest, but even if it had, he had since discovered plenty of reasons of his own to continue with it. If she had served first, he had only been too willing to engage in their covert tennis game, each extraneous glance, each small interaction, representing a return into the other person's court. Their language was coded but unambiguous in his mind, and the way she had looked at him and spoken after the recent meeting had only solidified the fact. He liked the candour of her manners, the freckles above her nose and the way she wore the same sweatpants all the time and carried around a calculator.

The inexplicability of her surname and pale skin only heightened her appeal. But it was because he liked Sara that he did not deem it wise to engage. There was no vacant space in his life for these feelings to be expressed. He had no money of his own and several years of his degree to complete. He couldn't get married, practically speaking, and *practically speaking* was the only vocabulary he had for marriage. Besides, his parents would never agree to him marrying a girl they did not know while he was still at university, and there was very little Naeem had done in his life without their agreement.

The bedroom door opened and Meherin entered. She did not knock or announce her presence; Naeem had learned other parents did these things from watching television. She walked over to where he was seated, her gold bangles jangling against his desk as she leaned against it.

'Come downstairs now, we're about to eat dinner. You know it's rude to be up here on your own when our guests are downstairs.'

'Just go ahead and start without me. No one cares if I'm there or not anyway.'

Naeem knew he was being petulant and, in doing so, he was conceding any advantage he could have maintained. His mother was gratified when he behaved like a child, because she then felt justified in speaking to him as one. He hated this about family, how they triggered patterns of behaviour a person had long shed in every other sphere of life.

'I don't think that's entirely true, and you know it,' Meherin said. The corners of her mouth turned up with the faint markings of a smile.

'Fine, I'll come down, Ammu. Just give me a minute.'

Meherin's smile now extended across her face, her teeth a shocking gleam of white against her plum lipstick, her eyelashes stiff with black mascara. Some of Naeem's cruder friends made remarks about his mother's looks, and while he laughed it off, it made him uneasy, if only because he knew his mother would revel in their compliments.

'That's more like it, Rocket. I made your favourite mango chutney. Come get it before Uncle Mahboob eats it all. You know how greedy he is.'

She pressed her lips to his forehead, taking care not to smudge her lipstick, before exiting the room. The old nickname grated. Long ago, he had requested not to be addressed by it, but his mother persisted in seeing people not as they were, but as she wished them to be.

Naeem picked up his phone once again, waiting for an epiphany on what to say to Sara. Whenever he reached an impasse in his studies, he would prostrate in dua to Allah to eradicate all obstacles from his path, but a dua did not seem appropriate under the circumstances. If his faith were more robust, he would not even ask Allah to fulfil a specific request, just for whatever He willed to come to pass. He would desire whatever outcome Allah decreed for him and would fear nothing but Him. Instead, Naeem yearned for so many things and was afraid of so many things he felt he would implode with the strain of it all. His phone buzzed in his hand and he wondered if it would be Sara, castigating him for his silence, but it was Ridwan.

Mum's dragging me to yours, dude. Have the cha ready when I arrive.

He would have to go downstairs and await Ridwan's arrival; to do otherwise would be churlish. Naeem walked down the staircase and into the lounge room where the uncles were seated. He disliked these gatherings, the way the parents jostled to announce their child's latest achievement, the merits of each person's child compared and analysed like they were cars in a showroom. It was a nasty sport, even if he was victorious at it: a near-perfect HSC score, gaining entry into the state's best medical school, even the bonus of strong Islamic accolades. In the living room, the television was blaring, and the pink lipstick girl's father was crunching, open-mouthed, on piles of muri. The talk was of the hospitals the men worked at and their private practices, of politics and money. Always money.

Professor Kazi owned a small block of flats with Dr Ahmed in Homebush and they were discussing issues with the ventilation and the fact the tenants at number six were hanging their washing on the balcony despite being told not to.

In the kitchen, the women had broken away from the men and Meherin was stirring a pot of carrot halwa. Naeem grabbed the wooden spoon and chanced a surreptitious lick. The purring Miele oven lent the kitchen a cosy warmth, the black granite benchtops gleaming from the regular attentions of Najwa, their Indonesian cleaner. His mother would not have a non-Muslim cleaning their house, saying that she did not believe cleanliness could be learned from people who used nothing but dry toilet paper to clean their bottoms.

'Eh, what are you doing? Put that down,' she said. 'These children, they have no patience. Can't wait a minute, everything must be now now now. Facebook this and Instagram that,' she declared.

'Nobody uses Facebook anymore, Mum,' Naeem groaned.

Meherin laughed. She liked bantering with him in front of the other women, playing at being the hip, stern mum. There were roles to assume in company and he obliged Meherin by playing along. Nevertheless, he enjoyed watching her in the kitchen. She was so quick, so busy, seizing the spoon from his hand, turning a knob on the oven and dolloping a scoop of thick strained yogurt into a metal bowl seemingly all at once. Professor Kazi only entered the kitchen to brew milky tea or cook green chilli and coriander omelettes on weekends, his movements shuffling and precise, his thoughts elsewhere.

Ridwan arrived with fanfare, shaking the uncles' hands and having a word with each, a thundering slap on the back. To know how to enter a room was a skill Naeem had not yet mastered. It required a certain effervescence he did not possess, the ability to engage each person in turn without being drawn into protracted conversation. At gatherings such as these he was liable to become stuck on the end of someone's monologue, wishing he could abscond but not knowing how.

'So Samia and I are on the outs again,' Ridwan said once they were in Naeem's room. 'She's a bloody bitch, I tell you. I caught her chatting to that madarchod from Randwick Boys after she swore she hadn't spoken to the guy for months. This might be it for good.'

'Sure, sure. I've heard that one before.' Naeem shook his head. He took a seat at his desk chair, tapping his foot to make the chair rotate as Ridwan sprawled across his bed. Ridwan had developed a slight paunch over the past year, the result of too many corporate lunches at the investment bank he interned at, but his upper arms were still gym-defined and his face handsome and lean, as though the fat had not worked its way that far upwards yet.

'Seriously though, the girl has zero respect for me. But what can I do? Ammu has her wedding lehenga all picked out already. Might as well just roll with it, hey? These girls, they're all the same anyway, might as well get on with the one I already have. You'll be in my shoes in a few years, bro.'

Ridwan tended to speak as though they were the same entity. There were photos of the two of them at Naeem's first birthday party and they had gone through school together, but Naeem was not Ridwan. He would not work at Goldman Sachs or call girls bitches or remain entangled with a girl because she was attractive and studied dentistry and their mothers were both married to doctors. It was possible that Ridwan really did love Samia. He bought her expensive jewellery and had cried on the previous occasion he had unearthed evidence of other boys, but he also seemed wedded to the convenience of their relationship, the way their parents expected the two of them to get married.

He would not confide in Ridwan now. 'I don't have time for girls, bhai, you know that.'

Although Ridwan would listen intently, Naeem could not bear to offer up his heart to Ridwan's indelicacy, his steady evolution into the men their fathers expected them to be.

'Just don't get with an Indian girl, they're too much hard work. Remember Anjali from first year uni? She was texting me every hour on the hour, man. Or maybe you prefer white girls? Like father, like son?'

'Bhaiya.' Tasnia appeared at his door. 'Ammu said you should both come get some food.' Tasnia spoke as Meherin had taught her to, nodding in deference and departing with the other young girl in tow. She looked like Meherin, with Professor Kazi's jutting chin rounding out her face, a combination that would suit her in later years, but which now looked misshapen.

'Dude, what the hell is wrong with you?' Ridwan stage-whispered downstairs. 'Afreen has been eyeing you up all night and you're just not giving the poor girl a look.' He turned his head towards the girl in pink and back again as he dished himself a tandoori chicken wing, then another.

'I told you, I'm just not up for it right now. I have way too much to worry about as it is. Besides, why is it always girls with you?' Naeem laughed as they carried their plates towards the dining table, but it was true. The boys could not stop themselves from talking about girls. It was the same whether they were religious or not; the religious ones just took more care to conceal it. Naeem prided himself on his self-control, succumbing to masturbation only when an infrequent and dire need arose. His MSA friends grumbled about how powerful the lure of girls and masturbation and pornography were and while Naeem listened, offering words of practical advice on occasion; he was repulsed at how highly sexed they all seemed to be. Why was sex so important, so central to their thinking? He could go for many days and weeks without thinking about sex at all. Masturbation was more about servicing a bodily need, like clipping his toenails or pressing a bruise, than deriving any real pleasure.

'It's not always girls, c'mon, bhai. I went to that fiqh course you told me about last weekend. It was really awesome, alhamdulillah.'

Ridwan could accomplish this casual shift in and out of religion. Naeem's faith was heavy and constant, which concerned his parents, who were religious up until the point where it conflicted with their ambitions. They were pleased that they could put him forward as an example to others, that they would never have to worry about him stumbling home smelling of perfume and booze, but they did not approve of him being involved in any Islamic activities outside of their own frame of reference and were particularly suspicious of his Lebanese friends, viewing them as responsible for tarnishing the reputation of more respectable Muslims in Sydney.

As Ridwan chatted on about the course, tearing at his paratha and scooping up a chicken wing with it, Naeem thought again of Sara, of how the green of her eyes had held his as they had conversed after the meeting. He longed to discover so much about her, but he could not proceed with whatever it was they would be doing. It would injure, taint them both. It was far better to extricate himself now before they became entrenched in secrecy and wrongdoing. He would be doing her a favour. He possessed the sparkle of outward accomplishments, but underneath it all lay only him, and Sara was only able to like him because she did not know him.

'And here's my son, hiding away in the corner. What are you boys up to?' Professor Kazi boomed in his navy Saturday suit, a grin etched across his face without spreading to his eyes.

Ridwan smiled and began engaging Professor Kazi on something relating to the recent drop in the stock market. Naeem reached for his phone one final time. He pressed the block and delete button, before turning back and facing the other men. It was done. He would have to put Sara Andrews out of his mind.

4

Sara

Sara pinned her hijab in the mirror, pulling its ends over her chest. The pin slipped from her hand and onto the bathroom floor. Her mother, Soraya, had not wiped it recently and Sara could feel the dust on her hands as she searched for the pin. She eventually retrieved it from behind the toilet, threading it through her under-piece as she grabbed the ends of her hijab and tossed them over each shoulder. The MSA was doing a chalking session, marking the floors with slogans and the walls with posters advertising Islamic Awareness Week, 'building the hype', as Ziad had called it, and she had turned down an extra shift at the tuition centre she worked at and instead arranged to pick Abida up at the train station to chalk together.

It was entirely possible that Naeem would be present today. She had typed up so many drafts of her message to him, revising it over a period of several days, her finger hovering over the send button. He had read it immediately, but he had not responded. She had waited and waited but when his profile disappeared a few days later, she realised it was because he had blocked her. A quick incognito search from her phone had confirmed it. Her first reaction had been to cry, alone in her bedroom. She had endeavoured to be brave and it had provoked such a cruel, unwarranted response. But after the initial shock she found her sadness becoming tinged with curiosity. The blocking was so inexplicable, so final. It was an oddly personal act between two people who had exchanged a few words at most. She latched on to the very specificity of it as proof that she had had some effect on him. She longed to know what he was thinking and resolved to speak to him today if the opportunity arose. She had been brave once, and although it had not produced the outcome she had wanted, she was more accustomed to the feeling of it now.

When she arrived at the station, Abida was already waiting.

'Assalamu alaykum, my love,' Sara said, opening the car door.

'Wa alaykum salam. Are you ready for a jam-packed day of thumbtacking posters around campus and avoiding getting bottles thrown at us? I know I am,' Abida said, flashing a stockinged calf from beneath the hem of her abaya as she settled into the passenger seat and closed the door behind her.

Sara laughed. Abida's proclamations distracted her from the tight knot in her stomach. Abida would start on a rant now about Australia's settler colonial history, its settler colonial present. She would pound her fist against the glove box without realising, apologise, then do it again. But instead Abida just laughed too, although hers was short and guttural.

'Laugh all you want,' she said to Sara, 'but they might actually throw a bottle at you for a change, white girl. You're looking particularly Muslim today.'

Sara ignored her, turning the key in the ignition and reversing out of the packed carpark. Abida would sometimes use what she knew of Sara to jab at her insecurities, the way Sara imagined siblings did. These jabs were administered as affectionate badinage, but the real sting was that most were true. Sara had in fact dressed with more care and conservatism than usual, donning a striped maxi dress she had purchased on sale and a proper wraparound hijab instead of one of her floppy, lopsided turbans. She wanted to appear as the other MSA girls did, to eliminate any doubts that Sara Andrews was truly one of them.

'I am definitely looking forward to lunch,' Abida said. 'I asked Ahlam to get manoush from her uncle's bakery and I told her to put aside two of the labneh and za'tar ones just for you, your favourite.'

'You always know the way to my heart. I'm going to return the favour and pump some T Swizzle for you.'

This was where they understood each other best, in the bits of their lives which did not make sense to other people. Most of the core people in the MSA didn't listen to music, or if they did, they wouldn't admit to it. Abida didn't listen to mainstream music either, but Sara knew that her one weakness was Taylor Swift.

'"We Are Never Ever Getting Back Together", please. An oldie but definitely a goodie.'

'This song always reminds me of our school disco –'

'And Emma-Louise hooking up with Matt King in the bathroom and we all heard him moaning in the toilet and thought he was being attacked.'

'Trust you to remember that. Such a gutter mind you have under that jumbo hijab.' Sara grinned, turning up the volume as they hit a rare, unclogged section of Parramatta Road and moved closer towards the city. She thought of Naeem again, imagining him driving his car as she was, getting closer and closer to where they would be meeting.

'So what do you think of me running for MSA President if Mustafa does quit? Do you think I could actually pull it off?'

Abida was in continual pursuit of a new scheme, some cause to petition or champion. Over the years Sara had handed out pamphlets, attended working groups and stayed up until the early hours listening to Abida rehearse pitches and poems. She consoled Abida through the fits of self-doubt as they inevitably emerged, knowing that underneath all the swagger, Abida was brittle. Sara thought of Abida's preoccupied mother and the way she smelled of bleach and garam masala; three girls to the one bedroom, the way Abida's father left the family for spells of several weeks while on Tablighi Jamaat proselytising missions to remote islands in the Pacific. She loved Abida for her evident strength, but she loved her even more for the vulnerabilities she knew it masked.

'I told you, I think you could definitely give it a go and then see how things unfold.' Sara had learned that the most judicious course of action was to neither encourage nor discourage Abida's proposals. If they failed, Sara would be censured for her lack of foresight, and if they were successful, she would then be upbraided for not having displayed requisite faith in them from the outset.

'I know, I know. It's just hard to know whether it would be worth all the hassle. The MSA is such a sausage fest and most of the guys are complete freaks when it comes to speaking to girls, let alone taking orders from one,' said Abida.

Sara nodded as they got out of the car. The group had arranged to meet in front of the musallah. On the way there, Abida was preoccupied on her phone, her fingers sliding across the screen as they walked. Sara was consumed in her own thoughts of Naeem. She was grateful now for the many years she had been friends with Abida, the space it allowed her to think and not have to explain herself. One of her least favourite parts of befriending new people was that it necessitated a show of unswerving interest, to be seen to participate and pose a stream of questions. The fact that she and Abida could so frequently sit or walk or drive together, both consumed in their own private contemplations, was one of the surest indicators that their friendship was sound.

'Assalamu alaykum, sisters. Great to see you both.' Mustafa walked ahead of them, bearing large canvas bags of materials.

As much as she tried, Sara could not feel comfortable referring to anyone as sister or brother; it seemed too cult-like and familiar. She did concede, however, that Mustafa managed to imbue the term with a level of respect and warmth she had not thought it could possess.

'He always has such nice adab, mashaAllah,' Abida whispered in her ear, nodding with approval at Mustafa's manners. Adab was one of the many Islamic terms Sara understood in the context of someone else's sentence without being able to explain or use it herself. It was easier to remain silent, let the others proclaim their knowledge of Him and His vocabulary.

Just ahead of them, several MSA members were already assembled. She looked for Naeem among their faces but he wasn't there. To one side, Ahlam held a styrofoam coffee cup and conversed with a chirpy Malaysian international student named Fitri and either Mariam or Lina Kamaleddine. Sara could not always tell the twins apart. Both possessed the milky skin she associated with red hair, had their hair been at all visible beneath their stretchy khimars.

Now on the other side of the quadrangle, Mustafa stood with Ziad and the burly Afghan boy, Wahid. Together, they looked like an advertisement for one of the government graduate programs that Abida derided for their tokenism: Mustafa with his clear black skin, Ziad pale with burnt caramel hair, Wahid with his dark brown hair and dark brown skin.

'Bismillah. Assalamu alaykum everyone. We're just waiting for a couple more people and then we'll get started with our chalking and posters. Islamic Awareness Week is still some time away but, as you know, we need to get in early and start getting everyone on campus talking. May Allah reward you all for giving up part of your weekend for this. Let's start with Al Fatiha before we go ahead with the day's proceedings,' Mustafa said.

Sara bowed her head and cupped her hands, murmuring the familiar words. Al Fatiha, the opening. She recited it every day, every few hours. The words could be leaden and cumbersome in one prayer, smooth and rhythmic in the next, an ongoing wrestle of the tongue. Sara had taken great care to learn its meaning in

English but still loved that millions of the faithful could speak it daily, reverentially, without ever comprehending its meaning.

When Sara glanced up from her palms, Naeem was standing on the fringe of the group. He had appeared so quietly that she did not think anyone else had noticed. His hands were clasped in front of him as he prayed. He was dressed in a striped black-and-grey jumper, his hair brushed back behind his ears, which protruded a little. If he was aware of her presence, he offered no indication of it, reaching for the posters Mustafa and Ziad had stacked on the floor.

'All right, let's get started,' Mustafa said.

Abida reached over and grabbed a handful of posters. Sara assumed the two of them would pair off, but Ahlam tugged at Abida's arm, leaving Sara to stand on the other side with Fitri and Lina/Mariam. It didn't occur to her to protest. She did not want to obstruct the intimacies of others, guarding her own as fiercely as she did.

'Let's head towards Law Library first and then make our way in?' Fitri's manner was brisk. She wore bootleg jeans and a frilly pink top that did not quite cover her bottom. Sara tugged at her dress, checking it was fixed in place, that she had not exposed her ankles as she walked.

'Sounds good, sis. Let's head off before it gets too late,' Mariam said.

'Sorry, I didn't catch your name, sister. What was it again?'

'It's Mariam. And you're Fitri, right?'

Mariam began to walk beside Fitri, leaving Sara to follow along in their midst. In these environments, she often felt like an appendage to Abida and that when they were apart people did not have much to say to her. She knew that much of this was her own doing. She papered over her anxieties by making herself as small and noiseless as possible. Whenever people learned her name, they asked the same erroneous questions about when her parents had converted to Islam and where they had migrated to South Africa from. She did not know the right words to explain that a British forebear had taken what he wanted from his maidservants, that their descendants had retained their religion in secret but not their names or languages or even where they had come from. Her MSA friends were Bangladeshi, Lebanese, Turkish, Somali. Their identities seemed rounded and full with language and dress and dance, where hers had been hollowed out centuries before.

Fitri and Mariam were talking as they walked. The campus was emptier on weekends and the walkways seemed wider, cleaner. The walls were crammed with posters for pub crawls, quiz nights and Marxist reading circles. Mariam was talking softly as she pinned her poster, making the case for hand-slaughtering animals as Fitri protested that stunning was more practical and still halal, still permissible. Mariam was gentle, but implacable. Sara wondered where Naeem was now and who had thought it clever to include a 'try-on-a-hijab' event as one of the scheduled activities for Islamic Awareness Week. It appeared to her much like a game of pin the tail on the donkey.

Once all the posters were secured the girls walked back over to the lawn outside the musallah. The conversation had now shifted to Fitri's irregular menstrual cycle and spotting, which rendered ascertaining the times at which she would be excused from the daily prayers and Ramadan fasts difficult. Finally, Sara had something to contribute as she had watched a lecture from a shaykh on this precise topic on YouTube, which she promised to send to the girls. She sat down, smoothed her dress. Through it she felt the pleasant tickle of the grass against her legs. The boys were walking back now.

Mustafa distributed the parcels of manoush. The oil from the za'tar soaked through the paper, coating her fingers. She bit into it, savouring the tang of the oregano as she looked around. The atmosphere was more relaxed than usual; people seemed too tired and hungry to bother much about the customary gender segregation. She watched Naeem, who sat cross-legged on the grass as Wahid delivered an impassioned monologue on some topic. Even as she watched Naeem, Sara could not say why she was doing so. He had not been kind to her, and she had more than adequate reason now to deem him rude and immature. She did not know why she had selected him and not Wahid, who was more handsome, or Mustafa, who was both witty and kind. There was no logic to it, and this unsettled her.

She was too old for a crush. She knew about kissing, she knew about sex. Some of this knowledge had been accrued by her own choosing, some through listening to her school and university friends talk about their sex lives and how much, or how little, they were getting. In sex education at school they had learned that the average Australian had sex by the age of seventeen, and here she was, two years into university, sneaking surreptitious glances at a boy with whom she had exchanged a few lines of conversation. But by the standards of many, Sara knew she was already doing too much. *The first look is permissible, but the evil lies in the second.* This she understood and accepted as correct, but she could not prevent herself from seizing this tiny consolation.

The girls were now discussing the schedule for Islamic Awareness Week and its headline events. Abida was talking to Mustafa, asking something about US airstrikes in Somalia. Abida could talk to the boys about anything, she was not craven like Sara.

Sara began to despair of having an opportunity to speak to Naeem. He had not once glanced in her direction or acknowledged her presence in any way. What was he thinking, if anything? He stood up now, dusted crumbs from his sweater and walked towards the bin on the other side of the lawn. Sara placed her hands on the ground, swung out her legs beneath her and followed him.

When Naeem saw her walking towards him, he angled towards the bin, seeming to inspect its contents before turning around and facing her. He looked the same as he always did. There was something irritating about how unflappable he appeared, and Sara longed to jab a hole through the façade. She thought again of how he had blocked her without warning. He was not as composed as he seemed; he could be frightened.

'Hey, salam,' she said.

'Wa alaykum salam.'

There was a conspicuous pause, the cackle of Fitri's laugh echoing across the lawn.

'I'm sorry –'

'There's nothing to be sorry for. You don't owe me anything. But if you didn't want to talk to me, you could've just said so rather than blocking and deleting me without saying a word.'

Sara unclenched her fist. She had not been conscious of the motion until she had to undo it.

Naeem looked down at the grass. Then he raised his head and looked somewhere to the left of where she stood, towards where the group were sitting.

'I'm sorry for blocking you. That was silly of me.'

'Why did you do it then? Are you too religious to talk to girls?'

Naeem sighed. It was not a dramatic sigh, just an exhalation which lingered slightly, suggesting that he was not unaffected by the brusqueness of her speech. To Sara he seemed to be a person who valued structure, and she had to wonder at how he had allowed himself to become involved in such an untidy situation.

'I'm sorry. I don't know what else to say. I'm not really sure why I did it, but it doesn't matter anyway. There's nothing to be gained from us talking. We're not exactly going to be best friends, are we?'

'I guess not.' Sara nodded, unwilling to impart anything further than those three words.

She had to contain the hurt, direct it inwards. If she did not, she would cry in front of these people, and they would observe that the two of them were not engaging in the type of polite and incidental conversation that they should have been.

'Okay. Take care then, Sara. Salam.'

Naeem walked away, and Sara stood next to the bin, wondering what she would say later to Abida, whose surprise at the sight of Sara conversing with one of the MSA boys was palpable.

5

'We really need to ditch this try-on-a-hijab thing. Our hijabs are not some kind of spectacle or prop. To reduce hijab to a piece of cloth anyone can just plonk on their head is to completely devalue the spiritual dimension of why we do what we do, and the struggles we face each and every day as the visible targets of Islamophobia and racism. This is why I need you girls to make your voices heard and tell the MSA boys point blank that we are not going to run the session during Islamic Awareness Week.'

Abida paused and tucked her skirt beneath her ankles, noting that her sock had developed a hole where her left big toe was. This was irksome as she owned precisely four pairs of socks. Every piece of clothing she owned was important, every piece of it carefully rationed. She would have to pinch one of Hamina's or Farah's pairs from the next round of laundry Ammu did and stash them in the top drawer where they seldom thought to look.

'I don't see what the big deal is. In Malaysia my non-Muslim friends loved trying on my hijabs. Some of them watched hijab-styling videos with me on YouTube and one even ended up converting a few years later,' Fitri said.

'If people are going to convert because of a hijab-styling video then frankly I'd rather not have them convert at all,' Abida said. 'It's all just commodification and rampant consumerism dressed up as modesty. Besides, we accept too many weirdos into the fold as it is.'

Ahlam giggled. She wore a green turtleneck jumper over fitted black jeans, black winged eyeliner etched on with kohl. From these accoutrements, Abida gleaned that Ziad was somewhere about on campus today. They were sitting around in the musallah as they often did in between lectures and tutorials. It was their home at university more so than any other place. The room divider between the boys' side and their own, which had been temporarily pulled aside for the MSA meeting, was now erect and the room was crowded with girls praying in rows, and occupied with various activities. There were mismatched donated cushions strewn about the room and a girl with fluffy pink socks was dozing on one in the corner, while two Saudi Arabian international students pored over an open architecture textbook on the floor as they chatted in Arabic. Abida loved this space, loved that in here they were not marked by their difference but by their similarity.

'You posted an article about white privilege and converts to Islam on Twitter last week, so can we not go there again?' Sara said. 'But I agree with you, this hijab event is silly and we should really do something else.'

Sara was sitting by the window, her hands clasping her knees, her hijab-turban tucked underneath her hoodie. Abida hadn't seen Sara since the chalking session a few days ago. Sara had been quiet on their drive home, and when Abida had asked if everything was okay, Sara had said that her stomach was feeling funny after too much manoush.

Abida appreciated Sara's agreement about the hijab event but wished she had not felt the need to reference Abida's online post. She liked to maintain a distinction between her online self and her real-life self. It was easy enough to appear intelligent and well-informed online. Anyone with a Twitter account and an avid readership of *The Guardian* could craft the veneer of being insightful. Abida could devote hours to drafting a post that achieved the crucial balance between intellectual analysis and trying too hard to sound clever. The trick was to quote the right, preferably long-dead people: Said, Fanon, Du Bois; Žižek only ironically. If anyone disputed her propositions, she could take her time in devising a response or claim that her initial remarks had been misconstrued. But to engage in prolonged, detailed discussions with people who challenged her was far more complicated and could expose her shortcomings in knowledge, something Abida was very keen to avoid.

'Okay, but what do you think we should do instead? We need an activity to fill up that slot,' Mariam said. She was eating a raw carrot, not sliced up into segments but wholly intact with only the stem removed. Her lunchbox was packed with a mandarin and Lebanese bread smeared with za'tar and labneh, wrapped in clingfilm. Such practicalities eluded Abida. When she had been in primary school Ammu had placed an assortment of items on the kitchen counter and left her children to grab what they could while she nursed a baby in some other part of the house. By the time Abida was in high school she was already preparing lunch for one or more of her younger siblings.

'I don't know,' Abida admitted. She had been thinking about it for several days but had not arrived at a conclusive answer. Her mind was teeming with disparate ideas, each vying for primacy.

'I'm sure we can think of something. It shouldn't be too difficult,' Sara said.

'Why don't you come up with something then?' Ahlam smiled at Sara as she spoke, but there was something in the brevity of it, something in the twist of her lower lip as her mouth resumed its resting position, which suggested to Abida that Ahlam did not very much like Sara. She presumed Ahlam's dislike related to the way the MSA boys ogled Sara even though she was not especially pretty – *the girl with the green eyes*, she had overheard one say – in addition to the way Sara did not prattle with inshaAllahs or kiss anyone's cheek in greeting, things she really ought to have done to ingratiate herself and appear as the others did.

'I'm no good with stuff like that. That's why I'm friends with this one, the future lawyer, she does the thinking for both of us.' Sara prodded Abida with her foot and winked. Abida recalled when Sara had gifted Abida an old laptop of hers and said that she had no use for it so Abida wouldn't feel grasping and poor when she accepted, how Sara had prodded her and winked in the same way as when they had joked that they would die with their bodies untouched when Ella Garcia had narrated the specificities of her first time in the playground when they were fifteen.

'Sex. Sex. It's everywhere on campus, but we never talk about it. Why is that?' Abida said suddenly.

'What exactly is there to say about it? That we're not allowed to have any?' Mariam did not pronounce the word. To say it would be to acknowledge how it burrowed in the recesses, how it was everywhere and nowhere at all. But Abida felt the idea take hold. Finally, she had thought of a topic worthy of consideration.

'Yeah, so people can feel even sorrier for us than they already do?' Ahlam said. 'This girl in my sociology elective last year said you haven't really lived until you've had someone's tongue down your throat whose name you don't know. Sorry to be so graphic, but that's what people really think. They think we're sad, repressed losers because we've never had sex.'

'We're not repressed losers just because we haven't had sex. Besides, we don't know that no one in here has had sex. That's just an assumption we're making,' Fitri said.

'It's an assumption we're told we have to make,' Abida said. 'You know, thinking the best of your brothers and sisters in Islam and all of that. But that's not to say there isn't loads of Muslims going at it right now, and I bet you anything that it's mainly the boys who think they can get away with it. You know why? Because we still have this gross obsession with women's virtue, whatever that means, which totally doesn't come from our religion – sin is sin no matter who does it, right – but just from people's sick patriarchal minds. I think we could do a really interesting panel discussion on the way women are held accountable for the same things men always do and double standards and all of that kind of stuff.' Abida's mouth was working ahead of her brain, and she was afraid the other girls would think her puerile.

'Woah. That's pretty heavy.' Mariam was frowning, her fine reddish eyebrows scrunched. 'I don't think we've done anything like that before and I'm not sure how the brothers would take it.'

'Do we care how the boys would take it?' Abida knew this would be viewed as a provocation. This had not been her precise intention, but she faced the other girls now as though it had been. She frequently backed herself into a corner like this, where she became more and more strident to defend an idea she hadn't even held in the first place.

'I don't know what you're playing at, Abida,' Ahlam said. 'For what it's worth, I think the topic sounds interesting but I'm with Mariam, I don't think we'll get the boys onside and that's the whole point of having MSA group discussions, so we can all consult and agree on things. Otherwise, why do we even bother to have meetings and group chats? Also, it doesn't fit with the theme at all, which you came up with.' Ahlam smoothed the skirt she had donned over her jeans. It was one of the items of aged yellowy cotton outerwear they stored in the musallah cupboard for anyone who did not feel they were sufficiently covered up to pray. Abida thought of how she navigated the lawns and walkways in her abayas, while girls like Ahlam pranced around in their H&M jeans and then waltzed in here and wanted to vocalise their thoughts on all things Islam.

'Leave it with me. I'll sort it, and don't worry, if it blows up you can all say you knew nothing, okay?' Abida picked at her sock hole, refusing to make eye contact with any of them, even Sara. These MSA girls came in types, each more prosaic than the last: those whose studies and vocational pursuits acted as a means of passing the time until they commenced their real life as wives and mothers, the agreeable girls who spoke in a string of God-fearing platitudes, and the cool girls whose photos of themselves attracted hundreds of likes. She loved them, she would do anything to preserve and defend their sisterhood, but she did not always like them.

'Look, I gotta get to class,' Mariam said. 'But I'll catch you later, inshaAllah. We can talk about it some more. There's no need to rush into anything.' She leaned in for a hug and kiss, which Abida received impassively. She was not like them, not in thrall to marriage and boys and a passive, benevolent Allah. Her Allah commanded justice, He demanded it to be exacted.

'I'll walk out with you. I have a lecture starting soon too,' Fitri said. They walked away, putting on their shoes in silence before disappearing into the corridor.

Sara shuffled closer along the carpet to Abida. She whispered in her ear, her breath hot and smelling of coffee. 'Don't worry about all of this shit. You do what you think is right and it'll all be okay. I'd better get going too, Mum wants us to do facials this afternoon before I go to work and I've already put her off as long as I can.' Sara rolled her eyes at her mother's attempts at mother–daughter convivialities. Soraya, with her spiky blonde hair and beautician's parlour, was certainly an incongruous mother for Sara. But Abida had learned long ago that families were just a group of people lumped together by acts of unprotected sex. She would have loved a mother like Soraya, one who was interested in talking rather than simply bandaging scrapes and feeding her children.

Abida rested against Sara's shoulder, then released her and watched her lace up her sneakers and walk out of the room.

'Anyway, enough about all of this,' Ahlam said, moving closer to Abida. 'I think Ziad is around today. I saw him outside just before with Naeem and Wahid.' She gripped Abida's hand, her buffed fingernails forming a perfect, shiny arch.

'I'll go talk to him now.' Abida pulled her hand away, noting the indentations Ahlam's fingernails had left below her knuckles. She had committed to doing this for Ahlam, and she would fulfil her responsibilities regardless of the irritation she felt. This was what she did best, help other people sort out their lives. At least it distracted her from her own. She stood up and rotated her sock to cover the hole, then slipped her shoes on.

The corridor was busy with students coming and going from prayer. She saw Ziad standing with Naeem and Wahid and walked towards them. Naeem was the first to note her presence. He was another dreary variation on a theme, one of those Sydney Bangladeshi boys with impeccable academic credentials and endless finances at his disposal. The world was a trampoline to them; they had only to bend their knees and they would be propelled into the sky, their landings gentle and buffered. She knew of Naeem's family, of course: the father, the former bon vivant who had made a first marriage to an American and a second to a beautiful Bangladeshi woman almost half his age; the mother, who was said to have excised her husband's flasks of whisky and commandeered his life and lucrative medical practice. Abida was sure Naeem knew nothing about her; her family were nonentities living in a rented fibro house in Leumeah, far from the surgeons and their behemothic mansions in the Hills.

Naeem stood alongside Ziad and nudged Wahid, who was standing with his back to her. Wahid half-turned, and when he saw it was her, aborted the full rotation he probably would have done for Sara or Ahlam. Abida could now accept her ugliness as a factual proposition. It had not always been this way. In her early adolescence, she had scrubbed and scraped at her uncooperative chest until it was pink and raw, willing something to emerge there. But the real confirmation of her ugliness had arrived not through looking inward but looking outward, noting the manifest distinction between how you were treated as a pretty girl and how you were treated as an ugly girl. This had been at its most explicit during high school, when Brendan Chalmers had circulated a nifty spreadsheet in which the girls in their grade were ranked according to their looks and corresponding likeliness to put out. Abida had found that adults were merely less crude in their methods. She was skinny in an unfashionable way with a flat nose and small eyes and blotchy dark brown skin, and so she had come to anticipate a half-turn at best.

'Salam, guys. I need to have a quick chat with Ziad, could you give us a sec?'

Naeem nodded, stepping aside. Wahid hesitated, and in his hesitation she was sure she read disapproval of unchaperoned conversations between boys and girls, but eventually he followed Naeem, the two of them walking a few metres away to the entrance of the boys' side of the musallah.

'Everything okay, sis? What do you need to talk to me about?' Ziad tugged at the zipper of his hoodie, his eyes trained towards the floor as a stocky boy in an Adidas shirt passed them and went inside the musallah.

'Well, it's about marriage actually. I've been thinking about it, and I think there's a sister who could be a great match for you. What do you think of Ahlam?' She had intended to provide a more extensive preamble, but she hoped the directness of her approach might at least render Ziad more acquiescent.

'Er, well, that's a bit random. I guess I haven't really thought about it, to be honest.'

'I'm sure you've thought about marriage. It's said to fulfil half the requirements of our religion, after all. Everyone's thought about marriage at some time or other.'

Ziad did not respond, his zipper catching on his polo shirt as he tried to pull it closed. Sensing she had frightened him, Abida decided to change her approach. She lowered her voice and leaned in towards him, close enough to introduce the notion of familiarity, but distant enough to not appear improper, conscious still of Naeem and Wahid's presence at the shoe cabinet.

'I know she thinks very highly of you, and I think the two of you could be very compatible in all areas, inshaAllah. She's a wonderful girl, and I have no hesitation in recommending a brother of your calibre to her,' she continued. She would not outright declare that Ahlam had commissioned the endeavour – she understood the parameters of the girl code, respected its underlying principles – but she did not see any harm in providing Ziad with some incentive.

'She is a very good girl, mashaAllah. I wasn't sure she'd consider someone like me. I still have a whole year to go before I finish my degree and I'd have to wait a while before I would be ready to support a wife. I'm not exactly prime husband material.' The apology contained in Ziad's smile, the gentle flaring of his nostrils, impressed Abida in its perspicacity. Very few people were able to mind the gap: between what someone might expect of them and what they had the capacity to offer; between the person they were at present and the person they might yet become. Undoubtedly, Ziad had promise.

'That really shouldn't be an issue at all. Leave it with me and I'll get back to you with her answer, and we can take it from there, inshaAllah.'

'That's really thoughtful of you, sis. May Allah reward you.' Ziad grinned over at her before joining the other boys.

She saw Wahid clap Ziad on the back before they entered the musallah together, but Naeem paused. He looked in her direction and she thought he was going to speak to her. But he too turned away and disappeared into the musallah.

Abida wondered what he had been seeking, what meaning she had been intended to glean from that glance. She decided to think no more of it. The machinations of people like Naeem Kazi did not interest her. She would return to the musallah and formulate a plan with Ahlam. But it was growing late, she would have to return home soon. Sara would be home already; she lived closer to the city. Abida had an hour on the train ahead, twenty minutes of walking after that unless her older brother Maroof picked her up. The train would be one of the old ones without heating or air-conditioning. They seldom put the new ones on her line. She had written to the state transport authority about it last year, asking why that was, but when they had replied that the distribution of trains was purely an operational decision, she had decided never again to waste her time asking such questions. Rich people got nicer things. Some things were so obvious they didn't need to be said.

6

It was said that Allah was at His most receptive in the last third of the evening, when only His most prodigious servants arose from slumber to call upon Him. There, in the absolute stillness of the night, the tears trickled down Naeem's face, catching in the strands of his beard. He was ashamed, kneeling before Allah in His glory. Naeem was ashamed of how much he had longed for Sara, how much he still longed for her, but he was even more ashamed that his fear was not of Allah alone as it ought to be. He was most afraid of other humans and their heavy boots and truncheons, of being condemned and humiliated and judged. He was afraid of what savageries people were capable of. His faith was resolute but untested, and he could not be sure it would survive privations.

Naeem knew he was not alone in this fear; the internet was awash with conspiracy theorists convinced that the end was nigh. The Sydney Muslim community was full of people who sat on their computers and shared posts on the CIA being the true masterminds of terrorist attacks, people who compulsively tracked the signs of the end of times. He didn't wish to be associated with such people and yet he could not dismiss his fears. He scoured the comments section on news articles pertaining to Muslims, tracing the steady deterioration in public sentiment towards them.

Two days after he passed his driving test he had heard on the car radio that fifty-one per cent of Australians held an 'unfavourable opinion of Islam' and he had very nearly veered into an oncoming car. From that time onwards he had only listened to recitations of the Quran or driven in silence.

Naeem could not foresee when exactly it would disintegrate into fire and blood. They would come for Muslims sometime, but for now his pathway was clear. He would study medicine until he finished, and he would become a doctor like his father. He would read the Quran and socialise with his family friends and the MSA. He could immerse himself in these tasks, but when an anxious spell overtook him, he could only motivate himself to continue by thinking of how it could assist him when the situation became critical. Doctors were often afforded special privileges in detention camps; memorising the Quran would preserve religious knowledge where no one could get at it. If he stretched the fantastical just a little bit further, his protection could be extended not just to his family but to Sara, although she most likely detested him now.

It had been a little over a week since he had seen Sara at the chalking day, and he was already regretting the finality of what he had said.

On Tuesday afternoon he headed into the university for one of the regular MSA barbeques. Naeem was rostered on at the hospital where he was meant to be shadowing doctors through the paediatric ward, but his supervising doctor had cancelled on him for the third time. Medical students were even more of an encumbrance than interns; interns could at least be given low-level administrative tasks and trusted to do their own Google searches.

He wondered if Sara would be at the barbeque. Although he enjoyed the ceaseless political debates among the brothers, the muscle flexing and the semi-competitive displays of piety, he was also drawn to MSA events because they offered the only opportunity to see her. His impulses relating to Sara were entirely contradictory: flee, or collide. He wanted to test if he could resist acting on either impulse and behave as he would with any other MSA girl: aloof and polite, unaffected by lust or any other base emotion. He did not know her; he had merely imagined her.

The barbeque was being held on the most popular lawn on campus, adjacent to the main library where the MSA stalls were set up. The weather was stifling and sunny, so there were large crowds of boys and girls lounging around in cropped singlets and shorts.

'Bro, the struggle is real. I can't look anywhere without seeing some girl's legs,' Wahid lamented, as the two of them wheeled the barbeque towards the back end of the lawn.

'Just lower your gaze, pretend the girls aren't there and focus on the sausages.' He waved a pair of tongs at Wahid, tutting in mock disapproval.

'Easy enough for you to say. You're practically a monk. Do you even know what a girl is? You know, half the population, nice manners and smiles, not jerks like us?'

Beneath Wahid's brawn lay a real sincerity and desire to better himself. He had confessed to Naeem that his father's secret drinking habit, now curtailed to the occasional glass of wine at parties and weddings, had sent his mother into fits of grief and hysteria for years. Unlike other rich Afghans, who drank alcohol as a marker of their sophistication, his father had virtuously abstained until the Soviets had dragged him away one night and returned him the next, the blood still dripping from his nose and underneath the ridges of his fingernails.

'I'm not a monk, dude. You could say they're just not my type.' He raised his eyebrows suggestively before reaching for Wahid's upper arm, bulging through the sleeve of his hoodie. This play at homoeroticism was common among the boys, starved of female company and bonding over the difficulties of their self-imposed celibacy. Naeem sometimes wondered if there were any credible appeals amid the jokes. He reasoned that there must be. At King Abdullah College they had heard rumours of a boy in the year above who had been caught in the change room with another boy, but no one had confirmed it before both boys had been spirited away by their parents.

'Hey, hey, break it up, brothers. Let's not give anyone the wrong idea here!' Mustafa reached out and shook Naeem's hand, grinning, before placing several bags of pink chicken and brown lamb sausages on the bench.

'The sisters should be coming in a minute with the bread rolls and sauce, inshaAllah. We're expecting a big turnout, so we'll get the two of you to start up the barbeque and the sisters will hand people bread rolls as they start to arrive.'

Mustafa was that rare type of leader who could give orders people wanted to follow. It helped that he was a middle-of-the-road Muslim, not opposed to any factions and even welcoming to the Shia kids, who had previously been harangued in the musallah for praying on tissues and stones. He was the son of Somali refugees, a cool guy who looked as comfortable in a thawb as he did in smart chinos and shirts. Naeem wondered whether he would ever inhabit his own body with such ease.

'Aye aye, captain.' Wahid saluted Mustafa just as a large swarm of MSA girls appeared bearing bread rolls and utensils. They seemed to crowd together and form one amorphous mass, their skirts and dresses skimming the grass. There were two pairs of legs in pants, the taller of which surely must have belonged to Sara. Naeem averted his gaze from her knee region and back to the browning sausages.

A line began to form almost immediately. Naeem worked with speed, flipping row after row of sausages. He loved moments like these, when he was part of the crowd but invisible to it. He was able to observe all its happenings: the girl in the green tank top lingering as Wahid placed a sausage on her plate, the friendly Chinese girl and her pasty white Australian boyfriend requesting an extra chicken sausage each. But despite the chaos, the happy throng of people around him, Naeem could not restrain himself from noting Sara's movements. She was handing out napkins along-side Abida, her face more open and animated than it had been when they had conversed the previous week. She had come to this event knowing that he would be there; surely she could not hate him as much as he feared.

'Bro, I think we're almost out of sausages.' Wahid was panting from the exertion and the heat of the barbeque, his broad forehead dotted with beads of sweat.

'Well, at least the crowd is thinning out now. I thought the trumpet had been blown for the Day of Judgement the way people were carrying on.'

Wahid offered a smile, but he did not laugh. Naeem knew he was not funny, but he did not want others to know this too. He worried suddenly that Sara also knew this about him, if she thought of him at all now. He looked over at her, noting the brown flannel shirt, the straight, thin eyebrows which did not seem to be plucked. She did not look like anyone else there. Their eyes met for one long, conspiratorial moment before he jerked his head away from her line of sight, thinking of the oft-repeated Muslim joke that since only the first look was within the scope of permissibility, it was best to use it up on a nice long stare. This thing, whatever it was, was not going to recede of its own accord. Now that he had travelled some distance beyond their conversation after the meeting, he could recognise it for what it was: a beginning. He needed to talk to someone, and the only person he could think of was Ridwan.

When his schedule allowed it, Ridwan attended the occasional MSA event with Naeem, but he had no interest in their political or religious discussions and mixed with boys and girls alike. At school they had not been allowed to sit with girls in the playground. They had been told to speak about academic matters only and to look at the ground when they spoke. Now Naeem saw photos of Ridwan on social media with girls and wondered how he had shaken off those years like confetti.

Naeem excused himself from the barbeque, walking away from the lawn and dialling Ridwan's number.

'Naeem, bro! What's up?'

Naeem could hear the din of a food court in the background. He exhaled and forced himself to continue.

'Not much. Are you on your lunch break?'

'Yep, just getting a salad. This gym and diet thing sucks, man.'

'When are you at uni next?' Naeem spoke quickly before he lost his nerve. 'I need to talk to you.'

'I have a class at five this afternoon. I can probably catch you for a bit before then?'

'Sounds good. I'll be in the library so just call me when you're nearby.'

'Sure, I'll see you then.' Ridwan hung up, not bothering to preface his goodbye with an inshaAllah.

Naeem muttered it to himself, more out of habit than annoyance. He preferred Ridwan's casual irreverence to the fervent preaching some of the other MSA boys indulged in.

He walked back towards the barbeque, which Wahid and Mustafa were scrubbing with rolled-up sleeves, their fingernails coated with grease and tomato sauce. The girls had departed, Sara with them.

'I have to go to the library. Are you guys okay to finish up here?'

'No worries, doc,' Mustafa said, shaking his hand again and pulling him in for a brief embrace, smelling of cologne even through the grease.

Naeem spent the next few hours annotating his anatomy textbook on the uppermost level of the library, where it was quieter and less students came to chat and flirt. He was disciplined enough not to think of Sara. He was just about to make more flash cards when his phone buzzed.

I'm outside the library. Get your big butt down here.

Naeem chuckled. The bespectacled girl with high Slavic cheekbones opposite glared at him in disapproval.

He walked down the staircase and out onto the lawn where Ridwan waved at him. 'About time, Rocket. I don't have all day, you know.'

Ridwan pulled Naeem into his arms, patting his back hard before releasing him. His charcoal suit was perfectly cut and he smelled of peppermint aftershave. Like Mustafa, Ridwan seemed to have moved easily from boy to man, leaving Naeem to wonder why he could not seem to get there too, wherever *there* was.

'It's good to see you, man,' Naeem said. 'What's new?'

'Oh, you know, people to see, assignments to fudge my way through. You're looking good. A little on edge though, I have to say.' Ridwan cast an appraising eye over Naeem. 'It's a girl, isn't it?'

Of all the things he liked about Ridwan, his ability to get straight to the point, to cut through the bullshit of ordinary conversation, was his favourite. He smiled and raised his palms in a gesture of surrender.

'Yeah, it is,' he said, almost bumping into a boy on a scooter before motioning for Ridwan to sit down next to him on the low concrete wall.

'Who is this mysterious lady who's finally tempted you away from the straight and narrow? Is she in the MSA? Now I know the real reason why you're always hanging out there.'

'I'm not tempted, and that is not why I hang out with the MSA,' he said, irked. Ridwan had summed up the situation with customary alacrity, which rendered Naeem all the crankier. Was he so transparent?

'Hit a nerve, have I? All right, I'll shut up. Just tell me a bit about her and Uncle Ridwan will give you some advice.'

'Her name is Sara. She's South African, I think.'

Naeem contrived a level of imprecision in his description, as though he had not researched an online post from several years ago in which Abida had tagged Sara about the recent increase in Muslim tourism to South Africa.

'Are you trying to kill your parents? A Black girl, chi chi chi!' Ridwan waggled his head in Bollywood-esque censure, but he was correct once again.

Naeem's parents would not state it outright – not in the specific words that would identify their prejudices for what they were – but on their scale of eligibility, a white girl, while shameful, would be less objectionable than a Black girl. Other common ethnicities among Sydney Muslims would be further categorised: Arabs were disliked for their perceived boorishness, Indonesians and Malaysians deemed smiley and inoffensive enough, Turks and

Bosnians at least fair and European in appearance. They liked these people as his friends, they liked these people on television and in other people's homes, but not in their own home and not as a prospective wife for their son.

'She's not Black. I don't really know what she is, to be honest. But she's different to the other girls.'

'That is the stupidest, most predictable line in the book, and just for your information, the whole "different to other girls" thing is considered an offensive thing to say, but I'm going to let it slide and ask, different how?'

'Well, she's tall, almost my height exactly. She doesn't dress in nice clothes and she wears this leather backpack. She's studying engineering, so she must be a gun at maths. She always looks really focused but also off on another planet and her eyes are green, like grass before it's been watered.'

The words rushed out of his mouth. He had resisted speaking about her and now he couldn't stop. He was startled at his own amassing of information, and he looked over at Ridwan, waiting for him to make a disparaging wisecrack, but none came.

'Wow, dude, you are in way too bloody deep.' Ridwan sounded almost reverential.

'What do I do? I've barely even spoken to her.' He omitted that he had already squandered an opportunity to speak to Sara, that he had been too timorous to type a few words on a screen to her.

'Okay, say you do speak to her. You speak, and it's all butterflies and rainbows, what then?'

'I don't know what then,' Naeem said, lamely. He just wanted Sara to like him in return, wanted them to converse and get to know each other without it necessitating any 'what then's.

'You don't do the whole girls thing, bro. You never have, not even in school when everyone else was at it behind mum and dad's back. No offence, but I always thought you'd just wait for your parents to pick someone out for you to marry and get it done that way,' Ridwan said.

'Do we have to jump straight to marriage? I'm telling you I think I like this girl, that's all.'

'There's no such thing as *like*. You're not me or one of the other Bangladeshi boys who have girlfriends on the sly who they'll marry when they eventually get tired of sneaking around. I know you. You're either going to let this die now, or you're going to marry this girl.'

Naeem shivered. Ridwan was looking down at his phone, checking the time, but his words had sounded oddly prophetic. He had an image of the path his parents had drawn out for him so long ago, and himself veering madly off course and straight into a pothole. He did not do potholes, those were for other people.

'Listen, I gotta get to class. But keep me updated, okay? And send me this girl's profile so I can look her up and see what's got your knickers in such a knot.' Ridwan stood up, straightening his collar before gripping Naeem's hand.

'Okay.' Naeem waved Ridwan off, gently pulling his hand away and contorting his face into a smile. He had no intention of allowing the nooks of Sara's face to be scrutinised and dissected by Ridwan's usual bluntness. He could predict exactly what Ridwan would say, his face scrunched up in assessment, *Well, she's all right, I guess. A bit on the average side, but she looks like a white girl in a hijab, if that's what you're into, bro.*

He was becoming infatuated. This was the work of Shaytan, surely. Ramadan was due to commence, and he needed to recalibrate and perfect his acts of worship. To this end, Naeem drove home and proceeded upstairs to his bedroom, taking his Quran down from its shelf and kissing the pearly damasked case. He would recite until his eyes strained, until he had earned his penance for the things he had done, for the things he was still doing. But after thumbing through several pages in quick succession, he found himself thinking of Sara again. He had prematurely eliminated the possibility of her from reach but that could be undone. He reached for his phone, found her profile and unblocked her before returning to the Quran and continuing from where he had left off. He had hit the ball back; it was now over to Sara once again.

7

Ramadan was a time when things just seemed to happen. People were more energised, more alive, not in spite of the absence of food and water but because of it. In the rush to prepare the special Ramadan leaflets to distribute, to order catering for on-campus iftars and organise shifts to man the da'wah stall, Sara felt more anchored and distracted from the awkwardness of her encounter with Naeem. She needed these people and their acceptance. If she couldn't be accepted here, she had no hope of being accepted anywhere. She didn't approve of everything people in the MSA did or said, but she longed to be subsumed, to be carried along like baby Moses in the river.

On the first evening of Ramadan, the MSA was preparing for one of its largest annual events: a communal, interfaith iftar and taraweeh prayer session under the stars. It was the very kind of cutesy thing required to dissipate the tension which had been simmering on campus following a mass shooting by a Muslim gunman that had happened in America. There were online comments about it on the university forums, warnings on the MSA group chat to be extra cautious of racist attacks when walking around. Abida had written a long post online about the hypocrisy of the Western media and although Sara had liked and shared it, Sara could not understand why some Muslims experienced the urge to comment each time one of these incidents transpired, whether in condemnation of other Muslims or to point out, smugly, that gun violence in the USA really was rather appalling. She preferred to insulate herself, concentrating on private acts of worship and on repenting for still thinking of Naeem when she knew she should not. They had reached an impasse and there was nowhere left for them to go, but her thoughts and feelings would not be extinguished.

The day of the event was a pleasant blur of frenetic activity. Sara folded napkins, distributed bin liners and counted paper plates and forks. She posed with the other girls in front of the pile of plates and Abida shared the photos on the group chat, saying they had to show the boys who did the real work. She did not need to think, only to proceed from task to task. She was a pair of hands to sort, a shoulder to hoist upon. She had not yet seen Naeem, but he was scheduled to be leading the taraweeh prayer later in the evening; she would hear his voice even if she could observe nothing of his face.

As the sun set, Sara took a seat alongside Abida and Ahlam and two very sombre girls from one of the Christian evangelical societies. Despite the chill in the air, the courtyard of the Education

building was packed with people. Sara performed a quick calcu-
lation and estimated there were between one hundred and one
hundred and twenty people present, and although the space buzzed
with noise from all corners, there was a palpable and deferential
silence once the adhan was called. The call to prayer assumed an
added significance in Ramadan, a signal to pick up a fat succulent
date, whisper a prayer, and chew it, the first sustenance to enter
the body in many hours. The space seemed to explode with chatter
and movement: rugs were pulled out, maghrib prayer commencing
for those who could join, the non-Muslims left to contemplate
whether it would be against the ecumenical spirit of the evening
to begin eating their plate of biryani.

Sara did not usually enjoy praying outdoors; a gust of wind and
her hijab would end up in her mouth. So she did it with as much
speed as she could, returning to her place next to the girls, who
were now engaging in the type of polite, restrained conversation
that people who were convinced of the rightness of their own
convictions and the wrongness of those of others could manage.
She listened to them compare Christianity and Islam's stances on
adoption without much interest. She focused instead on finishing
her biryani and then collecting discarded plates and placing them
in black garbage bags.

The adhan for isha prayer was called, marking the end of formal
proceedings for the night. The non-Muslims were handed takeaway
boxes of biryani and sent along their way, while several of the MSA
girls felt it was getting too late and decided to leave as well. They
felt nervous at the prospect of being out late in the city, and their
parents liked it even less than they did. Sara offered to drop Abida

and the other girls at home after taraweeh, which they gratefully accepted, taking their places next to her on the prayer mat.

Taraweeh was always challenging, as much for the imam as for the congregation. Ingesting food and drink after a day's deprivation rendered standing, bending and prostrating cumbersome, especially when the imam opted for the full set of twenty rak'at rather than the shorter set of eight. She had assumed that hearing Naeem's recitation would make it more bearable, and while his Fatiha was sweet and light, he began to falter once it was completed. His tongue tripped over the verses; again and again he forgot which verse followed and had to be prompted by the low rumble of the front row. Sara was mortified on his behalf and found respite in the silence of sujud, her forehead and nose pressed against the ground. She wished someone in the congregation would step in, but he was forced to labour through prayer after prayer until he reached the end of the eighth rak'at. She caught a glimpse of him in a white thawb, his bare feet poking out underneath, before he was swallowed in the crowd.

'Poor guy, subhanAllah. It must be so difficult to remember everything when you're up there.'

Sara could not discern if Ahlam sounded kind or condescending, deciding that sympathy was a strange combination of both. She shook her head as they rolled up the woven plastic prayer mat for the boys to carry back to the musallah.

'I know, especially in front of all those people. It can't be easy,' Abida agreed.

'Maybe he should have practised more then,' Sara said. The other girls looked at her and she was aware that she had been too forceful in her pronouncement. She was unaccustomed to discussions of this nature, where others spoke about Naeem and she was expected to participate as if he was someone she could be impartial about. She knew Abida would ask her about it later and she would have to think of something to fob her off.

'He practises all the time. Mustafa was saying brother Naeem is always reading the Quran in the musallah when he's not in the library or at the hospital.' Ahlam spoke with finality.

Despite her embarrassment, Sara felt a pinprick of jealousy that Ahlam had procured information about Naeem that she had not. Perhaps Ahlam also harboured feelings for Naeem and she hadn't realised it. According to Abida – whose cynicism was piercing and cruel, but usually accurate – overlaps of romantic interest were frequent in MSA circles. There were only so many of them; in the search for a Muslim boy or girl to love, they were bound to bump up against each other. Abida had put it much more plainly. *Sloppy seconds*, she labelled it.

Sara looked at Ahlam and waited for her to continue.

'Anyway, girls, I want to tell you something.' Ahlam leaned in as Mariam joined them, linking arms as they walked towards Sara's car across the deserted campus. A lone boy with a Velcro headband holding back his afro walked in front of them.

'What is it?' Sara opened the car door and turned the key in the ignition, Abida seated in the front next to her. She could guess what Ahlam's news was. It had to be something related to a boy. There was little else that would be imparted with such ceremony.

'Well, brother Ziad has expressed interest in getting to know me through Abida.'

Sara was surprised, not at the information but that Abida had known and withheld it from her. She looked at Abida, who shrugged almost imperceptibly. They had always operated on the principle that it didn't count as divulging if they only told each other.

'That's awesome, alhamdulillah. What's going to happen now?' Mariam shifted in the back seat but was otherwise unaffected by the announcement.

'We're going to meet up for coffee with Abida chaperoning. If it goes well, he'll come over and meet my parents,' Ahlam replied.

The complexities of the marriage process eluded Sara. Abida understood it all instinctively and had tried many times to explain it to her. You could 'get to know' someone, but you couldn't call them your boyfriend. You should never be seen in public with anyone you were getting to know unless you were already engaged. If he told his parents about you, he was legit, if not, he was just stringing you along like an fboy. Everything was shrouded in secrecy, but the more clandestine something was supposed to be, the more people seemed to talk about it.

'That's so exciting. How are you feeling about it?' Even as Sara asked the question, she thought of Naeem. She attempted to imagine her parents meeting his, the ceremonious conversations they might have about the weather and the ambitions of their respective children.

'I'm hoping this is the one, girls. I've already gotten to know three guys before and it didn't work out. I just can't take another failure.' Ahlam sighed, sinking into the seat before directing Sara to take the next turn on to Auburn Road. There were still large masses of Muslims out on the street, purchasing kebabs and avocado cocktails for a post-taraweeh treat.

'Amen, sister. My parents are always trying to get me to meet random guys and I can't stomach it,' Mariam said.

'Yeah, I had to say no to so many guys before my parents even let them in the house,' Ahlam said. 'They're going to love Ziad after the parade of losers they've subjected me to!'

Sara remained silent, looking out the window at a woman in niqab holding a bottle of fresh carrot juice in her gloved hand. She could add little to these exchanges about things Muslim parents do. She felt her difference again, the way her heritage was so fractured that even her parents had no idea how other Muslims behaved. Her parents had dated for years in Cape Town. They had gone to the movies and the park, and no one had said it was wrong. Soraya and Amin did not mention the topic of marriage at all, joking that their daughter must have her pick of the boys in her engineering cohort as one of its very few girls. They commented on her comings and goings with mild interest; if she was at home, they would venture out for ice cream or to a movie as a trio, and if not, Soraya and Amin went on their own.

She was relieved when the girls were duly dropped off at their homes, with Ahlam requesting their dua for a successful outcome with Ziad, and Abida saying that it was going to work out, no doubt about it, Ziad was keen as mustard. Sara promised to make dua, but her mind clambered its way back to Naeem as she drove along King Georges Road, her window open to allow in the cool night air. He would be suffering, of this she was sure. He would take care to present the same reticent façade to others, but Sara imagined him sinking into an anguished sujud in solitude, asking Allah for forgiveness for failing His Book and His Words. She longed to be his source of comfort, despite knowing he would neither request nor accept any with ease.

The house was silent when she entered, but her parents had left the hallway light on so she would not have to fumble in the dark. Sara whispered a dua for their continued good health, closing her bedroom door quietly and turning her tall foldable bedside lamp on, her fingers now stiff from cold. She rubbed them together before sitting on the edge of her made-up bed and reaching for her phone and navigating to the message she had sent Naeem all those weeks ago.

He had unblocked her! He had thought about what he had done and decided against it. Although she supposed he could have said something to her, apologised for what he had done, she felt vindicated. Something had compelled a change in his behaviour and he had reopened a door she had presumed closed.

Sara sat on her bed, crossing her legs beneath her and settling herself against her pillow. In her haste, she accidentally swiped her way to her own profile rather than Naeem's, zooming in on her current profile picture, a travel snap of Angkor Wat she had taken last year. She was indifferent to social media, checking it once or twice a week as opposed to the hourly foraging her friends did. She swiped across to Naeem's profile, his profile picture was one of him and someone she took to be his younger sister, also taken some time ago judging by the length of his hair. It had pleased her to learn that he too was inactive online. She would have found him far less appealing if the quotidian details of his life were displayed for all to see.

She had two options: to say something, or to wait for him to say something. Neither option was appealing. After some minutes Sara decided to initiate, thinking that at least this would bring about some conclusion.

Salam, Naeem.

He began typing a response, and she allowed herself to believe that he had been waiting for her.

Salam, Sara.

There was an expectant moment of cyber-silence. Sara was unsure of what to say next. She knew how to talk to boys, but not how to talk to *the boy*. She uncrossed her legs and ran a hand through her bobbed hair, feeling the blunt choppiness of its edges where her mother had trimmed it. She would have to continue this conversation, clumsy and inelegant as it was. *Did you have a good time at the event tonight?*

It was good, alhamdulillah.

Alhamdulillah.

The same banal filler Muslim phrases, trotted out at timed intervals. Sara did not know what it was she was undertaking, initiating conversation with this boy with whom she had shared approximately two minutes of strained conversation. She was aware of the desire but not of its origins.

A reply came through from Naeem: *Who am I kidding, I was a fucking mess tonight.*

Her heart thumped inside her chest, a bird trapped in a room with a low ceiling and all windows latched. To swear was to invite intimacy, to mark a clear departure from convention. Naeem would not speak to her in this way unless he was experiencing the same inexplicable pull. Sara thought of how best to respond to him, not wishing to repay his confidence in her with glib words of reassurance. *I felt so bad for you. I can't imagine what it's like to try and recite the Quran from memory in front of so many people.*

I've done it so many times before, but tonight was just terrible. I just couldn't seem to get it together and the words froze in my mouth, Naeem replied.

I can't say I know what that feels like, but I'm always embarrassing myself, so welcome to the club I guess? Sara attempted to divert his wretchedness, feeling the inadequacy of her offerings as she did. She could not provide him with the absolution he was seeking; she could not allow herself to picture comforting him in a manner which would do so. They were confined by both their inexperience and all the things they didn't know about each other.

I'm sorry about blocking you. Sometimes I do things because I'm scared of what might happen if I don't. Do you know what I mean? Sorry if that doesn't make any sense.

Sara's heart now thumped with such urgency that she was certain her parents would be awoken at the other end of the corridor. There was something dangerous about the way he was unburdening himself to her, the angst and exaggerated melodrama of these revelations. It was far too easy to do through this medium, at this late hour of night when they were both ensconced in their separate bedrooms. They were play-acting intimacy without having read the script. But it was thrilling, nonetheless. She began typing a reply.

8

Abida

An unscheduled MSA meeting had been called. Abida supposed that Mustafa had, at last, made his decision to stand down and that an election would now be forthcoming. It was generally understood that Ziad would not volunteer for the job. He wouldn't believe himself capable of it; he had already proven to have a very apt grasp of his own limitations. Besides, Abida knew romance preoccupied people, blunted the once sharp edges of their ambitions. Abida was assisting Ziad and Ahlam, facilitating their meeting, which she would be chaperoning, but she knew it would detract from their ability to do anything else.

Since her discussion with the MSA girls Abida had been busy. She had contacted a psychologist, Dr Rania, whose videos on love and intimacy and assertiveness for Muslim women she had long admired. She had found an

Islamic scholar in Pennsylvania, Ustadha Halima, who specialised in traditional Islamic sources on marriage and sex and had agreed to appear via video call. She had sought out speakers who were grounded in Islamic orthodoxy – she wanted none of those whose minds she viewed as colonised and embarrassed by the tenets of their faith – and she had been pleased to find them. She had pretended that the MSA had agreed to have a conversation about sex and patriarchy. *We need to drive this conversation ourselves or white people will keep doing it for us*, she had said. When she had told Sara about what she had done, Sara shook her head and said Abida was well and truly in her renegade era.

Sara had not responded to her text message about whether she was attending the meeting, and if so, whether they could drive into university together. She and Sara lost each other occasionally in the smog of everyday life, resurfacing without explanation and talking for hours once they did. They exchanged hundreds of messages, then they did not talk at all. None of it blunted the closeness she felt to Sara. Although Abida felt that she had been at least responsible for crafting the person Sara was today, she felt, in doing so, she had imparted something of herself too. She had played at being Sara's teacher before she had known her own mind, and Sara had shaped Abida in turn.

As she waited for the train to arrive at Leumeah, Abida ensured not to make eye contact with the two white teenaged boys kicking a glass bottle back and forth with boredom and barely-disguised animal ferocity. Leumeah was not as unkempt as Lakemba or Auburn, but beneath its wide streets and yellowing fields lay a very real sense of menace which those areas, for all their stray cats and bearded loiterers, did not possess. There were still white Australians here, and they were angry at being too poor to get away from the masses of Bangladeshis who had moved into the area, lured by the promise of large blocks of land to build their mansions on for a fraction of the price of the eastern suburbs.

When the train arrived, the boys got on and sat just two places in front of her, their feet splayed across the ripped seat. Abida kept her phone in her hand, recalling the spate of recent racial vitriol on Sydney trains and buses documented on phone cameras and circulated via popular news outlets. Although she did not like conceding it, even if only to herself, she knew that some small part of her would derive perverse pleasure from being the subject of public racial abuse. Not only would it provide confirmation of her academic understanding of Australia as a racist country, but she could post about it online, maybe use it as a springboard to write for a publication lambasting Australia for its inability to curtail its fear and loathing of anyone who wasn't white. You needed a real tragedy to be heard amid the online chatter. But to her slight disappointment, the boys were far too preoccupied with lifting up their singlets and filming the results to pay her any attention. Abida plugged in her headphones and played a recitation of the Quran, leaning her head against the grimy window and closing her eyes. She felt sluggish, bereft of the usual spiritual uplift Ramadan afforded.

When she entered the musallah she was surprised to see Sara sitting alongside Ahlam and the twins, Lina and Mariam. She gave the others perfunctory kisses and squeezed her chair in beside Sara's.

'You didn't reply to my message! I didn't think you'd be here,' Abida chastised.

'I'm here now, aren't I? I must have forgotten.'

Ordinarily, Abida found Sara's plainness of speech pleasing. Other people, Muslims and non-Muslims alike, made statements they did not mean, like promising to catch up at some unspecified time in the future. Sara did not do any of that, but Abida wished that on this occasion Sara could have at least apologised, even if they both knew it was disingenuous.

Any further conversation was prevented by the appearance of Mustafa, his smile wide, his eyes grave.

'Assalamu alaykum, guys. I called this meeting to discuss a few things. First, thanks for making the time to come here on such short notice and especially during Ramadan, it's much appreciated.'

He cleared his throat. Abida attempted to catch Sara's eye and make a ghoulish face at her, but Sara was resolute in looking towards the front of the room where Mustafa stood.

'As some of you may know, I'm going to be starting full-time work shortly, which means I'll be dropping to part-time study. As we're all aware, the MSA presidency is a full-time commitment and one which requires a lot of time and energy. Unfortunately, I won't be able to give it the time and energy it deserves and since Ziad has declined to step in, our constitution states that we'll need to have an election for a new president much earlier than anticipated. But I'm giving you plenty of notice. We have the winter break coming up in a few days, which at least gives us some time to plan, and I'll be staying on until after Islamic Awareness Week.'

Ziad bowed his head, as though his declination had condemned the MSA to mutinous bedlam.

'It's been an absolute honour and privilege to have led this MSA, but its success has always been due to the quality of the brothers and sisters we have here and not any one person. I have no doubt that whoever the new president is will lead the MSA on to bigger and better things, inshaAllah.'

It was a gracious speech, but throughout it Abida had been distracted by the realisation that this was it, the juncture at which she would assume leadership. This was her opportunity to shape the conversations of the Muslim kids on campus, to mould and influence the agenda the MSA pursued with the university community and beyond. Her event was just the beginning. She could expand their consciousness beyond a narrow focus on da'wah and proving the existence of God and on to the greater Muslim world, like the faded glory of the Sokoto Caliphate in West Africa or the deadly mass deportations of the North Caucasian Muslims by Stalin during World War II. She could talk about orientalism, privilege and power and lateral violence. There was so much to absorb, so much to discuss and debate. The MSA was small beginnings, but beginnings nonetheless. Female MSA presidents were still a rarity, and she could galvanise the other girls into seizing the momentum and giving the boys a much-needed knock from their pedestal.

She was aware of Mustafa's measured voice droning on and on about a general election and candidates being required to nominate their choice of deputy by a certain date, but these logistical considerations did not interest her. The closing dua interrupted her thoughts, and even then, she did not follow the standard plea for increased knowledge, substituting it with her own private supplications. *Oh Allah, please let me be a means of bettering and reviving this ummah. Use me as an instrument of good and do not let me be led by the pursuit of worldly glory or fame.* Several young Muslim journalists, lawyers and wannabe talk show hosts had ridden on the frenzied wave of interest in all things Islam to feed their own careers, and although Abida was cognisant of her own hunger to be recognised, she loathed their cynical opportunism.

She wanted to take Sara aside and together devise a detailed plan that would see her elected, but after the meeting concluded, the MSA girls had resolved to go for a walk around Darling Harbour. Abida found it amusing how some of them were still giddy at the novelty of coming into the city, but she knew that, in several years, their trips to the city would be biannual outings on special occasions with husbands and prams in tow. The city wasn't a place for them, it was a place for towers of money and tourists, while migrant workers were tucked away deep in the bowels of restaurants and nail salons. They belonged in the suburbs, far away from the lustre of the harbour.

As they strolled around the backstreets of Chinatown towards the water, Abida spotted some of the Korean melon lollies her school friend Connie Zhou had introduced her to. She wandered inside the supermarket while the other girls stood outside, intending to stash them away for iftar and share them with her siblings. Some of the MSA girls were choosy eaters and didn't like to go inside unfamiliar supermarkets. Abida watched them, a group of girls in hijab, thinking of how scenes such as these were used as evidence to allege that Muslims didn't integrate. She decided she didn't care; the willowy blonde girls who sat together on the lawns in their identical jeans and bandeau tops were doing the same thing. It was never commented on when white people surrounded themselves with other white people, only when Muslims did it.

'It's so sad that Mustafa is going. He was such a great president,' Lina said. She wore a silvery hijab, which nicely offset the red of her eyebrows. Mariam favoured pastel shades and Abida wondered how they had demarcated their preferences on the colour spectrum. They were the only set of twins she knew. She wondered if being a twin could be effective training for marriage in learning to accommodate the whims and quirks of another human being. Over the years, she had learned to manage, cajole and supervise her younger siblings, but she did not know how to interact with them as equals.

'He really was, but I'm sure the next person will be just as good, inshaAllah.' Ahlam sounded defensive, as if anticipating that someone would mention Ziad's unwillingness to take on the role.

'It'll be Wahid's turn next. He's already spoken about it to Mustafa and I don't think any of the other boys want the job,' Mariam said.

None of them seemed to have considered the possibility that they too could stand for election. Abida decided to speak now, before the inevitability of Wahid's presidency asserted its hold in their minds. They passed the walkway into the main harbour where a man sat and played the didgeridoo, a group of tourists filming him on their phones.

'I'm thinking of running myself, actually,' Abida announced.

She had expected, even hoped for, someone to challenge her. She welcomed the prospect of arguing them all, Sara included. Abida had not yet forgiven Sara for her lack of remorse in the meeting or her lack of solicitousness on the walk to the harbour. The two of them shared a history of intimacies, but right now Sara was behaving like she was merely one of the rabble.

'Really, Abida? Would you actually want to?' Ahlam seemed perplexed.

'I think the MSA needs to take a new direction. We're part of a global ummah and it's falling apart, but all we do is sit around and have barbeques and bake sales.' Abida's tone was scornful. In truth, she enjoyed the fuzzy cuteness of the MSA bake sales, which showcased Mariam's excellent non-gelatinous version of lamingtons, but she needed to make her point somehow.

'What's wrong with the bake sales? They're one of our most popular events!' Ahlam continued, as they surveyed the boats along the harbour, the row of restaurants and bars with throngs of businessmen picking at bowls of salad and grilled fish.

'That's not what Abida means,' Sara said. 'She just means that we have more pressing problems that cupcakes aren't going to fix.'

'I'm aware of that. Just because I don't get into arguments with people about toxic masculinity and neoliberalism doesn't mean I'm some airhead. I just think it's easier for some people to point out problems constantly than to actually do anything about them,' Ahlam said.

It seemed far more conducive to good humour for everyone to focus on the scene ahead rather than respond. Abida smiled at Sara, who was shading her eyes in the sunshine. She wanted to roll her eyes and have Sara roll them in return, to exchange conspiratorial eyebrow raises. She could convince herself that she wasn't being bitchy so long as Sara joined in. But Sara was busying herself with reading a sign on the types of boat rides on offer and their respective prices, suggesting that they take a short trip across the harbour, to which the others agreed.

As they queued up, Mariam used her phone calculator to ascertain what they each would owe for a group boat trip. Abida reached for her wallet, which contained coins and a fifty dollar note Abbu had gifted her last birthday, still crisp. She placed the coins in her palm, counting the gold ones first and then the silver, down to the ten cent coins, but she was still three dollars and forty cents short of fourteen dollars.

'Don't worry about it, I've got it,' Sara said, wafting a twenty dollar note across Abida's coin stack.

'Thanks,' she muttered, not looking at Sara.

The girls boarded the boat at the end of the jetty, Lina and Mariam and Ahlam now talking about one of Lina's friends who was showing an interest in converting to Islam but whose boyfriend was a staunch atheist. The man operating the boat, handsome and young with a pomaded pencil moustache, looked at them with blatant curiosity, watching the way Abida held her skirt down as they gathered speed. The city rushed by them, the magic of its cloudless skies and clear waters – blue everywhere. There was a reason why her parents had chosen to come here, so glossy and sterile, the ugliness of its conquest washed away out of sight. But they returned to shore a few minutes later, and Abida thought again of the election, and how Wahid would be sure to garner support from all sectors of the MSA.

'I'll drive you to the station,' Sara said, wrapping her arm through Abida's as they walked. They passed a butcher's window in which ducks and chickens were strung up by hooks, grocers with rambutans and dragon fruit piled in pyramid-like formations. The two of them had walked like this so often across the playground, through the hallways and outside the freestanding classroom the teachers had allowed them to use as a prayer space. But it had been some time since they had done so, and Sara had grown even taller, so that their shoulders could no longer bump against each other's. Abida had ceased growing years ago, but she was three centimetres taller than Ammu and shorter than Abbu by just two.

They bid the others farewell and clambered into Sara's car on the far edge of campus. Once inside, Abida felt strangely shy. She wanted to be assured that Sara would support her, but she did not know how to broach the topic. In the end, Sara spoke first.

'If you're serious about running for president, then you should just do it,' Sara said. She wasn't wearing a turban again, her hijab puffed up like pizza crust in its voluminous layers around her head.

'I am serious about it,' Abida replied. 'But you know as well as I do that the boys love Wahid's weightlifting and the girls will vote for Wahid because they think he's hot, not because he'll be any good.'

She didn't really know what it was Wahid stood for, other than the fact that he had been the instigator of the high wooden screens separating the women from the men at jumuah prayers on Fridays. To her, this suggested tyranny, something to rail against.

'I don't really know too much about Wahid, but you and I both know that these things are always just popularity contests.' Sara cut in front of another car, merging lanes down the highway.

'You're right, but I'm still going to try my hardest,' Abida said, grim in her recognition of how difficult it would be.

'I'll back you all the way, you know that. Just don't get too invested in it, okay? I don't want to see you get hurt if things don't work out,' Sara replied.

It was too late for such warnings. Abida simply could not permit this opportunity to be frittered away. She would do whatever it took. This was bigger than her, bigger than the MSA. If she could dissuade Wahid from running at all, then they could bypass the cumbersome and time-consuming business of nominations and voting.

She was just about to ask Sara how she could raise this with Wahid without appearing domineering when Sara began to speak.

'Random question for you. What do you think of Naeem?' Sara stared ahead at the road, but her index finger tapped the steering wheel, once, twice.

'What do you mean, what do I think of Naeem? What's there to think about him?'

'As in, what do you think of him as a person?'

'Yeah, I figured you meant as a person. As opposed to what? Animal, vegetable, mineral?' She laughed, but Sara didn't join in. She wondered now if this was the cause for Sara's preoccupation, but she dismissed the idea as ludicrous. Sara was far too cerebral to have a crush on someone unattainable like Naeem. He was bound by prescription upon prescription, his every move curtailed by the expectations of others. She was certain that his mother would have already assembled a list of suitable candidates from the girls they deigned to socialise with. Besides, Naeem was brown and Bangladeshi and Sara was not. These were indisputable facts. Those who said they did not see colour were simply holding their hands over their eyes. She had assumed Sara would marry closer to the age of thirty, barefoot on a beach somewhere to a white convert, or someone born Muslim but whiteish, like a Turk or Bosnian. Maroof had once dated a Turkish girl at university; Abida had helped him compose messages to her, advised him on what brand of perfume to buy her.

'You know what I mean,' Sara said.

'I really don't. Please don't tell me you're about to confess that you're in love with him, or even worse, that you think I should get with him?'

'Is he really such a bad guy?'

'No, he's a nothing guy. One of those guys who never says anything interesting and never puts a toe out of line or Mummy will step in. The only thing I can say about him is that, aside from that one time, he does recite the Quran really nicely.'

'He does, doesn't he?'

They had arrived at the station and Sara pulled over. Abida looked at her and read her hesitation in the feigned distraction.

'You know you can tell me anything, right?'

Sara nodded. Abida knew this was what the delineations of friendship demanded, this profession of a space that was snug and devoid of judgement, but she was afraid of what Sara might reveal, and how this revelation would alter the fundamental parameters of their friendship. For all these years, they had been on the same trajectory, traversing each step into adulthood concurrently. They had gotten their period the same year, just before their thirteenth birthdays. They had the same friends at school and they had chosen different courses at the same university. But if Sara liked Naeem and Naeem liked Sara, Sara would proceed where Abida could not follow, into the realm of those whose feelings ran beyond reason or duty.

'Maybe you should get with him after all,' Sara said. 'You're always matchmaking everyone, it's time someone repaid the favour.'

They both laughed now, conscious that they were skirting around something unsaid. It was a heavy and physical presence sitting between them. Abida knew that if she pushed just a little harder, Sara would relent and tell her whatever it was. But she didn't feel equipped to process it just yet. Ordinarily, she had no trouble facing uncomfortable truths, but certain truths were sacred: her faith in Allah and His commands, her knowledge of power and race and class, and her faith in Sara. She leaned over and kissed Sara's cheek, catching her familiar scent of almond before unfastening her seatbelt and getting out of the car, still smiling at Sara's uncharacteristic suggestion, before running at full speed towards the platform where the train awaited.

9

Naeem

Several hours after his wondrous conversation with Sara, Naeem had been awoken by Ammu for sehri. He did not enjoy forcing himself to eat in the early hours of the morning, but Meherin enforced the pre-dawn meal with the fanaticism of a drill sergeant. She could not tolerate her children going without food or drink with only the previous night's meal as sustenance, despite the Australian fasting days being many hours shorter than those in the Northern Hemisphere. She had embarrassed Tasnia by not allowing her to fast the entire month until the previous year, when all her classmates at King Abdullah College had been fasting since they were six or seven.

Naeem managed to down three Weet-Bix with luke-warm milk under Ammu's watchful eye, trying to hug the magic of last night to his body, but the glaring lights of the dining room and Tasnia's slurping soon eroded any trace of it. By unspoken mutual agreement, no attempts at conversation were made; they were all too sleepy and cantankerous. The house's efficient central heating system meant that it was never cold inside, but the particles on the window attested to the cold outside they would all have to face in just a few hours. Professor Kazi, in his waffle gown and slippers, pushed a boiled egg around on his plate in a vague approximation of eating. Naeem suspected his father did not enjoy sehri any more than he did, but it was far easier to comply with Meherin's wishes than to raise objections. He suspected that Meherin was aware of her family's lack of enthusiasm, but was satisfied with the outward perform-ance of duty, picking up Professor Kazi's plate from in front of him and scooping the egg into her mouth, whole.

After praying fajr, Naeem fell back asleep, a heavy slumber without dreams. When he woke up once again, it was almost noon and he had missed his morning lectures. He was annoyed but unconcerned, knowing that his success in his studies lay, for the most part, in his ability to memorise large chunks from textbooks and regurgitate them at will. He checked his phone and saw that Sara had sent him a message over two hours ago, asking how he was. He read the message three times, noting his grip tighten over the phone. Thoughts of Sara had long ceased to be an analytical exercise; he now experienced them as a physical sensation, an insistent rumble inside a body emptied of all food and drink. Naeem thought this portentous, but he was determined not to abscond this time. He whispered a bismillah, and typed, still sprawled in bed.

Salam, Sara, it's so nice to hear from you. I'm great, alhamdulillah, how about you?

When she did not reply at once, Naeem despaired, his fingers slackening their white-knuckled grip on the phone. He had not bothered to sound nonchalant, like he spoke to girls at 3 am all the time. He exited the message, navigating to his Quran app and letting its words engulf him. It eased his anxieties, as it always did. He did not so much read as allow the words to dissolve onto his tongue like fairy floss. But within minutes, a reply from Sara popped up on his screen, which his fingers swiped across greedily.

I'm also great, alhamdulillah. Are you tired after our chat last night?

They were only words on a screen, but he imagined Sara smiling, a little bit bashful. He had permitted himself a comprehensive scan of her photos last night for the first time. Her eyes were not the leafy green his imagination had rendered them, but a catlike brown-green which appeared somewhat at odds with the soft pliability of the rest of her features. He could understand how others would declare such a face plain, but its very simplicity appealed to him. He was gratified that her posts displayed good sense and a certain level of restraint. Sara's few photos were mostly travel snaps, angled, sometimes blurry, shots of unnamed foreign markets and squares. This also impressed him, as he often thought that the main reason people travelled was to be photographed in front of recognisable landmarks, and to have those photographs plastered all over other people's social media feeds. Living my best life, making memories. These were the phrases used by people of his age, masking the constant fear that someone, somewhere, was having more fun.

Better now that I'm hearing from you. But I'm not tired, don't worry!

Don't get ahead of yourself, mate, I never said I was worried. She followed up with a winking emoji.

Oh, so we're in emoji territory already, Naeem thought, grinning, turning to the wall and cradling his phone against it. *What are you up to, anyway?*

I'm in a statistics tutorial, dying of boredom. My friend Ravi is actually snoring a little bit next to me, that's how boring it is.

Naeem was stung by her offhand mention of a male friend, hypocritical and petty as he knew it was. He did not consider any of the female peers in his medical degree to be his friends. He was respected, even admired, for his academic prowess, but he was not labelled a friend in the way people who got drunk together were. The Bangladeshi girls he knew were the secret girlfriends of his male friends, and the MSA girls were just faces he avoided looking at beyond what was required.

When he did not reply, she began again. *Well, he's not really a friend, just one of the hundreds of guys I'm surrounded by as a girl in mechanical engineering. So, what are you doing?*

She had interpreted his silence correctly and was attempting to placate him. He did not want her to feel she had to justify any part of herself. That was a public exercise; he wanted her private, uncensored self.

I'm still in bed, actually. Is that terrible? he replied.

No, it's not, you lucky thing. It's so cold today, I wish I was in bed too.

At these words, his penis darted up expectantly, as if summoned. Naeem stared down at the bulge in his pants, appalled at the acuteness of his lust, whose comparative nonexistence he had so prided himself on. He typed a quick *gotta go, talk to you later*, then buried his phone under his fluffy eiderdown and ran downstairs, the house vast and empty and smelling of furniture polish and coriander. A drive would settle his nerves, assuage his lower self, his nafs. He rummaged around for his keys, picked up a laundered jumper from the latest round Najwa had done and went out to his car, his nose dripping from the jolt of cold air.

As Naeem had anticipated, the unceasing stream of traffic forced him to focus. He drove without aim at first, then towards King Abdullah College in Burwood, where Tasnia would be finishing school in an hour. His parents entrusted school drop-offs and pick-ups to a Bangladeshi family who lived in a neighbouring suburb and whose two children also attended King Abdullah College. There was a train station two blocks away, but Meherin did not believe public transport was safe or hygienic. The only time they caught the train was to watch fireworks displays in the city with other Bangladeshi families, their bags stuffed with plastic containers of pre-prepared sandwiches and fruit juice poppers for the children.

Naeem parked in front of the school, which he had not visited since his graduation two years earlier. His Quran teacher Shaykh Hassan kept asking him to visit and he had been invited to man a stall at their careers fair last year, which heavily promoted medicine and other sciences, but he had declined. In their estimation, Naeem had achieved the ultimate feat in securing a place in a medical degree. Their teachers had pushed them to be academic superstars, upstanding citizens, helpers of beleaguered old ladies with shopping; they had to be seen to earn their place in a country that was not their own, despite what their passports said. But he could not in good conscience stand before students and glibly advise them to follow their passions, nor could he tell the truth and advise them to just do whatever their parents thought they should do.

Naeem heard the school bell ring and waved as he saw Tasnia emerge, her face crestfallen at the sight of him. The Bangladeshi family she was dropped off by had a shaggy-haired son, Sabir, who was in the year above her. Nevertheless, she recovered quickly, recounting a long and elaborate blow-by-blow account of a goal she had scored in soccer and how Hatice Keskin, her Turkish Cypriot best friend and occasional arch-nemesis, had labelled her a dumb bitch for not passing earlier. Naeem managed a few appreciative ooohs and ahhhs, but Tasnia sensed his preoccupation, falling silent and placing her feet, shoes and socks discarded, on the dashboard.

Naeem did not want to tempt himself by returning to his bedroom, where his phone still lay tucked under the covers. Instead, he busied himself with unnecessary tasks around the kitchen: wiping down clean surfaces, reshuffling cutlery in drawers. When Meherin arrived, bearing packaged samosas and parathas, she immediately retreated to her room due to a headache, which he knew was real because she hadn't bothered to wait for him to display any sympathy. Professor Kazi arrived soon after, and together they heated the samosas in silence and reheated yesterday's pulao on the stovetop.

The front doorbell rang, an insistently upbeat musical jangle Naeem's parents had been proud of when it had first been installed just over a year ago, but which now made all of them wince.

'That'll be Chachi and Chacha. Get the door, won't you?'

Neither Professor Kazi nor Meherin had mentioned that they were expecting guests, but this was in keeping with their general attitude that children did not need to be informed of their parents' plans. This was dressed up and reframed as a kind of casual, family-first brand of congeniality, but Naeem recognised it for what it was. On this occasion, however, he was pleased at the prospect of seeing his cousin Sadia.

Chachi and Chacha bounded into the house, Sadia trailing several steps behind with a box of jelebi. Chachi sniffed the air, dog-like, before proceeding into the kitchen, seizing the pair of tongs from Professor Kazi's hand and swishing the puddle of oil around in the pan. Professor Kazi's expression was neutral, but Naeem suspected he did not like Chachi behaving in such a proprietary manner. Much of Naeem's upbringing had been a schooling about putting objects and behaviours and even people in the correct place, except that what constituted the correct place in one setting could be entirely different in another. It was not so much outright fakery as permitting many different selves to coexist within the same body, ready and poised to be assumed when necessary. In this way, his parents did not have to pretend to be devout Muslims, nor did Professor Kazi feign his man-about-town bonhomie; he simply saw little utility in extending any of it to the family unit.

Meherin appeared, her eyes bloodshot, but otherwise composed. They partook in their iftar, the radio blaring with the adhan. The first bite into a date seemed to drop right into the pit of his stomach, filling it with a burst of warmth.

'I think I'll go to Lakemba mosque tonight for taraweeh,' Naeem said, attempting to appear only mildly interested. He had learned long ago that his parents did not like it if their children were invested in an idea prior to their approval being sought.

Neither Meherin nor Professor Kazi glanced up from their heaped plates of rice, mashing the grains into balls with their fingers and scooping the assembled piles into their mouths. He and Tasnia used forks and spoons, more out of ineptitude than ideological opposition to eating with their hands, and their parents indulged their choice as a marker of their own tolerance. Naeem wondered if Sara knew how to eat with her hands, or if she was one of those people who used a knife and fork to carve up a slice of pizza.

'Eh, boy, you don't want to be in the mosque with the smelly old uncles, with their short pants and food getting caught in their beards. Especially not Lakemba, with all of those Arabs,' Chachi said, miming a beard with the aid of two fists jammed under the jowls of her chin. While observant of religious fundamentals, Chachi possessed a deep-held suspicion of the outward symbols of religion, notwithstanding her daughter's hijab. She was an admirer of Sheikh Hasina and the Awami League in a kind of garbled attempt at feminism, sidestepping the fact that Hasina only led the country because her father had before her and that she jailed anyone who opposed her rule. But Chachi's antics were not without their uses; outside opposition was sure to galvanise his parents into acceptance.

'You go ahead, Rocket, and make dua for us while you're there. Now, who wants tea?' Meherin began collecting their dirty plates, a signal that the conversation was not to be continued. Without prompting, Sadia rose and went to the stovetop to commence brewing their tea, Naeem following behind her.

'How are you always so nice? Tell me your secret, please,' he said.

Sadia swirled the pot around, the air fragrant with cloves and cinnamon. Even though she was twenty-nine, she had the face of a schoolgirl, rotund and smiley, but her judicious manner was exactly what you would expect from a pharmacist.

'I'm not, Rocket. I just know when to pick my battles, that's all. What's been happening with you?'

'Not much. How did the meeting with that last guy go?'

'Let's just say I don't think there will be a second meeting. The guy admitted he only prays when he feels like it and that he thinks girls in hijab need to, and I quote, "loosen up". Honestly, I don't know where my mum finds some of these guys.'

Chachi had entered the kitchen and overheard Sadia's last sentence; she sighed against the clang of scraped plates and walked away. Her elder child, Faheem, had made an advantageous match with the daughter of an Awami League stalwart and had then relocated to Dubai on an engineering contract procured by his wife's uncle. Chachi had believed she would be joining them soon thereafter, but it had been four years and Sadia was still unmarried, Chachi's suitcase remaining unused in the cupboard behind the stairs.

'You should stop going along to these meetings,' Naeem said. 'These guys are losers and you are so much better than all of them.'

'I don't enjoy it, but I do want someone to share things with and I don't really know how else it's going to happen. Family and friends are nice to spend time with, but then they go home and plan their life with someone else. You know what I mean? I know you're still young but you're old enough to understand.'

'I do know what you mean.'

Naeem longed to trill Sara's name, to tell Sadia that this elation was unlike any he had experienced. He knew she would listen without reproach. But she would also ask when he would want to marry Sara and when he would be speaking to his parents about her. This, he thought, and not abstaining from drinking alcohol or eating pork, was what really distinguished Muslims from non-Muslims: everything a Muslim did was permeated with a sense of urgency. They were mindful that the life of this world was temporal and the life of the hereafter infinite, and it showed in everything they did. They didn't do gap years, they didn't go off and try to find themselves or live in a shared house at the age of thirty. Everything counted, every action had consequences.

'Oh, you do? This sounds interesting.' Sadia raised her eyebrow, pouring the tea into a row of mugs.

'I will, when there's something to tell. But I'd better get going, it's a long drive to the mosque.' Naeem smiled and almost went to hug her goodbye, but cousins could marry, and people who could marry could not touch each other. Neither set of parents would mind if they did; he knew they deemed it odd and overzealous that Sadia did not remove her hijab in his presence.

Lakemba Mosque was not smelly, but it was crowded with people of all descriptions, such as those sitting in Naeem's row: a tall Black man with a toddler son who sat admirably still, a teenage boy with dyed reddish streaks running through his spiked hair, an elderly man with a professorial beard who was helped into a chair by the teenage boy. Naeem thought often in moments like this of how vulnerable they all were, how anyone who despised them could walk right into the mosque and shoot the place up like they had in Christchurch. He assessed the closest exit point, then pressed his face to the carpet to distract himself.

Once the prayers began, his fears dissipated in this rapture, his soul elevated to where all was right. Here, he spoke to Allah and he felt Allah speaking to him through His Book and His Love. One set, then another, hands and forehead to the ground, stand back up again. He lost count of how many sets they had performed, aware only of the melody of the imam's recitation, his own tongue whispering along the words so familiar and dear to him.

Outside, it was all fuss and beaming headlights, the beeping of horns and people congregating in groups across the middle of the road despite the queue of cars attempting to depart. The rapture died and the temporal came to the fore again. He thought of Sara and what she was doing at this moment. Naeem sat in his car, rolled the window down and reached for his phone. This was the worst possible time to be doing this, just as he was departing the mosque, but he had to send Sara a message. He began typing.

We should both take some time out to focus on Ramadan, but what do you say we meet up once it's over?

He deleted the message, then retyped it and hit the send button, just as the traffic began flowing again and he could drive back towards home.

10

Sara

The night of power is superior to a thousand months.
The verse was a reminder to heed the last ten nights of Ramadan, for no one could be certain which of the odd nights laylatul qadr would fall on. The strongest evidence suggested it fell on the twenty-seventh night, and so, on this night mosques overflowed with those in search of absolution and the granting of the most secret of desires. The angels were said to descend, the barrier between the divine and the earthly rendered penetrable. Even the most indifferent and sceptical of believers were not immune to its sway; they would enter the mosque and press their humbled faces to its floors in sujud before departing, never to enter its doors again until the subsequent Ramadan arrived.

No two mosques undertook their laylatul qadr liturgies in the same way. Some favoured long, sobbing duas, invoking Allah to extend His mercy to all suffering Muslims, from the Uyghurs to the Rohingya to the Palestinians, while others fostered a more upbeat, almost celebratory atmosphere, distributing food packages filled with sugary treats. Sara's parents favoured the small, homely mosque run by Bosnian Muslims in the nearby suburb of Penshurst as their laylatul qadr venue of choice. Abida had joked that it was because Bosnians were the closest Muslims came to being white and Sara would fit right in. Sara had marked the previous laylatul qadr with Abida and her two younger sisters at a mosque in Bankstown, and although she would not have conceded it, had deemed the heaving masses of people and frenetic crying fits too overwhelming to attempt again.

'What do you think of my abaya?' Soraya appeared at Sara's door, donning a black abaya with butterfly sleeves her sister in Cape Town had gifted her.

'It's nice, Ma. But you know the Bosnians wouldn't care if you rocked up in jeans anyway.'

Sara sometimes tired of her mother's vanities, inserting malicious asides into their conversations then admonishing herself when Soraya brushed right over them. She could not tell if Soraya did this because she was patient or because she simply didn't notice, but it amounted to the same thing: her mother was a much nicer person than she was.

'Could you take a photo of me in it so I can send it to Aunty Ayesha? I kept telling her I'd wear it and I haven't up until now.' Soraya handed Sara her iPhone. Sara's mother possessed a childlike love for gadgets and her phone was always the latest model and her messages jam-packed with emojis.

'Sure, just stand a bit to the left. Why don't we get Dad to come in the photo too?'

'Because Dad will ruin the photo, that's why.' Amin's thickset figure appeared from around the corner, pouncing on Soraya from behind, who giggled and mock-pushed him away. Sara's annoyance returned as she snapped a photo and passed the phone back to Soraya. Her parents didn't know how to behave with any level of propriety. It was the most sacred night of the year, and they were engrossed in their silly posturing and posing. They car-danced to the Bee Gees on road trips and watched reality television. She much preferred the stoicism of Abida's parents, their dedication to their faith and their children.

The mosque was walking distance from their house but Soraya said they would drive. Sara continued to sulk in the car while Soraya and Amin chatted about Aunty Ayesha's upcoming birthday party in Cape Town and whether they could video call in. They asked her if she wanted to go to South Africa after her final exams and when she said she didn't care, they could go alone, they laughed and said they could but they'd have a lot more fun with her there. Sara's parents feigned obliviousness to her shifting moods, which forced Sara to dissipate them in a fit of remorse. *Heaven lies under the feet of mothers.* She was not the daughter she ought to be. She needed to repent, commit to improvement of the self. As they walked into the mosque, Sara grabbed Soraya's peachy-scented hand and held it in hers as they parted with Amin at the men's entrance.

The women's section was half-full at most. Most of the women were elderly babushka types, with thick woollen socks, indeterminately shaped floral skirts and silk scarves knotted under their chins. There was a thin smattering of thirty-something women with young children in tow, but just one or two girls Sara's age. Across the room, Sara watched her father enter the mosque and sit down next to a man with a furry kufi atop his head, his gnarled fingers clasping a set of prayer beads. She enjoyed peeping through to the men's side, something she was not able to do in many mosques due to the thick partitions and sectioned-off rooms. She did not object to the partitions and the cosy femaleness it allowed for, but she found it far easier to follow what the imam was doing when she could see him. Many mosques now had video cameras installed in the men's section to allow for this, which provided occasional moments of comic relief when someone did not realise they were on camera and began scratching at some body part.

Following the standard set of taraweeh prayers, a group of young children dressed in sparse laundered tunics assembled in the empty space between the men and women. They began singing in Bosnian, a mournful tune, not the cheesy Allah-loves-you children's fare Sara had been anticipating. Soraya was recording it on her phone, whole tufts of her dyed hair creeping out from underneath her loosely coiled hijab, much like the Iranian women Sara had seen on television. She wondered where the men and women her own age were in this community, if the children were mourning their absence and were soon to join them in their secret hideout. Perhaps their parents encouraged their absence, confident in the knowledge that they would have plenty of time to repent and thumb prayer beads with rheumatic fingers.

The children sung one more song, a faster, more spirited song in the same unfamiliar curvature of their mother tongue. They did a pretty little curtsey before running to their mothers and fathers, zooming between and across the gender divide as if it did not exist. Such things were adult concerns, adults with their fixation on lines and borders. At least children marked their possessions with less officiousness. Sara had not had to learn to share; the closest she had come to a sibling were the many miscarriages Soraya had endured. She reached for Soraya's hand again, thinking of Naeem. She thought of who their children would resemble, whether they would inherit her stubby toes, what the median point of her mousey hair and Naeem's black hair would be.

It was laylatul qadr; she could call upon Allah and He would be nearer than ever. Would it be so terrible to trouble Allah about a boy? Her requests of Him had so far been minimal: passing an exam, increased patience in her dealings with her mother. It did not concern her whether these requests were granted or not, as the very act of asking delegated the outcome to Him. Too many people mistook religion as a contractual relationship: ask and you shall receive, perform certain acts and reap certain rewards. To Sara, this was sheer arrogance, to think that God's reason for being was to simply hold up His end of the deal. It was much easier to be a believer once you understood that He owed you absolutely nothing.

Sara cupped her hands in front of her and spoke into them. She told Allah that she thought she was falling in love, that she wasn't sure if it was love because she had never experienced it before.

She had cut her nails too short so that her fingertips smarted when she touched anything and the crease between her thumb and index finger was a mottled grey due to her indifference to moisturising, but she could at least align her fingers, pinkie to pinkie. She called upon Him by her favourite name, Al Samad. On the MSA group chat, Ahlam had asked once which of the ninety-nine names of Allah everyone liked best, and most people had come up with fluffy ones like Al Kareem, the Generous, or Al Mujeeb, the Answerer of Prayers, but she valued His all-encompassing strength most of all.

When she raised her head, she saw that there was cake being passed around. She was handed a large piece in a napkin by one of the singing girls, her tunic now strewn with syrupy crumbs.

'Thanks. I really liked your singing!' The girl chuckled in response, revealing a tongue rendered blue by some sucking lolly, before moving on to the next person.

'She's a beautiful girl, isn't she?' Soraya broke off a piece of the cake, a semolina concoction coated in icing sugar and desiccated coconut.

'I suppose so,' she said. Her mother was forever commenting on people's appearances, not with malice or judgement, but with almost unthinking appraisal, regardless of how she felt about the person in question. Saying Aunty Ayesha was pudgy did not in any way diminish Soraya's regard for her, but that same regard was not enough to compel her silence.

She sent Abida a message and Abida responded with a video of a man flipping a slice of knafeh in the air, the strands of vermicelli and cheese oozing as he poured sugar syrup over it. The next video panned to the crowd of people around the stall with the caption,

Check it out, the Ramadan markets have officially been colonised by all these white people. Come rescue me, girl.

Sara kissed her mother on the cheek and asked if they'd be okay to walk home while she took the car. Soraya nodded and Sara walked to the car alone. She drove for some minutes until she was close to Lakemba. The streets surrounding Lakemba were full, cars parked and double-parked across driveways. After several minutes of circling she found a spot and began walking towards Haldon Street. The street was smoky from the streetside kebab stalls and lined with people despite the lateness of the hour, the bins crammed with styrofoam boxes and plastic bottles. She followed the map Abida had sent her and eventually found her at the bridge overlooking the train station, surrounded by a family with two prams and four children, the father holding up his phone as he showed the crowds to whoever he was speaking to.

'This is even crazier than last year,' she said, her body pressed against Abida's as the mother pushed the pram past them and through the crowd.

'I told you, all the white people have found out about it now. That's what happens when they start advertising it as a "cultural experience" on *Broadsheet* or whatever they read. See, look over there, those guys could not get any more peak inner west,' Abida said, pointing to a group of men. One wore a vintage camera around his neck, his beard the same shade of chestnut as his hair.

'You're right, they're everywhere.' Sara looked around for a pathway through the crowd and they began to walk in the middle of the road, where it had been closed off to cars.

'They made fun of our stinky food and our ethnic ghettoes for years and now they want a piece of it. Could not get any more ironic.'

Abida began to warm up to her theme; she seldom required much encouragement to get going. She spoke for several minutes more about how white people enjoyed watching them like lions in an enclosure, but only at a distance they could safely retreat from. She pointed out each white person as she saw them, assigning them names that grew more theatrical as she went along. Olivia, James, Bartholomew Howard the Second, Henrietta Fitzherbert Montague. Sara laughed as she bought them a camel burger and a sugarcane juice from one stall, a roti and shami kebab from another. They sat on the footpath together, next to the numerous police vans and began to eat.

'Oh look, there's some of the MSA boys,' Abida said. She tore into the roti, scooping up the kebab and rolling it in coriander chutney before placing it in her mouth.

Sara looked up from her burger and stifled a sharp intake of breath. She took a sip from the sugarcane juice and the saccharine liquid on her tongue was soothing. On the other side of the road, in a puffy black jacket and a kufi on his head, was Naeem. He was walking alongside Mustafa and Wahid and several other boys she recognised from MSA events.

'Should we go say hi? I wouldn't mind talking to Mustafa about the structure of the colonialism debate,' Abida continued. She got up from the footpath, placing the roti tray under her arm as she reached for her bag.

'I'll stay here and mind our food,' Sara said quickly. She would not know how to interact with Naeem with so many people around them. The thing between them was too fragile, too new, for any acknowledgement of it to be made. But it was too late. Mustafa had already seen them and waved as he started walking in their direction. Sara stood up.

'Assalamu alaykum, sisters, how are you doing? What food did you get? Give us some recommendations please,' Mustafa said. He was smiling at them, his hand placed over his heart in greeting.

'Wa alaykum salam. The roti and shami kebab is awesome. Highly recommend,' Abida said.

Naeem was standing slightly behind Mustafa, together with Wahid. His hand raised and fell in a gesture which might have been a wave or simply swatting at something buzzing adjacent to his head. Wahid whispered something in Naeem's ear and pulled out his phone, which they both looked at. Sara had not expected any special gesture from him but she felt disappointed nevertheless. He was in front of her, close enough to reach out and burrow her hand in the billow of his jacket, but he was wholly inaccessible.

'Good to know,' Mustafa said. 'We might go check it out now. Enjoy the rest of the night, ladies.' He nodded and smiled at them again before walking towards the stalls.

'God,' Abida said, 'he always makes the other boys look like the socially inept weirdos they are. Would it kill Wahid and Naeem just to be normal and polite for once?' She reached for the sugarcane juice Sara had been drinking, sucking the last of the liquid noisily through the straw.

'I'll get another one, this one's finished,' Abida said. She walked past a group of teenage girls in avocado-patterned oodies towards the sugarcane stall, and Sara watched her go, trying to focus on the waves of people around her and not where Naeem had gone.

Her phone vibrated in her pocket. Naeem had sent her a message, saying he was sorry that he couldn't have said hi and spoken to her, that it was so good to see her and that it had made his night. *It had made his night.* She read the message once, twice, again and again. There was nothing contrived about the words he had written. He was not trying to play it cool; he trusted that she would not think less of him for it. He had apologised unprompted for not being able to speak to her and, in his haste, he had missed a space between the words 'my' and 'night'. The mere sight of her had affected him, and she hugged the knowledge of it to her chest, a festooned trophy she would stash away until it could be displayed. Her phone vibrated again. He had sent a date and time in a week's time and asked if it suited her to meet him then.

It was still laylatul qadr for seven more minutes. She pressed her hands together and whispered a prayer to Allah to thank Him for all the blessings He had bestowed upon her, to ask Him for forgiveness for any sins she had committed, but most of all, to quicken the days and hours until she would see Naeem again. She was wiping her hands across her face just as Abida returned with the juice in hand, exclaiming that she had just seen a well-known influencer filming herself dancing next to the knafeh man.

11

Abida

Abida had selected her clothing with care, donning a polka-dotted blouse she had fished out of a Zara sale bin, a stiff black skirt from a Muslim-friendly store in Lakemba, and a blazer she had borrowed from one of her family friends who worked at Ernst & Young. Still, the effect was less than pleasing: the blouse would not remain tucked in the skirt, the blazer was too broad across the shoulders and the skirt too fitted at the hem, requiring her to take tiny steps like some snobby debutante. She was grateful for the jacket, ill-fitting as it was; it concealed the sweaty patches that had accumulated under her armpits. Most of the clothing in her wardrobe did not fit well, but she had so wanted to make a good impression for this interview. The future MSA president was not unemployed; the future MSA president had plans and spreadsheets and their shit together.

Connie had provided her with the address for Carrington Feltham Emery, but the buildings on Pitt Street were all a similar boxy grey. Abida did not come into the business district of the city often and felt disoriented by the height of the buildings and the lack of obvious signage. She paused in the doorway of a building to search for the address on her phone but moved away with alacrity after realising the building was a hotel by the hour. While she wasn't priggish about sex, she did not like being so close to the building, as if she could be infected by the immediacy of its activities. She knew this was nonsensical, but these aversions could not be shaken off with ease, in the same way she felt her stomach contract with instinctive disgust when she smelled bacon being cooked. Religion was transmitted through text and speech, but it could only really be understood inside the body.

Abida located the correct building with two minutes to spare, an unimpressive blocky structure six storeys high with a bright, unmanned foyer. She studied her reflection in the elevator, applying chapstick to her cracking lips, and was still absorbed in the examination of a fresh pimple when the door opened to the fourth floor. She turned around and walked out onto the landing, hoping no one had seen. A receptionist with auburn hair swept into a raised bun sat at the front desk, staring at her screen and typing. A vase of indifferently arranged flowers sat on the counter in front of her, emitting no fragrance but injecting colour into the palette of beige and grey.

'Good morning, I'm here for the paralegal interview?' Her voice sounded unfamiliar to her own ears, diffident and squeaky.

'Hi there, just take a seat and I'll let Mr Emery know you're here.' The receptionist smiled, but its toothy radiance was general rather than specific, sweeping right over Abida, the couch and flowers, and back towards the computer screen.

To alleviate her nerves, Abida picked up a newspaper from the pile atop the circular glass table. The headline was about refugees on Manus Island staging a protest against the conditions of their detention, an issue she had been following with keen interest and posting about online, but she did not want to appear to be too interested, not here. She placed it down and picked up one of the financial papers instead.

'Ms Hoque? I'm Steve Emery, nice to meet you.' He was a tall man, well over six foot, his body crumpling in half to extend his hand to hers. Abida reached out and took it. She could count on one hand the number of times she had shaken a man's hand: her school principal, when he had presented her with her graduation certificate; two boys in her Foundations of Law tutorial who had seemed to go out of their way to shake her hand despite her attempts to wave at them across the table.

Abida followed Steve through a maze of desks and cubicles before they arrived at a room with frosted glass walls and a large rectangular table laid out with notepads and a jug of water. He indicated for her to take a seat opposite him, which she did, attempting to clutch the end of her skirt underneath her so that it wouldn't catch.

'One of my fellow partners here, Caroline Feltham, will be joining us shortly, but I'd like to get started. Could you tell me a bit about yourself? Let me pour you some water first.'

Steve chuckled, which Abida returned with a smile and a brief outline of her credentials, her participation in a moot tournament during the previous semester and her distinction average. She paused and sipped from her glass. Although the month of Ramadan was ongoing, she had her period and had decided that she would eat in public this year, despite the ongoing debate about whether Muslim women were advertising their menstrual cycle by doing so. She tried not to gawp at the chunky gold band on Steve's finger; Muslim men were prohibited from wearing gold jewellery, and she did not think it looked very good against the thickness of his fingers.

'Well, let me also tell you a bit about our firm. We're small, but we do a wide variety of work here: property, commercial disputes, a bit of industrial relations and intellectual property. There are four partners including myself, and sixteen solicitors. We like to have a bit of a laugh as we get our work done.'

'Unfortunately, I don't think a sense of humour seems to be a common trait among law students.'

Steve chuckled again. He had a heavy dusting of freckles across his cheeks and nose, seeming to suggest afternoons on a sailboat, something the North Shore kids at university spoke about when Abida asked them about their weekends.

'I guess things haven't changed much since my day then. So you're in your second year of studies?'

'Yes, and I'm taking Property Law this semester actually, so I'm getting up-to-speed with all the reforms to the *Real Property Act*.'

Steve nodded in approval just as a woman walked into the room.

'Sorry to barge in so late! Hi, Abida. I'm Caroline Feltham, one of the partners here.'

Caroline's hand was warm against hers, gripping it tighter than Steve had before releasing it. At least she was a woman and Abida did not have to reproach herself for the physical contact. She had observed women like Caroline before, women of an uncertain middling age in sleeveless shift dresses and round-toed nude pumps, with manicured toenails and fingernails. Abida had buffed her nails with care prior to leaving the house, but the edges were short and unvarnished as always, since wudu could not be performed over polish. There had been a burst of breathable nail polishes appearing on the market of late, which bemused sales assistants who served the bevy of Muslim women who purchased them in every shade.

'Nice to meet you, Caroline.'

Caroline smiled, but, as with the receptionist, the smile was brief and ambiguous in its aim.

'We're pretty informal here at Carrington Feltham Emery, as you've probably gathered from Steve. We like to maintain a collegiate atmosphere.'

There was something in the word *collegiate* which smarted, but Abida could not quite discern why. She crossed her legs and attempted to relax her back into the chair.

'So, Abida, what makes you want to work here with us?'

Abida had conducted research on the firm, memorising the names and facts of two of the cases they had been involved in this year, which she had found by trawling through pages of Google results. She regurgitated these with deliberate emphasis, taking care not to waffle and to make eye contact with both Steve and Caroline.

'Well, that's certainly very impressive,' Steve said. His manner was still affable, but his gaze was directed towards his notepad and the jug of water on the table.

'Yes, very impressive. We like that you've taken such an interest in our work. Tell me, Abida, do you have any lawyers in the family?' Caroline continued to smile, the pearls in her ears catching the light as she turned in her chair.

'No, I don't actually. My older brother is studying accounting, though.'

'I see. Well, I think we're about done. We'll have a look through your academic transcript and get back to you by close of business on Friday.'

It seemed appropriate to stand. There was more shaking of hands, flashes of teeth and the reordering of chairs against the plush carpet.

Caroline escorted her to the door, Steve having retreated somewhere back into the maze of desks.

'It was great to meet you, Abida,' Caroline said. 'You have a lovely name, where is it from?'

'My parents came to Australia from Bangladesh, actually.' She hated that she spoke in this way, the demarcation it signalled between parent and child. They had gone to, so that she could come from, except that it hadn't worked: no one thought she was from Sydney anyway.

'Ah, I see. I can't say I know much about Bangladesh, but my husband and I were in India a few years ago and we had such a wonderful time. Such a fascinating country. Well, you have a good day then, Abida.' Caroline gestured with a smooth flick of her hand that it was time for Abida to depart, and Abida found herself in the elevator, still unsure of what had transpired but certain that she had missed something of note in the exchange.

She felt she had earned something greasy and disgusting to eat. She walked down Pitt Street, past a comic book store and a Thai grocer and a sushi train restaurant before arriving at a sprawling underground food court below a department store. She spotted an Oporto, which she knew stocked halal chicken, and ordered herself a double burger meal with a can of Solo. She thought the Indian boy serving looked at her with curiosity, but upon inspection his nametag said Mahesh – not something recognisably Muslim. He probably knew enough to realise that it was still Ramadan and that a girl in hijab was not supposed to be eating in the middle of the day.

It was not time for lunch, but the food court was so crowded that Abida was forced to take her tray and sit opposite a man in a suit who was eating a bowl of wonton soup. Although she would have preferred having a table to herself, she was relieved that she would not have to eat her meal in the company of someone eating a kale salad or one of those overpriced yogurt boxes with clumps of muesli strewn through it. She checked her phone and saw a message from Dr Rania confirming the first panel discussion question on the development of the brain in late adolescence and how this differed for men and women. This would then follow on with a discussion about the discourse on sexual intimacy for men and women and traditional Islamic sources covering the issue.

She was particularly pleased with the question she had devised on navigating Muslim dating apps as a woman; she had heard stories from the older MSA girls about the gross men on there and was keen to hear more. She typed out a quick reply to confirm, then reached for her food.

She bit into her burger and felt a glob of mayonnaise run down her chin. Abida left it there for a moment longer than necessary, savouring the deliberate look of disinterest the man in the suit had adopted and replaying the conversation she had just had. She had not been called any names or been sworn at, like her mother had been several years ago by a man in the supermarket. She had not been spat on, like Ahlam had narrated in tears at the beginning of the year, nor had she been mocked or insulted or even stared at, the most benign of behaviours she had come to anticipate. She could not fashion the incident into something for her friends to rally around and share online, the way they did whenever politicians said something galling about Muslims. In fact, there was nothing overtly sinister about what had happened at all, except that she had been rendered so compliant, so eager to please these people and appear unruffled by their questioning.

Even the question about her background, one Abida was accustomed to and irritated by, had not caused her to divert from her bland acquiescence, despite knowing that there was nothing sexy about being from Bangladesh. If she told people she was from Afghanistan or Iraq, people would nod with knowing sympathy, *yet another mess of a country we tried to liberate.* That Churchill had condemned three million inhabitants of the Bay of Bengal to deliberate starvation and death in the latter years of World War II was of no interest to anyone at all. It was nowhere to be found amid her high school history classes on the First Fleet or the Weimar Republic, and to try and assert it would be pointless. But what had frightened Abida most was that for all her fancy book-reading and bluster about white privilege and Western hegemony and war crimes, when she had been questioned about her family and her background she had not thought to protest. In that moment, she had really believed that they were entitled to their questions because they were rich and white and successful, and she was not.

The realisation stung, but wallowing was for people without responsibilities. She turned her focus now to the next item on her schedule, the meeting she would be chaperoning between Ahlam and Ziad the day after Eid. First, she sent Sara a message asking if she would stand as her deputy for MSA president. Just because she could not impress some corporate white people did not mean that she was unfit to lead her own. She did not have to accept their measures of success simply because she lived in a world they designed. There was no response from Sara but she pressed on, asking Ahlam where she wanted to meet Ziad and what time. Ahlam suggested a cafe in Auburn. Abida thought it an indiscreet choice; generally, she deemed it best to meet in a suburb where neither of the parties could be spotted by anyone they knew. But she did not press the point, agreeing to meet Ahlam behind the cafe so they could enter it together.

In the carpark, she greeted Ahlam. Ahlam was wearing a panelled silk maxi dress and appeared outwardly composed, but her hands were clammy. When they entered the cafe, Ziad was already sitting up the back, looking boyish in a flannel shirt buttoned almost all the way up.

'Assalamu alaykum, girls. I've ordered apple teas for all of us, hope you don't mind!'

He looked so pleased with himself that Abida could not fault him for ordering without asking them what they wanted.

'Thanks, Ziad! I love apple tea!' Ahlam spiked her sentences with exclamation marks in an echo of his.

'No worries. Thanks for coming to meet me today,' he said, looking at the wall behind Ahlam's head, where a Turkish peasant shoe was displayed in a kitschy nook. The cafe had been featured numerous times on guided food tours of the area and television specials on Sydney's ethnic cuisine hotspots. The food was terrible, being both starchy and bland, but no one came for the food.

'Maybe we should get started by you telling us a bit about what you're looking for in a partner?' Abida attempted to sound authoritative, but Ahlam kneed her under the table, hard. She had provided Abida with instructions on the script she was to follow, and the question Abida had just asked was supposed to come much later in the conversation, once they had discussed the weather and their respective Eids and the statement the MSA had released on a Quran burning somewhere in Scandinavia.

'Umm, well,' Ziad began, 'I guess I'm looking for someone who's pretty chilled and is into Islam, of course. I'm very close to my family so someone who's close to their family too would be good. I'm not looking for anything crazy or out of this world. Just a good person, you know?'

'I'm super close to my family,' Ahlam said, 'especially my nieces and nephews. I'll show you a photo of my little niece Sophia in a tutu on Eid, she's so adorable, mashaAllah.' She reached for her phone and displayed a photo of a cherubic pigtailed girl pouting her lips in what appeared to Abida to be a disturbingly adult way. Sophia was a popular name among young Muslim couples seeking something pronounceable, but with a hint of tradition. Everyone's child was a Sophia or an Ariana now.

'Oh, she's so adorable, mashaAllah. I have a niece who's around the same age, I'll show you a photo of her too.'

Ahlam leaned in and cooed in appreciation, the two of them bent over Ziad's phone, just as the waiter appeared with three identical glasses of tea on a tray. Ziad passed the first cup to Ahlam, who held his phone in one hand and stretched out with her other hand to take the cup from his. Abida watched them as they smiled at each other. She was conscious of something shifting, and although she could still feel the tapered edge of Ahlam's knee under the table and hear the words she was now speaking to Ziad, Abida nevertheless felt that the two of them were somewhere else altogether, somewhere she could no longer reach. She sipped her tea, licking her lips as the liquid passed through them and into the back of her throat.

12

Naeem

Naeem had selected a cafe in Dural at random from a guide to good Sydney cafes he had looked up online. He knew people at university who regularly consulted such guides, and he supposed brunch was the sort of thing Sara might like. Naeem ate out on very rare occasions. His parents ordered in halal Thai noodles or Turkish pide once or twice a month, but they would always bring it home to eat out of plastic containers, adding their own sauces, fresh chilli and generous squeezes of lemon juice. When they did eat out at a restaurant, it was most often in a large group to celebrate someone's birthday or anniversary. Meherin would pencil and lipstick her mouth and wrap her sari in waves over her shoulder. The food sitting on the table was a decorative prop against the real show of everyone dressing up and the uncles jostling for the bill, which no one wanted to pay but everyone had to be seen and heard demanding to pay.

He had spent every night of the final ten nights of Ramadan at the mosque, sometimes even sleeping and eating there and reading the Quran for several hours each day. Naeem had gone to His House in search of absolution, but the lack of sleep and extensive prayer sessions had drained his last reserves of energy. As he splashed his face in wudu and inhaled the smell of the mosque carpet, trying in vain to sleep for just a few hours before waking for further prayers, he had thought longingly of his bed and even of his mother and father. He presumed he had been good for so long that something inside him, a rattling gear, had worn loose and malfunctioned.

On laylatul qadr, which ought to have been the peak of his engagement with his Lord, he had instead contacted Sara and planned to meet in person. She had responded with eagerness, uncloaked in niceties. They had been chatting late into the night in the days since, and the content of their conversations had become increasingly forthright. In the freshness of her curiosity the details of his life and upbringing were rendered novel and exciting. He had not known he could interest anyone in this way.

They learned of similarities: they both thought the MSA was inane but soothing in its protective handhold on campus, both were born in Sydney but felt extraneous to it, both had attended co-educational schools. Differences presented themselves too: his education private, hers public but selective (he was impressed that she had received no tutoring but had still passed the entrance exams), no siblings at all for her versus his one sibling, and he enjoyed reality television while Sara detested it. At the tail end of one very late night conversation, he even found himself telling her about Katherine, the medical student his father had married and divorced in Boston all those years ago, of the photo of her he had once found in a box before it had been secreted away. Sara had listened to him with such care and tenderness that he had been certain that he was in love with her.

Naeem had arrived at the cafe several minutes prior to the agreed time. Although it was a weekday, the snug space was packed with hip twenty-somethings in mismatched, casual ensembles and scruffy waves of brown and blonde and red hair. He noticed that, aside from the kitchenhand whose face hovered in and out of view, he was the only non-white person in the whole cafe. This was a check Naeem did without conscious thought, searching for Muslim-sounding names on rosters at the hospital or in tutorials, not so that he could befriend them, but just for the comfort of knowing he was not the only one. He did not feel as though he belonged in places like these, despite their shelves of pot plants and fashioned air of homeliness. He was too conspicuous, too tucked into his shirt and pants with none of the carelessness affected by those at surrounding tables. He tried to study the menu, hoping Sara would arrive soon.

'Sorry I'm late, I couldn't find parking anywhere.'

Sara stood over him, removing her anorak, revealing one of her grey oversized sweaters and slouchy, cuffed sweatpants. Naeem had expected she would wear something unusual, decorative, but he decided that he was glad she had not. He was unsure of whether he ought to stand in greeting, but there did not seem to be any point in doing so. They were not going to shake hands or embrace, and so he placed his hand over his heart and, after hesitating for a moment, Sara returned the gesture. Naeem had always liked the Muslim substitute for a handshake between the sexes, but with Sara, the gesture felt more meaningful, his heart to hers across the brunch table.

'No worries,' he said in response to her late arrival. 'Did you find the place okay?'

'It was fine, I just plugged it into my GPS, but you know Sydney traffic, it's always a nightmare.'

'Yeah, I make dua every time I get into the car to make it to my destination in one piece!'

Naeem knew he was being facile, but he was uncertain of how else to behave. He had been picturing this moment for so long, but their conversation was so commonplace, so wholly free of subtext. Their late-night chats seemed incongruous, the things they had said to each other reflective of little more than pre-adult angst now that they were facing each other. Sara appeared unconcerned, reaching for a menu and signalling to the waitress with her right hand, a thin silver ring on her middle finger.

'Are you ready to order? Sorry, I should've asked you before I called the waiter over.' Sara bit the side of her lip and appeared so contrite that Naeem experienced the urge to grab her hand and squeeze it. Before he could answer, the waitress appeared at their table. Sara ordered the poached eggs with dukkah and labneh, and after deliberating for a moment, he requested the same. The purple-haired waitress did not write the orders down, asking if they wanted sourdough or rye bread before departing.

'So, how was your Eid? I know we spoke about it already but tell me everything.' Naeem settled on another Muslim filler topic, wondering how they would pierce through the quotidian and just be at ease with each other. He did not wish to be her friend, to exchange quips and banalities while he fantasised about her by night. He had perceived Sara's longing to be as intense as his, but now her poise suggested otherwise.

'It was pretty quiet. We went and visited some South African oldies my parents know, but aside from that we just ate a lot. You know, making up for the entire month's deprivation in a day type of thing.'

'I know what you mean, my mum force feeds us like we're half-dying of starvation.' This year Meherin had done so with even more ferocity than usual, claiming that he had lost weight from all his hours at the mosque, which was most likely true. Naeem had not enjoyed the orange biryani the mosque had provided for its worshippers and had scooped up small handfuls of it for subsistence only; there had never been enough plastic cutlery to go around.

'I've been meaning to ask you properly about your background. You're South African, right?' Naeem continued, trying to manoeuvre the conversation to more substantial topics.

'Yep, my parents were born in South Africa, which I guess makes me South African too.' She put on a decent imitation of a South African accent as she spoke, crinkling her nose and cheeks.

'I don't really get it though, with your last name and all,' Naeem continued.

'It's one of those nasty little colonial legacies. We have Indo-Malay slave ancestors who were brought to the Cape, which is where the Muslim bit comes from, but, as always, the white masters couldn't keep their hands off their servant women.' Sara shrugged and Naeem felt he had failed some sort of test. He could not think what it was though. He was curious about her and had not thought to pretend otherwise.

'As far as I know, my family is Bengali through and through,' he said. 'Pretty boring compared to you.'

'I don't know why Muslims always think it's so interesting to have a bit of white blood in them,' Sara replied, this time betraying a definite hint of irritation.

'I don't think it's interesting because of that. I just find you interesting in general,' he said, more boldly than he felt, meeting her eyes. Sara looked straight back at him. Naeem tried not to allow his breathing to spike, but the sustained eye contact felt more intimate than anything he had ever experienced. It was too intimate for this setting, his knee now twitching to conceal the growing bulge in his pants. He had worn his loosest pair of slacks in anticipation of this occurring, but he was afraid to look down and see if it was visible.

Their lengthy stare was interrupted by the waitress bearing plates of eggs and toast. But the look had unravelled Naeem's squirmy insides and the reticence they had both felt obliged to feign. They ate their eggs in leisurely silence now, punctuated only by the clinking of forks and the hum of chatter from the tables next to them. Naeem chewed on a forkful of runny egg and crunchy dukkah, looked over at Sara, and then ate another. The transfer of fork to mouth seemed to happen independently of his hands, for surely his hands were too close to hers to perform such an ordinary task. She kept hers close to the centre of the table, as did he. There was no mistaking the symbolism of the gesture.

They lingered over their empty plates, a smear of yolk across his. He had not planned what would transpire. He had come here driven by compulsion, not in pursuit of a defined outcome. Naeem wanted the shame to stay where he could control it, on the prayer mat, alone with Allah. He could not withdraw now. *Do not come close to zina.* The wording of the verse in the Quran specified not just that sex was prohibited outside of marriage, but that any act which preceded it was also prohibited. He was behaving like a horny teenager; it was so predictable and banal, all this pent-up desire, the very stereotype he had sought to avoid.

'I'd better go check on my parking,' he said. Naeem was aware that he sounded abrupt, possibly even combative. He rose from his chair, knocking over the jug of water from their table as he did. He did not stop, walking towards the counter and offering his credit card as though he couldn't hear the waitress wiping up the floor behind him or Sara's chair knocking against the table.

Naeem walked out of the cafe, Sara still behind. 'Are you okay?' He heard the brittle edge to Sara's voice, but he continued walking at speed.

'Please. Please turn around, Naeem,' she pleaded. They had arrived at his car now, on the side street adjacent to the cafe. She had not addressed him by his name like this before. Naeem felt the word dance on her tongue, and at once craved the taste of it too, his resolve to leave dissipating. But he could not lean across and reach for her. That was something people only did when they were unconcerned by who would see them. He was not far gone enough to forget that touching in suburban daylight would be rash. Instead, he gestured towards the car to indicate that they should sit inside. After pausing for a moment, then another, Sara opened the door and got in.

Inside, the air was hot and close, his obsidian prayer beads hanging from the mirror. Naeem rested his cheek against the cool of the side window, attempting to consolidate his shambolic thoughts. He felt a hand brush against his. He curled his fingers around hers, cool and slim. Sara responded by running her index finger up and down his, their palms pressed together. He could not look at her, his cheek still pressed against the window. They continued to run their fingers up and down, up and down, the contact between their palms unwieldly, but neither would pull away.

'Look at me, Naeem.' Her voice was gentle, but Naeem could not comply. Eventually, she reached over with her other hand, her thumb on his left cheek, her other four fingers (were there only four? there seemed to be far more) against his other, until his face was angled towards hers.

'I don't do these kinds of things,' she said. 'Not with anyone, ever. I'm going to go out on a limb here and guess that you don't either.' Sara's smile was wry as she released her hold on his cheek but continued to stroke his hand. In her smile, Naeem detected that she had seen the bulge in his pants and was not disgusted by it, only amused.

'Really? What gave it away?' Naeem answered in the same tone. They burst into laughter in unison, and the act of laughing together felt just as substantial as the touch of her hand. He had laughed before, of course, with Ridwan at school, with Tasnia when they splashed about in the pool, with Shaykh Hassan at school when he had recounted how, as a boy, he had stolen his father's favourite kufi and pretended it had gone missing. But laughing with Sara provided a release that nothing else had, the release of sharing an unguarded part of himself with another person. Naeem had never let anyone witness, or touch, this part of him; he unburdened himself before Allah alone. But as all-encompassing as He was, none of His characteristics seemed to involve a sense of humour or this animal lust, heavy in the pit of Naeem's belly.

Naeem reached for Sara's other hand, arranging and rearranging both until they rested against his knees. Her knuckles seemed to protrude from her hands and her wrists were now exposed, bony and pale. He wanted to kiss the blue of her veins there, but he could not incline his head at the right angle. They sat facing each other, silent again. This time, he leaned towards Sara, pressing his forehead against hers. Naeem felt a tightness inside his chest, a constriction he knew preceded tears and sobbing. He was ashamed of his transgressions even as he committed them, but he did not know to stop. He did not feel equipped to cry in Sara's presence, so he leaned in to her with his lips instead.

13

Sara

Naeem had not requested that she visit his house, not in those exact words. He had instead informed her that he would be at home by himself all day, and she had replied that she too was free for the day. This mutual avoidance had formed an essential part of their charade: if an act remained unnamed, it did not need to be justified or atoned for. They had been in constant contact since their meeting at the cafe only days before, but they had not once referenced the touching. Instead, they shared the minute details of their lives: the meals they were eating, the classes they were attending, the maths problems Sara was teaching to her students at the tuition centre, and most of all, how much they were yearning to see each other again. In this oblique way, Sara knew that they would touch each other again. She wanted it to happen, she could not pretend otherwise. When they conversed late into the night, the last thing she would remember before falling asleep was Naeem's voice in her ear, and if she was sufficiently focused, she could almost believe that he was there next to her.

Sara had anticipated that she would feel penitent and unclean following that moment in his car, but she had not. She had gone home and prayed as though she had not just committed a major sin, as if she was not drawing closer to zina. She had not yet begged Allah for forgiveness, observing a one-way silence on the topic and imagining Him to be respectful of it. This could not be true, of course, but she had realised from the outset that in order to continue seeing Naeem, she would have to maintain a fiction of this sort. She was certain that Allah would forgive her if she repented; He was the Most Gracious, the Most Merciful, but her friends were not. Abida would be perturbed and would not believe Sara capable of sitting in a car with a boy and pulling at strands of his hair. Sara could not resent anyone for being incredulous or holding her in utter contempt. She had not believed herself capable of such acts either, until she had gone ahead and done them.

As she drove towards Naeem's house, she contemplated her feelings for him. They had not yet pronounced outright expressions of love, but they were treading in its vicinity, whispering of their affection, half-asleep and tangled deep inside their conversation. But neither of them had discussed the logistics of marriage, which they both understood to be the sole legitimate mechanism for the pursuit of love. She resolved to raise it today, not because she was certain that she would marry Naeem, but because it would be the truest way of gauging his feelings for her. If he did not wish to marry her, she would be compelled to abandon him; this was what she had been told. A boy who touched you without entertaining the thought of marriage did not respect you; he would seek out your companionship and discard you when the relationship was no longer of utility.

She arrived at the address Naeem had provided. It was not an area of Sydney Sara was familiar with and it seemed very *Stepford Wives*, with wraparound porches and trimmed hedges. The house itself was imposing and far larger than it had appeared on Google Maps. She looked at her phone and realised that she had forgotten to reply to Abida's message about the deputy nomination, and although they had messaged back and forth since then, she had not said yes or no. She would reply later. She could not park her car in the driveway behind his as an ordinary guest would, so she drove further down the street and parked in front of an even larger house with stained glass windows. Sara stepped out of the car and scurried up the steep driveway, afraid of being seen by someone from behind a frilly curtained window, despite knowing no one who resided in the area. Naeem opened the door before she had even reached it; she suspected he was driven less by excitement but by their mutual fear of being seen.

He held the door for her, grinning at her with all of his teeth before closing it. Sara did not know how to greet him. To kiss on the cheek would be too casual, like the boys and girls at university who were no more than friends but would air-kiss each other's cheeks once, then twice. There was nothing casual about what was happening. She followed Naeem through a gleaming marble corridor and into what she presumed was a sitting room, judging by the white leather sofas and prominent glass display cabinet with a miniature crystal ka'bah inside. There were two vases full of arranged flowers and a general air of disuse, betrayed by the meticulous angles at which the cushions were positioned.

'Do you mind taking your shoes off? I'm pretty sure my mum can sniff shoes in the house from kilometres away,' Naeem said. He was dressed in grey trackpants and a shapeless old sweater, clothing which made him look younger and more relaxed.

She pulled her sneakers off her feet, one after the other. Her socks were mismatched, which seemed incongruous with the stiff formality of the sitting room. Naeem picked her shoes up and went to the front corridor, presumably to put them in a shoe cupboard, the house demanding that objects like shoes and umbrellas be placed out of sight. He was behaving as though she was an invited guest to a sewing bee. If they continued the farce any longer, he would be serving her tea and biscuits on one of his mother's Royal Doulton trays.

She attempted to settle into the couch, but all Sara could think about was how affluent Naeem's family must be to afford a house of this size in this suburb. She had been aware that he was wealthy without him telling her so, just as she recognised the wealthy students she encountered at university. From throwaway comments Naeem had made about his father's job and the cars his parents drove, she had deduced that his family were far more well-to-do than hers, but she could not have conceived of this form of palatial living. Her own home was comfortable, but Sara's parents tended to privilege experiences over things. Soraya was a poor cook and an indifferent housekeeper, leaving Sara and Amin to sort out piles of mail and mow the lawn when the grass began to tickle their calves.

When Naeem reappeared, he was holding a glass of what looked like the sort of cordial she had sometimes drunk as a child, a deep purple-red in colour. Sara snatched it from his hand, muttering a thanks, watching him as he climbed onto the sofa next to her and sat, his legs crossed neatly underneath him. The compact way in which he was sitting reminded her of one of Soraya's yoga poses, and Sara was struck anew by the absurdity of this life she was now inhabiting.

'Are you okay, Sara? You're looking a little tense,' he said. His voice was so beautiful; Sara wanted to ask him to read the Quran to her while she closed her eyes and lay down on the Persian rug on the floor. The couch she was sitting on was too rigid, designed more for the eye than the back and bottom.

'Yeah, I'm fine.' She was being churlish, just as she was so often with her parents. How could she convey to him that she was afraid of what they would do to each other, with each other? How could she ask him if he intended to extract what he wanted from her and then marry a girl who lived in a house like his own? She had always characterised herself as a rational person and she was annoyed that he had disturbed this fact.

'You know you don't ever have to do anything you don't want to,' he said. 'I would never pressure you into anything.' He was hovering very close to breaking their unspoken rule, if only by way of implication.

'That's good to know. How thoughtful of you.' Sara took a big gulp of the juice he had given her, thrilled at how biting and sarcastic she sounded. She wanted him to share in the confusion she was feeling instead of being so reasonable. She so infrequently snapped at anyone aside from her parents, it was a new sensation and she found it exciting.

'Hey, I didn't mean it like that, okay?' Naeem's eyes grew round and wary. Sara liked that she could have this potent an effect on someone, she who laughed on cue and swore in her head instead of aloud. She wanted to wound him, this boy who was afforded the protection of his parents' money and his show-pony piety.

'How did you mean it then? That you invited me over here for some cordial and sex?'

To Sara's dismay, a tear ran down Naeem's cheek, then another, bursting the parameters of the game she had been enjoying. She gathered him in her arms as he sobbed. He felt smaller and skinnier than she recalled, his shoulder blades jabbing into her chest.

'I'm sorry,' she said. Sara did not feel remorseful, not yet, but she supposed it was the thing she was supposed to feel and say. She let her hands give life to the lie, massaging his shoulders and neck the way she had seen her father do to her mother when they sat on the couch and watched old episodes of *Midsomer Murders*. As she did, she thought of how people must do this all the time: pretend with their bodies.

Naeem looked up at her, his eyes still sad but no longer leaking tears.

'I don't know why you'd cheapen what we have by talking about it in that way. You mean so much more to me than that.'

Sara liked it far better when he was recounting the events of his day or cracking one of his unfunny jokes. This day was not transpiring as she had envisaged. She had pictured them looking into each other's eyes, maybe watching a movie with their arms wrapped around each other, Naeem remarking that he would allow her to select the movie when they were married. She wanted to be wrapped up in the charade of them, the valid couple with their own space and predilections. But they were not a couple, not in any sense that she understood couples to exist. She needed clarity on the things they were doing and saying to each other.

'What exactly is it that we have? You haven't really told me.' She pulled away from him now, retreating into the recesses of the sofa.

'Do you want to get married to me, Sara?'

He had said it. It was not a proposal. It was too unrehearsed, too blunt to be considered one. Naeem was curious as to what her expectations were and how far she was willing to go, whether they could somehow transfigure this beginning into a sanctioned commitment.

'I know I want to be with you always. Is that the same thing as wanting to get married?'

'Well, I love you. Is that the same thing?' Naeem brought his face closer to hers. She could smell the cordial on his breath, its colour staining his teeth and tongue.

The mood shifted, tugged. Once it was over, Sara could recall very little of what had happened. She supposed her brain was protecting itself by erasing the shameful contents, and she was grateful for it. She knew only that she and Naeem had proceeded away from the sitting room and into his bedroom, and that once inside, the door had been shut and locked and the blinds drawn. All Sara could remember now was informing Naeem that his desk was as organised as hers. Other inconsequential details lingered: the persistent, high-pitched barking of a dog in a neighbouring backyard, the pleasing dimensions of Naeem's duvet, the stack of tabbed and colour-coded notes on his bedside table.

If she had been unsure of her love for Naeem before, his tenderness and intuitive understanding of her limitations had tipped her into certainty. His expression of love had now illuminated her own feelings, and she needed to tell him as such. They were now sitting on the varnished floor, Naeem's head cradled in her lap. When Sara pronounced the words to him, his face was suffused with such joy that she felt ashamed of pushing and prodding him earlier. He was so much softer and more vulnerable than she had perceived him to be. When she had interacted with him at MSA activities, he had appeared intent on his tasks and at times forbiddingly serious, but Sara observed now how he smiled with ease, and how sunny and wonderful it was when he did.

'What was it like memorising the Quran and becoming a hafidh?' Sara asked, her back and head resting against the side of Naeem's enormous bed. As with the rest of the house, Naeem's room was spacious and glossy but impersonal, as though all its contents had been bought as a set from a catalogue. Her walls were covered in raggedy posters of bands and printed snaps from high school and overseas trips; his were bare except for a laminated world map his parents had likely purchased from a school fair.

'My parents weren't that keen on the idea at first, but my favourite teacher, Shaykh Hassan, convinced them to let me go for it, that it was just a couple of extra hours each day. You'd be surprised at how easy it is if you start at a young enough age. You just read and read until it sticks.'

'It must have taken a lot of hours though, surely.'

Sara thought of herself as studious, but she was not especially good at rote learning. This was why she enjoyed mathematics: its real value was in its application. There were certain rules and formulae requiring memorisation, but what she liked most of all was a line or two of problem set against a big empty sheet of paper. She liked deriving the correct answer at its end, but she relished the process of drawing it out, each step building on the next even when the correct result was not yet apparent.

'What else does a six- or seven-year-old have to do?' he said.

'I don't know, kid things? Make mud pies, get chased around and kissed in the playground?'

She had not been speaking in complete jest, but Naeem snorted.

'First of all, Sara Andrews, I'm Bangladeshi, we don't make mud pies, it's too dirty and we have homework to do. Secondly, you know I went to an Islamic school, so there was none of this kissing business in the playground.'

Naeem rose to his knees, still laughing. The pang of irritation Sara had felt at being dismissed in such a way could not be sustained when he was so elated. Her moods had always been changeable, but she was unused to another person exerting such influence over them. She felt tied to him in a way she had only previously felt with Abida, that they had chosen each other, and there wasn't a thing anyone could do to alter it.

'Are you hungry, darling?' Naeem experimented with the word, failing in rendering it unaffected and natural, but the sweetness of his expression compensated for it.

'I am, actually. I think I've worked up a bit of an appetite.' She winked, and the long, knowing look he gave her by way of reply made Sara fear they would be lost for the afternoon. But Naeem kissed her hand and rose to his feet, stretching his arms and legs as though he had just woken from a nap.

'You stay put. I'll be right back with some food.'

He trotted down the staircase before Sara could protest. She would only have been feigning in any case. She wanted to remain in his room, which was comforting and smelled of him. The rest of the house, with its marble and leather and suede, would not be as accommodating. She had attempted to readjust her clothing, including her hijab, but she was aware that her overall presentation remained dishevelled. She reached for her phone and finally replied to Abida's message, saying that she would be a rubbish deputy, that Abida could find someone better. Abida replied instantly with a series of crying emojis. If it had been just one, Sara would have been concerned, but the hyperbole of Abida's response assured Sara that all was okay. She longed to tell Abida where she was and to hear Abida's incisive commentary on it, but she knew she could not.

She heard the beep of a microwave from downstairs. There was still time to adjust her clothing and wash her hands and face. Sara opened the door and walked along the corridor. The tiles were cold against her bare feet, her socks having long been kicked off under the bedsheet, and all the doors to the various rooms were open. This was not a house designed for concealment. She passed the room adjacent to Naeem's, which was identical to his but with overt splashes of pink and purple, the bed orientated in the same direction, map on wall. She presumed this was his teenage sister's room. The furthest room along the corridor was far larger than the others and looked out onto the garden. The room featured a walk-in wardrobe on one side and a white dressing table with bottles of perfume aligned like soldiers on the other, with a closed door in the corner suggesting an ensuite bathroom lay behind it.

Sara moved towards the double windows, distracted from her original purpose by the view they offered. The rectangular swimming pool below was covered by a tarpaulin sheet, the rich green of the tennis court just beyond it. She could not comprehend what was required to amass the type of wealth that would allow people to build their own private tennis court. She had been on a tennis court twice before, on a high school sports activities day. Most people she knew wore similar brands of clothing and owned similar models of phones; anyone could buy a Prada bag at a factory sale or pay off their iPhone month by month, but in their homes the wealthy could truly be distinguished from the others. She had liked Abida far more after visiting her home and seeing how cramped it was, how her mother seemed to be forever spraying and wiping without making any real dent in the layers of grime accumulated by its previous owners.

'I don't know why we even have a tennis court. My dad only ever plays with his doctor buddies occasionally and my mum wouldn't be caught dead breaking a sweat out there.'

She turned around and saw Naeem holding two white ceramic bowls piled high with rice and an unfamiliar spiky green vegetable swimming in a brown sauce. She was embarrassed to be lurking in his parents' bedroom, but he did not seem to mind, putting down the bowls on the dresser and pressing her to his chest from behind. They stood for a moment, looking out at the garden in silence. Sara could not guess at what he was thinking, and she couldn't see his face at all from the angle at which he held her, but the feel of his arms around her chest and his chin on her shoulder was pacifying. Whatever would come, they would face it together.

'When do you think we should get engaged?' She wiggled out of his hold, rotating her neck until their foreheads were pressed together.

'Definitely by the end of final exams this semester. That gives us plenty of time,' he said. He was so calm, so pragmatic. She smiled and turned back to the window, but she was no longer seeing the tennis court or the pool, only the expanse of their future, stretching out infinitely in front of them.

'I'm starving. Let's eat,' she said.

14

Ahlam was recounting the details of Ziad's first home visit to the other MSA girls as they sat at the event registration desk. She had already informed Abida in extensive detail that their fathers had discovered that they had a third cousin in common and how her niece had kissed Ziad on the cheek in front of both families, but she was now required to be subjected to it once again. Abida noticed that the tale was altered in this rendering; in the version she had been told, only Ahlam and her mother had been present when the niece had done her kissing trick and the third cousin had been by way of marriage and not birth. These alterations did not serve any particular purpose, nor did they detract from the overall gist of the story, but Abida felt the urge to correct them nevertheless. Ahlam then stated that they were already talking about when they might want to do their katb kitab, that the date would be set on the following visit.

'Ziad's pretty keen to get the katb kitab done, isn't he? What's the rush?' Lina teased, as if they did not all understand that couples were both eager to avoid falling into forbidden premarital relations and to be able to kiss and cuddle in their cars in the months and even years before they could afford to live together as a married couple. Some parents remained suspicious and guarded even after their children signed their Islamic marriage contracts and prevented them from going out at night with their husbands and wives until they made their final exit from the family home. Given the number of couples who broke up after the katb kitab but prior to the wedding, Abida thought that this could be viewed as prudent practice.

'We're not exactly in a rush, Lina. But as we all know, it's not a good idea to delay a marriage and we don't see the point in waiting too long since we already knew each other from the MSA,' Ahlam said, serene. As the sole girl at the table with imminent marriage prospects, she was in possession of the prized goods.

'I agree,' Sara said. 'What's the point in waiting around if you know that you like the person and want to be with them?' Sara crossed, then uncrossed her legs.

Abida did not understand why Sara was saying this and stared at her. It did not make any sense. Abida knew that Sara's parents had dated for years before getting married, she had seen the photos of them in frayed jeans as teenagers. Soraya had attempted to tell her all about it when Abida had gone over for a movie night years earlier and Sara had been mortified, shooing Soraya away with the tray of snacks she had prepared for them. Abida had been appalled at Sara's rudeness, at the way Soraya had not scolded her but had instead retreated with a sheepish giggle.

'Exactly. The thing is, there are no guarantees either way. You could know someone for years and it still doesn't work out,' Ahlam said.

'That's very true. You hear about it all the time with non-Muslims, living together for years before getting married, then getting divorced.' Lina straightened her name badge, just as the first groups of people began arriving for the talk about colonialism and the devastation it continued to wreak upon the Muslim world.

Abida was relieved at this diversion. She could not stand all this grandstanding, as if a few weeks of interaction with a boy had rendered Ahlam some sort of relationship expert. Unless you were married, you could not attest to marriage's peculiarities, and even then, like most things in life it seemed to be all grunt and guesswork.

'Is this Dr Omar Ali's talk?'

A girl with faux leather leggings and chunky snakeskin ankle boots peered over at them, her hand moving towards her hair as if she were now conscious that it was uncovered. The MSA girls were wearing identical teal hijabs for effect, the colour they had branded their Islamic Awareness Week materials with. They had all been instructed to change their profile pictures on social media to the Islamic Awareness Week flyer, a hideous, teal speech bubble filled with text designed by Ziad. Abida nodded and passed the girl the program for the evening, ushering her inside. They were expecting a crowd of several hundred for this first event. Abida felt the familiar buzzing in her stomach, the thrilling awareness that she was part of this world of ideas and intellectual discussion. They could talk about the Taliban without labelling them primitive barbarians, they could talk about whiteness and proximity to it. She had chosen to study law because that was what smart people who were not interested in the sciences did, but it did not enthral her in the way that these MSA activities did. In here, they had conversations that mattered.

Wahid was fussing about the room, testing the lapel microphone first, then the presentation clicker. He stood near the front stage with the speaker, Dr Omar Ali, a Somali–Australian academic from Brisbane whose online posts Abida had long admired. She had messaged him once about a post he had written on feminism and he had been thoughtful, cracking a joke with her as if they were friends. Thinking of this, she walked down to where they were standing together.

'Assalamu alaykum, Dr Ali. I'm Abida, I spoke to you online a few months ago?'

Dr Ali was handsome in his blazer and beige corduroy pants, young enough for her to scan his finger and be surprised at the ring on it.

'I remember. We were having a laugh at how afraid some Muslims, no, some people, are of the f word.'

He laughed again, inviting her to do the same. Wahid joined in, as though he were not one of the very people Dr Ali was referring to who was petrified at the prospect of feminism. Abida restrained herself from visibly rolling her eyes. The boys tried so hard to be cool whenever they hosted a visiting speaker, taking them out for burgers and shakes late into the night. She hated how they obtained such easy access to people she had to jostle to speak to.

Ziad signalled to them from the back, and they turned around. The room was just about full, and it was time for the talk to begin.

'I think that's my cue to start talking. Maybe I'll catch you afterwards, Abida.' Dr Ali had the politician's touch, inserting people's names in conversation to build rapport. Abida recognised the strategy but was not immune to it. She was glad he was married; her resolve to get through university without having a crush would have been tested otherwise.

She walked back towards the registration desk, intending to greet and help seat some of the stragglers. The other MSA girls had gone inside, leaving Fitri standing at the doorway as an usher. Abida heard Dr Ali commence, something stinging on the fallacy of the number of African nations not colonised by European empires. She was reaching for her phone, tucked away under a pile of papers, when Wahid cleared his throat behind her.

'Just a minute, sis. Just a minute of your time please.'

Wahid was wearing an ugly black jumper with an asymmetrical zipper and shoulder pads. Like the pretty girls in Abida's law classes who often dressed in gym leggings and pilled tank tops, there was something in his casual insouciance about his clothing which grated with her.

'Yeah, what is it?'

'I've heard what you're planning for Thursday. One of the speakers you got in touch with told me, before you think someone from the MSA dobbed you in. Mustafa is still our president, and he agrees with me on this. It's not going to go ahead. You can't just run an event without telling anyone, especially not something on sex.'

Wahid spoke the word with distaste. She knew then what she had suspected, that he was not one of the Muslim boys who had sex. He was too prudish, too uptight, probably keeping his pants and underwear on when he did whatever it was he needed to in the privacy of his bedroom.

'It's not about sex. It's about double standards and patriarchy, something you would know all about.'

She was livid, absolutely livid. They had no right to dispute, none at all. Only yesterday she had received a message from Dr Rania saying how much she was looking forward to the discussion and how 'pioneering' Abida was in organising it. The one consolation following the bland, polite rejection email she had received from Carrington Feltham Emery was picturing the expression on the MSA kids' faces when they arrived and realised what they were attending.

'Why do you always talk to me like this, as if I'm some kind of bogey man representation of the patriarchy or whatever else you're angry about? We could work together on things if you wanted. I'm not your enemy, you know.' Wahid spoke softly.

She saw the black of his eyes widen, the breadth of his arms hugged to his chest.

'You're not my friend, either,' she said.

'This is about the election, isn't it?'

She shook her head, but Wahid continued.

'It is. I know it is. Yes, I am going to run for president, inshaAllah, and I know you're going to run too. But we don't have to be nasty to each other because of that. I respect you, and I'm sure you'd make a great president. It's up to the group to decide.'

There was nothing to do but apologise and hope he would leave her be. Abida would attempt to be polite to him, but he was not going to elicit her sympathy when he was so undeserving of it. He accepted her apology with grace, hand on heart, before turning back to enter the room.

'One quick question. Who are you nominating as your deputy?' Abida asked.

Wahid smiled, and looked at her as if the answer were obvious.

'Brother Naeem, of course. He's so modest he'll probably say no, but I'll talk him around.' Wahid waved and departed.

For the rest of the week Abida avoided any further conversation with him, with any of the MSA boys. She fielded questions on polygamy, the Taliban and Malala, trying as she did to steer the focus back to colonialism, to the wreckage of the Muslim world in its continuing aftermath. She spoke to passers-by about the responsibility they all had to listen to and work with First Nations communities, the anti-Black prejudices many of the Sydney Muslim community had ingested. She skipped her commercial law tutorial to help moderate the panel discussion on Islam and conquest, watching with horror and then delight as campus security intervened to remove an older man who would not cease his yelling and swearing in the intermission. She avoided Mustafa, the apologetic smile he aimed in her direction. She asked Ahlam if she would be her deputy, and Ahlam said that she was too busy with her engagement planning to do it.

On Thursday, Abida conspired to be as far as she could be from the spectacle of the hijab event, the event she ought to have been running. She muted the group chat and attempted to concentrate in her constitutional law lecture, taking comprehensive notes on the power granted to the federal parliament to make laws in relation to marriage. Connie sat next to her, thumbing through her textbook as their lecturer, a thin woman with a raspy voice, spoke. The nominations for MSA president were to be submitted soon, and she still had no deputy. Abida had returned to the MSA constitution and learned that it was not mandatory to nominate a deputy, but she felt the isolation of her position without one. Sara had not shown interest in her campaign since their initial conversation and none of the other girls or boys had offered to stand with her. She supposed leadership would isolate her even further. She was ready for all it entailed; she would willingly accept the burden as long as it allowed her to address the burning injustices she saw around her.

Abida remained in the law library until it was early evening, now perusing the series of before and after photos of girls trying on hijabs people were sending through on the group chat. She flicked past photo after photo of blondes, brunettes and purple- and pink-haired girls smiling as their heads were swathed. But the person holding the hijab in one photo, twirling its ends around a girl with green streaks through her hair, was Sara. She picked up her phone, messaged Maroof to come pick her up on Parramatta Road, and then messaged Sara.

What the hell, girl. You went to that f'd up try-on-a-hijab day?
Sara responded immediately.

I know it's all a bit stupid, but it was actually pretty fun :)

Abida exhaled. Maroof's car pulled up with a girl in the front passenger seat. The girl had a curtain of glossy black hair and plump pink lips.

'I told you to be out here in ten minutes. I had to circle around and then come back,' he said, pulling away from the kerb.

'Maroof, don't be such a mean grump. I'm Maggie, by the way,' the girl said, extending her arm down the middle of the car towards Abida.

'Nice to meet you. If you know my brother, Maggie, then you know meanness is his default setting, but his bark is far worse than his teeny bite.'

Maggie laughed. Abida turned back to her phone and began to type.

If you think this event is just 'a bit stupid', then you have even less political awareness than I already know you do.

Abida pressed the send button. She reread the message once, then again. She had insulted Sara, not simply because of a political abstraction, but also because Sara had not supported her in the way she had hoped, in the way their friendship merited. The political was the personal, the personal the political. Only those with the luxury of power and privilege thought otherwise. She thought about deleting her message and typing something kinder, softer, but she saw Sara was typing already.

I'm not your puppet, Abida. You can't tell me which way to move. I'll make up my own mind and you don't have to like it, but you'll have to deal with it.

Your puppet? Excuse me?? What exactly is your problem?

Sara did not reply.

Maroof dropped her off a few houses down from theirs and drove off somewhere. Abida had not asked where they were going, and he had not volunteered the information. She listened to the revving of his car as it sped off around the bend before she walked up to their house and sat on the front doorstep. She could hear Tauseef crying from inside the bathroom as Ammu bathed him, the blaring of the Quran on the radio. She turned back to her phone. She thought about what to say next. It was a chess game, this business of arguing with Sara. Each move she made exposed her, each countermove made by Sara likely to weaken her defences even further.

She could escalate; escalation was something Abida knew how to do. Part of her longed to turn up the dial, take the conflict to the point from which there could be no détente. There was something so appealing about releasing the thoughts she had built over the years like a stack of dominoes she could topple with a single shove. She could tell Sara that she was a pushover, remind her that the only reason the Muslim kids at school and in the MSA had accepted her was because of Abida, that she was white-passing and should shut up on all matters of Islamophobia and racism because she had no clue. She had certainly hinted at all of it before. But when she looked up at the inky sky, the distant orbs of stars twinkling down at her, she felt her resolve crumble. Sara was her closest friend, and she loved her. She loved Sara.

She began recording a voice note to Sara. She apologised first, saying that she was guilty of treating Sara like a puppet on occasion, that it was a bad habit of hers from their school days that she would do her best to unlearn. She said that she was really just sad that the event had gone ahead because she did not think it fitting to the dignity of them all, that white people could not understand what hijab represented and the discrimination they received just because they plonked a piece of fabric on their heads, but that she was also sad because she valued Sara's opinion above all others and had wanted her to be honest and just tell her if she disagreed with her. She said she loved Sara and that she felt sad that she had not shown interest in her presidential campaign, and she apologised again.

After she pressed the send button, Abida looked up at the sky again. A half-moon had appeared from behind the clouds, and she basked in its glow for a moment before turning her key in the door and going inside.

15

Naeem

Just over a month in, and they had already established a routine of sorts. If Sara was not at work and they both had classes they did not deem essential to attend, Sara would come to see him in the early morning, once Naeem's parents had departed for work and Tasnia had been picked up for school. They would then proceed straight up to his bedroom. Despite the increasing frequency of these visits, Naeem's heart still rattled inside his chest whenever Sara appeared at the door, and continued to do so all the way up the staircase, only quietening once the bedroom door was closed. Naeem suspected Sara also felt this strain, speaking in whispers until they were inside the room's confines.

Afterwards they were more relaxed. Sara had enjoyed the ritual of eating together so much the first time that it now formed a regular component of her visits. They spoke about potential wedding venues, their favoured honeymoon destinations, debated the benefits of joint bank accounts. Their plans grew simultaneously more grandiose and more practical. Naeem set the table for her with a knife and fork and poured her fruit juice, refusing to let her wash the dishes when they were finished. Meherin cooked three or four dishes on the weekend, which the family ate throughout the week, ensuring that their fridge always remained well-stocked. Sara was acquainted with Bangladeshi cuisine through her friendship with Abida and seemed to enjoy the lau bhaji and daal and chingri bhuna Naeem served up, often asking him for second and third helpings. Naeem worried his mother would notice that their inventory of food was disappearing more rapidly than usual, so he was conservative in the amount he ate, chewing it to a mushy pulp in his mouth to ensure that Sara did not realise what he was doing.

One day, it rained, fat noisy drops which danced against the roof, and they remained in bed, nestled underneath the covers. They began recounting how it was that they first noticed each other, a narrative Naeem seldom tired of revisiting. This was what he supposed couples did: created and packaged their story, constructing a timeline in which everything else in their lives dimmed in comparison to their preordained meeting.

'I'd been watching you for some time, but I had no idea you had noticed me too,' Naeem said into the dark warmth. It was difficult to breathe and within a few seconds he would have to resurface and gulp in some air, but he resolved to stay with Sara until necessary.

'I'm not really sure why I did. You always seemed so serious and dignified, like the Queen Mother or something,' she said, laughing.

'I didn't know what to say to you. You made me so nervous and I'd hardly spoken to girls before, not properly.'

'And then at the MSA barbeque I remember looking at you and you looked back, and that's when I knew that, even though you'd told me we should stay away, it'd never work.'

'I wonder if anyone else noticed our little staring contest,' he said, suddenly fearful. Naeem hated people knowing things about him. He knew people already spoke about him, about his parents, about their house and their money and their perfect children. He did not want to give them any further cause to do so. Besides, he did not claim to comprehend the workings of his own mind so he could not stand for others to presume they did.

'I doubt it, there's always so much going on and everyone in the MSA likes everyone else anyway. I do feel guilty not telling Abida about us, though. She's going to be so upset at me when I tell her we're getting married. She's already annoyed enough that Wahid wants you as his deputy.'

'You know I have precisely zero interest in being the MSA vice president.' Naeem turned over, facing away from her. Sara had made several remarks like this of late and he didn't know how to respond. He adored Sara, could foresee no future without her in it. But he was enjoying her company so much that he did not want to spoil it by telling anyone else, especially not vociferous people like Abida or, even worse, his parents. Sara brought him an ease, a lightness of being he had never experienced. To tell his parents would be to depart this world of unbounded possibility and to re-enter the familiar world of constraints and quantification and comparisons.

Naeem could not guess at the precise form their reaction would assume, but he knew that it would be terrible. What he and Sara shared worked because it was unknown and undeterred by the noisy opinions of others. His parents would have much to say about how he was too young and too immature to know his own mind yet, that he was years away from earning a living and that marriage was not all about love or lust or whatever it was young people believed in nowadays. These points were all valid and he would have very little recourse against them. He did not want to imagine what the MSA boys and girls would say; they would exclaim and fuss and make dua for it to be their turn next. But he had told Sara they would be engaged by the end of semester, and he had to act now to make it happen.

'I'm going to tell my cousin Sadia about us. She's so good with parents, she'll definitely help to convince them that this is a good idea,' he said, reaching for his phone.

'What, right this second?'

He had only intended to check his messages, but Sara sounded so hopeful that he did not want to admit that he had meant some-time in the distant future. He turned to her. The way she was looking at him reminded him of the heart-eye emoji he had seen people use, love manifest in a single gaze. He would have to do it now or he would fail her. He avoided disappointing anyone but disappointing Sara was not like disappointing his parents; it was as though a cloud had obscured the brilliance of the sun when she was unhappy.

'Well, let me get out of bed first. Not exactly a good look,' he said, laughing. He adjusted the collar of his sweatshirt and went to sit at his desk on the other side of the room, motioning at Sara with his finger against his lips as he dialled on video call. He was surprised when Sadia picked up on the second ring.

'Hey, little bro. How are you doing?' She smiled, the pharmacy backroom behind her stacked with pillboxes and capsules.

'Doing good, alhamdulillah. How are you?'

'All good, alhamdulillah. What's up? I'll have to get back to the counter in a sec.'

'I won't take up too much of your time, apu. I just wanted to tell you something.'

'What is it?' Sadia placed both hands under her chin, propping her phone up against the table.

'Well, I've met someone. A girl, that is,' he said. He was unsure if he should smile as he imparted this news or remain stoic, an adult with serious intentions conveying serious adult information. He was aware of Sara sitting up in his bed, her back parallel to the wall.

'That's amazing news, mashaAllah. I'm so excited for you. Tell me all about her. I need all the details. Where did you meet her? Is she Bangladeshi?'

'We met in the MSA, actually. Her name is Sara Andrews. And no, she's not Bangladeshi. She's South African. Cape Malay. They're descended from slaves and prisoners from different parts of Asia,' he said, trying to repeat the details Sara had told him, the things he had found on Wikipedia.

He saw Sadia's smile falter. She was considering the information he had presented and in her hesitancy he knew he had not been wrong, that his parents and his family and his social circle would deem his relationship incomprehensible. A girl nobody knew from an obscure ethnicity whom he had met wholly of his own accord.

'I don't think I've ever met someone Cape Malay. Never even heard of it. Sounds interesting though. Have you told your parents about her yet?'

'Not yet. I'm telling you first. You know how they are.'

He saw Sadia pick up her phone again and hold it closer to her face. They did not openly discuss the peculiar dynamics of their family. He had never told her that he was afraid of his parents and that pursuing something just because he wanted it was foreign to him.

'It's scary. I get it. I'd love to meet her sometime, though, if you'd like me to?'

'I would love that. We want to get engaged by the end of semester so maybe we can do it soon, that way when I tell Ammu and Baba you can help me out and verify that she's a great person. Which she is.'

'I'm sure she is. She'd have to be, if you like her. I have to get going now, but let's make a plan for soon then, inshaAllah, okay?'

Sadia waved at him and he hung up. He felt rather than saw Sara creep up behind him, her face nestled in the crevices of his neck.

'See, easy peasy. Done,' he said. He was triumphant. He had not known he could be so brave. In loving her, he had unlocked a sense of daring that was as unfamiliar to him as it was electrifying. She was magical, his Sara. He reached for her and pulled her onto his lap, spinning the chair around and around until they were both dizzy and breathless with laughter.

16

Soraya asked her to go shopping on the weekend. She wanted to buy some new white sneakers, had narrowed it down to two pairs she had seen online, but needed Sara to help her decide between them. They could get some king prawn pasta for lunch afterwards, or maybe in between purchases. They could choose their seats and meals for the flights to South Africa, which was now booked for after Sara's exams. Soraya was so eager that Sara did not feel she could say no.

Sara put on the radio as she drove, hoping it would deter Soraya from constant chatter. She was afraid that something about the way she carried herself was different and that her mother would ask about it. For all her ostensible preoccupations with shoes and hair and *MasterChef*, Soraya was certainly not stupid. She had frequent bursts of insight into what Sara was thinking or feeling, all the more alarming for their unpredictability.

'How's Abida doing?' Soraya asked as they headed into the shopping centre. She had always liked Abida, admiring what she labelled Abida's 'laser focus'.

'You know her, she's got something brewing as she always does. She wants to be the next MSA president,' Sara said. She had forgiven Abida after their argument, had apologised in turn for her lack of support for Abida's campaign and promised to be more present. She knew she had been flaky recently, absorbed as she was in Naeem and the secret life they were building together.

'She'll make a great president of anything. She's a powerhouse. But what's this MSA thing all about anyway? You're always doing things with them these days.' Soraya placed her hand on Sara's arm as they got onto the escalator together.

'It's an on-campus group, Mum. Just a group of Muslim kids who do Islamic things together.' She was aware of the minimising words she had used, how feeble they sounded. She did not know how to even begin to tell her mother about the strange appeal of the MSA. It was so unlike anything she had been raised with. They walked into the shoe store and the teenaged sales assistant greeted them with a smile. Soraya immediately asked for the shoes she had seen online and sat on the couch in front of the mirror while they waited for them to be brought from the back room.

'That sounds nice. You're so good at keeping up your Islamic practices. You make Dad and I look like such infidels,' Soraya said, laughing. Sara examined their reflections: her hijab tucked in to her shirt, her mother's hair just covering the lobes of her ears, from which a set of gold hoops hung. She saw herself in her mother's face: the familiar arc of nose and cheek. She was seized with a desire to tell her mother about Naeem. She knew her mother would not castigate her for it, and although she wanted to tell Abida too, she did not know if she could say the same for her friend.

'Mum, I want to tell you something. There's –'

'Who is he, then?' Soraya continued to look at Sara's reflection as the assistant brought the shoes to her. She reached for the box, holding one shoe in her hand as she waited for Sara to speak.

'How did you know?'

'I know, honey. I'm your mother. I've seen how distracted you've been lately, and all those late-night phone calls. Now tell me a bit about this boy.'

Sara watched as Soraya placed the shoe on her foot, pulling at the sole before toggling it into place. Her mother did not seem surprised. She wondered why she had presumed Soraya would be. Sara had not been herself recently, and at her age, Soraya would have already been several years into her relationship with Sara's father.

'There's not that much to tell. He's nice. We met in the MSA. He's Bangladeshi. He studies medicine.' Sara heard the staccato pattern of her speech as she spoke. It was futile, this pretence of checking off items from a shopping list. Soraya would not be fooled by it.

'We could do with a doctor in the family. Maybe he can check out my bung ankle.' Soraya wiggled it in front of the mirror as she removed the shoe.

'Mum –'

'I'm just being silly. You know that. What does he think of my daughter? What's his name again?'

'I didn't say. It's Naeem.' In speaking his name, she abandoned all attempts at casual disregard. She could not look at her mother, only at the reflection of her face, the deepening of the crease in her forehead.

'Naeem,' Soraya repeated. She placed the shoes back in their box and began lacing her own back up, tying one lace into a bow, then doing the same with the other. She gave the box back to the assistant, shaking her head before turning to Sara.

'It's your birthday in a couple of weeks. You could ask him to come along for dinner with us if you like? He can meet Dad too?'

Soraya thanked the assistant as they walked out of the shop together, passing a toy store, then a mobile phone repair stand. Around them people were being ordinary, holding shopping bags and looking down at their phones as they walked. Sara had thought of Naeem meeting her parents; they had discussed it, discussed the laughter he would have to feign at Amin's jokes. But her mother's suggestion solidified the two of them in a way she had not experienced before. The secrecy of their relationship still occasionally made her question if it was real or if she was somehow fantasising the whole thing. She wanted it to be real. She knew that now.

'That sounds good, Mum. I'll ask him,' she said. She appreciated that Soraya had not asked her when they wanted to get married or even if they wanted to get married. Her mother was grounded in present realities, and this grounded her in turn. Naeem had said they would get engaged by the semester's end, and she trusted he would take the steps needed to achieve it.

They continued walking and Soraya asked more questions about Naeem, and Sara found that she was happy to answer. Her only misgiving now was Naeem's reaction to the news that her parents wanted to meet him. She thought he would be pleased but she could not always anticipate his responses. She decided to wait to tell him in person tomorrow. There was too much ambiguity in reading words on a screen and she wanted to see his face when she said the words.

When she arrived at Naeem's house they were unusually short on food supplies. She suggested making a tajine, which Naeem had not heard of or tasted, but they did not have the couscous or preserved lemons or harissa the recipe specified. She offered to drive to the supermarket, but he insisted on accompanying her. They went in her car, which was parked some distance away.

Upon entering the supermarket, Naeem scanned the aisles. She saw the craning of his neck, the shift in his gaze. She knew he was afraid someone he knew would be there and see them together. It bothered her that he was thinking of other people when they were together. As she proceeded towards the vegetable aisle, he seized the basket from her hand and carried it despite her protestations, and when they got to the counter, he packed the shopping bag efficiently and paid for the items.

When they reached his house, she had once again taken the lead, assigning him to peeling and chopping the onions and carrots as she began fluffing up the couscous with a fork. The air began to smell of cinnamon and garlic. She knew she would have to tell him about her mother's suggestion now but just as she was about to, his phone began to vibrate. They both saw that it was his mother, and he motioned to her with a finger on his lips before answering it. He walked away as he spoke. She could not hear what he was saying, only that his tone was both hushed and deferential. There was nothing about Soraya that would compel such a change in manner and she thought, not for the first time, that Naeem's mother must frighten him.

After a minute Naeem returned to the chopping board. He had chopped half an onion and he was now chopping the other half, lengthways, then horizontally. The pieces were uniform and he tipped them into the pan. They both stared into the pan as the onions sizzled and darkened in colour. She turned to face him.

'So I have something to tell you. I told my mum about us yesterday and she suggested you come to my birthday dinner,' she said.

'You did? Why didn't you tell me before you talked to her?'

'It just came out, okay? We were talking and I just blurted it out,' she said.

'What did you say exactly?' His hand on Sara's shoulder was unsteady, and he released his grip.

'Just that there was someone I've been talking to, and that you're special. That's all I told her,' she said.

'Okay, so what now?' Naeem's voice was raised as he tipped the can of tomatoes into the pan. If she did not know him as she did she would have said it was the voice of someone who was angry.

'She really wants to meet you. You know how it's my birthday in a couple of weeks –'

'No, you never said it was,' he said. They had in fact discussed birthdays some time ago, but she had not thought about it since.

'I don't even like birthdays,' she said, impatient now. 'But my mum had this idea that we could go out for dinner to celebrate – you, me, her and my dad – and I promised I'd at least ask you.'

'Do you want me to come?' He was so considerate. That was one interpretation of it, but the other, which she refused to consider, was that he was being cowardly, placing the onus on her.

'I'd love for you to meet my parents. I've told you, they're really laid-back, they're not going to interrogate you.' She was trying to minimise a threat her parents had never posed. The idea of parents frightening their children was foreign to her and she wondered if he knew that there were ways parents could impart their thoughts other than through intimidation.

'It's a good idea,' he said. 'We're meeting Sadia next week anyway. I'd love to meet your mum and dad, babe.' He placed his forehead against hers before returning to chopping the sweet potato and carrots into quarters.

Sadia worked at a pharmacy near Central station, close to their university. Sara knew these streets well, knew where to get vegan banh mi and milk teas studded with sago and black tapioca pearls. In the first few weeks of university she had been enthralled by the enthusiasm of the buskers in the station tunnel, the discount bookstore where Abida had bought a paperback copy of Edward Said's *Orientalism* for a dollar. The novelty had quickly worn off and she had become the same as everyone else, avoiding eye contact with anyone asking for money or singing jazzy renditions of ABBA originals.

When she arrived at the food court Naeem had named, she found that he was already sitting with a girl in a compact green hijab she assumed was Sadia. Sadia stood up to hug her. Naeem remained in his seat; they could not hug here. Sadia's white pharmacist's coat hung across the back of her chair. Her face and body were round, soft, and she had to stand on the balls of her feet to reach Sara. Sara could not discern any resemblance between the two cousins, Sadia's smile wider and less guarded than Naeem's, her teeth charmingly crooked.

'It's great to meet you, Sara. I've heard so much about you.'

'All good things, I hope,' she said, glancing at Naeem across the table. They were both contained within their own bodies, his hands knotted in his lap.

'Of course. Honestly, when he first told me he was talking to someone I didn't believe it. Naeem's never shown the slightest interest in girls up until now and, I might be biased, but there are definitely plenty of girls who'd love the chance –'

'Apu, you don't have to talk me up, Sara already knows what a nerd and loner I am, and she doesn't mind,' Naeem said, laughing. Sara saw the look they exchanged and was surprised at the jealousy congealed at the back of her throat. Here was a person who had a pre-existing claim to Naeem's affections, a person who could love him without shame. It reminded her of her friendship with

Abida, and with a pang she realised how much she wished she could share this moment with her. She missed Abida. Even as she drew closer to Naeem, she was aware that he could not satisfy her every need, that he was uncritical of the world in a way that Abida would find infuriating. She placed her hand on the table and tried to smile at Sadia.

'Why don't you go grab us some food and Sara and I can have a chat?' Sadia said to Naeem. 'I told you there's a really good Malaysian stall here, they do the best satays and peanut sauce.'

Sadia stuffed a twenty-dollar bill into Naeem's hand, retracting her fingers as she did so there was no risk of their hands brushing. Her caution with the possibility of physical contact shamed Sara, and she found it difficult to look at Sadia. Sadia did not know what she and Naeem had been doing. Sadia would surely not sit and smile with them if she did. Naeem placed the money on the table before Sadia could protest, and walked off. Sadia shook her head ruefully, smiling again.

'He never lets me pay for anything. Anyway, enough about my goody-two-shoes little cousin, tell me more about you. Naeem said you study mechanical engineering?'

Sara began with the modest script she had revised in the morning: selective school education, plans to go into motor sports or automotive design. She skimmed over her status as an only child, deliberated a little longer on her heritage because she knew it would be asked. She was never quite sure how to explain it; she knew nothing more than the broadest strokes of her ancestry, the family lore about the British great-great-great-grandfather whose fists had marked his Javanese servant-wife. This was the part of meeting new people that she hated. She was marked by her difference, by her inability to explain that difference.

Sadia nodded as Sara spoke and made encouraging noises when she faltered. She seemed a most obliging person and the things Naeem had said about her struggle to find a husband seemed strange, unlikely.

'So you and Naeem met in the MSA? I don't mean to scare you, but what I said before about Naeem is absolutely the truth. He's the golden child of our circle, the one all the mothers want for their daughters. And I love my aunt and uncle, but they're no walk in the park. Aunty especially, she's a tough cookie.'

These euphemisms frightened Sara, reiterated the things she had already surmised. The mother, beautiful and steely; the father, the big-shot psychiatry professor with all the money.

'I figured as much. Just between you and me, Naeem seems a bit scared of them,' she confessed. She felt disloyal for stating this, but she had been waiting for this opportunity for some time now, the chance to speak of Naeem to someone who knew him well.

'Yep, you've got that right. That's why I was so surprised when he told me. He knows what an uphill battle it will be to get his parents onside, but now that I've met you, I can see exactly why he's doing it. You're beautiful and you're smart, mashaAllah.'

Sara thanked Sadia as profusely as she could manage, not wishing to be ungracious, but she knew she was not beautiful, just green-eyed and fair in complexion, which many Muslims seemed to think was the same thing. Abida would have interjected now about the need to decolonise their minds and Sara almost said it now to Sadia in Abida's absence.

Naeem returned with a huge pile of satays, the cubes of chicken yellowed with curry powder and glistening with oil. Sadia chided him, saying he had bought too much and that she would have to return to work soon in any case, and then asked the question they had been anticipating.

'So what are you guys planning to do now? When do you want to get married?'

Sara bit into a skewer, the chicken sweet and salty and topped with kecap manis. She knew Naeem was relying on her to answer, but she refused to look at him, dipping her skewer into the bowl of sauce and filling her mouth with it.

'We think we could do our Islamic marriage next year and then live separately until I start my internship,' Naeem said. 'Either that, or we move in together a little sooner and live with our parents. I'm going to meet Sara's parents in a few weeks and I'll tell Ammu and Baba soon, inshaAllah.'

The outline of this plan was known to Sara. They had spoken of logistics so often in the early days and weeks, of how much money they would need to live on and whether they could live with his parents or hers to begin with. They had discussed whether they wanted to remain in Sydney or relocate to Melbourne, a city they both admired, and how many people from the MSA they would invite to their wedding. But they had lost this thread of conversation some time ago, allowing their discussions and their house visits to lull them into a sense of finality.

'I'll make dua for you guys. And let me know if you want me to help speak to your mum and dad, Naeem. I'm sure they'll come around, inshaAllah. They'll just need to freak out a bit first and then they'll be fine.'

Sadia reached for her white coat, and they all stood up to depart. Sara did not want to sit alone here with Naeem, switch back into their uncensored selves when they had just played at such respectability. She hugged Sadia and they walked off in separate directions – Naeem to the hospital and she back towards home. She finally had something to tell Abida, something Abida would understand and recognise as legitimate. Family meetings and endorsements were moving her and Naeem out of the compacted soil where no roots could take hold and into the loamy, fertile soil of the lowlands. Abida would be upset that Sara had not told her from the outset. But Abida would also bring her customary insights to the situation, and together they would navigate each step as it came. Abida would tell her what to do, then tell Sara it was up to her, that she was sorry for being such a tyrant. She could see the surprise in Abida's face now, the cacophony of her initial reaction. She smiled as she walked on.

17

Abida

They were packing and assembling with industry, forming a dedicated production line. Abida snuck a mint and surveyed the pile of one hundred jars they had already put together, all with the labels 'mint to be' and Ahlam's and Ziad's initials affixed to them. There were still another hundred to go. Abida had been enthusiastic at the outset, stuffing mints in jars from the hefty plastic sack Ahlam's father had procured from his store. But she was now bored of the shaking and sealing, hungry from the exertion and wondering when Ahlam's mother would serve them lunch. She could smell something meaty, the air fragrant with olive oil and sumac.

'I still can't believe this is actually happening, girls. It's just so surreal,' Ahlam said. Her hair was tied back in two plaits, her face bare of makeup.

'SubhanAllah, it's all unfolding exactly as you'd hoped. Isn't it amazing, the plans Allah has for us all?' Mariam was perched on the floor, her eyes trained to the pile of labels, her stack of assembled jars far larger than any of the other girls. Sara was the second quickest, her labels all symmetrical and aligned with their corresponding cork lids.

Abida leaned back into Ahlam's bed, running her fingers along the furry yellow throw draped over the quilt. She picked it up and swiped at Sara with it, and Sara squealed and moved away. She watched the reflection of the other girls in Ahlam's full-length bedside mirror, which was draped with silver and gold necklaces and a feather headdress. Abida's possessions were all stuffed in the single drawer allocated for her usage, its knob whittled down to a misshapen stub.

'It really is. But nothing would've ever happened if not for this girl right here,' said Ahlam, pointing over at Abida. The other girls whooped, and Abida got up and bowed with dramatic flourish.

'Thank you, thank you. If anyone else needs matchmaking services, I'm happy to take on some more clients.'

'Wahid's pretty cute. I wonder if he has his eye on anyone?' Fitri said as she shook out the sack of mints with vigour, causing them to spill on the floor, some rolling under the bed and the closed doorway. Abida fished for them, the underside of the bed as immaculate as everywhere else in the house. She thought people who cleaned underneath their beds were likely to be uptight weirdos; it did not surprise her that Ahlam was one of them.

'Hard to know, really,' Ahlam said. 'He doesn't give much away. Ziad said he's definitely open to getting married, though. But I think he's so focused on the MSA and his degree that everything else is taking a back seat for now.'

There was a knock on the door, the exchange of some indecipherable words in Arabic. Ahlam's mother, a plump woman in her late fifties wearing an abaya and pink fluffy slippers, beckoned to them.

'Come eat, girls. I know my daughter has you working hard so you need to keep up your energy.'

They trailed out of the bedroom and into the dining room, where the table was already set. Two platters of stuffed vine leaves piled with tomatoes and chunks of lamb were placed at its centre, rice and a salad with radish and crispy fried bread to its side. Abida met Sara's eye, and they both grinned. They had been cautious with each other since the day of the hijab event, both of them conscious that they had overstepped a boundary the other had drawn. Since then Sara had been more attentive, reminding the girls on the MSA sub-chat for girls only that the election was approaching, that Abida had been a prefect at their school and secured the Muslim students their own prayer space. But she had still declined to stand as Abida's deputy, and Abida knew that none of the other girls would agree. She would have to face Wahid and Naeem alone.

Ahlam's mother scooped intertwined bundles of the vine leaves onto their plates, the juices from the meat and rice dripping all over Abida's plate. She urged them to take more, to eat until they were full, and then some more. It was like this with any of Abida's friends who were not white Australians, this same flourish of hospitality and keenness to please, whether the food was dosa or spanakopita or momo. Only her white friends withheld, their mothers warm and chatty with nothing to prove.

'Wahid's getting really worked up about this whole president thing, isn't he?' Abida reached for the ladle to dish some more rice, aiming to sound mild and disinterested, but Mariam looked at her before speaking decisively.

'I hate to say it but the combination of Wahid and Naeem is going to be pretty hard to beat, Abida. Wahid is so dedicated and Naeem is pretty much a –'

'He's a saint, honestly,' Ahlam said. 'Remember when we did that collection for the Rohingya refugees? Ziad told me Naeem donated a thousand dollars anonymously and he only found out because he was administering the account. And the guy reads the Quran like an angel, mashaAllah. If I wasn't already taken, I might have married him instead.' She laughed, the green residue of the vine leaves caught in her two front teeth before she flicked her tongue over and across it.

The girls then moved on to discussing the MSA's upcoming charity campaign for the Horn of Africa, the bake sale they would hold on the lawns and what each of them would be making. Sara got up and gestured for Abida to accompany her, and Abida licked her fingers clean, then followed.

They walked past the kitchen where Ahlam's mother was shredding cabbage leaves while watching an Egyptian soapie, past the photo wall of Ahlam's siblings' graduations and several grandchildren, and into the backyard. There was a garden swing set against the door, and they both sat on it. Abida kicked her feet against the white concrete floor, and the swing moved with a creak.

'Sorry to drag you away, but I needed to talk to you about something,' said Sara.

'What is it? Are you okay?' Abida heard a wail, the exaggerated crack of a television slap, Ahlam's mother muttering something in Arabic at the actors.

'I should've told you this a long time ago, and I'm sorry I didn't. I understand if you're going to be annoyed at me, but Naeem and I are together.'

'Together? What the heck does that mean, together?' She knew what it meant in the metaphorical sense but in this moment the literal eluded her. She replayed what Sara had said. The apology had been offered without reservation, but there was a discernible element of pride in Sara's voice, which conveyed to Abida that her best friend had been contemplating how to announce this for some time. Sara had been living an entire existence that she had not known about. She shared everything with Sara, but Sara had withheld. She began to piece it all together: Sara's distraction and silence, her absence from conversations on the MSA presidential election. Now she understood Sara would never have agreed to be her deputy; that would have placed her in direct opposition to her lover boy. Sara had permitted Abida to stand alone while she had been intertwined all along. The injustice of it caused Abida to kick at the ground, the swing protesting as it rattled and pulled to one side. Ahlam had consulted Abida while getting to know Ziad, but she did not require her any longer, and now Sara would be the same. Abida would be discarded, superseded by this boy and his wealth and charms.

'We want to get married, obviously. You know what I mean,' Sara said.

'Sara, I don't know what Naeem has told you, but I'm your oldest friend, and I will tell you honestly that I think the chances of you getting married to him are slim to nil,' Abida said, softening her voice as much as she could. She saw Sara's eyes widen but she refused to grant false reassurances. Sara was foolish and Naeem smug, and the combination of the two was not to be borne. They had swallowed this fallacy of love, this grand notion that any two people could choose each other and the world would have to abide by that choice. She knew better. She would tell Sara so.

'I don't know how you can possibly know that.'

'I know guys like Naeem, and I know families like his. He's just a follower. They all are,' Abida said. 'I have nothing against the guy, but he doesn't strike me as the kind of guy to stir the pot by bringing home some random non-Bangladeshi girl when he has years of uni to go. His parents would put their foot down and force him to give you up. I'm sorry, but you have to know the truth.'

The absurdity of Sara and Naeem was even greater than that of Naeem marrying Abida, a fellow Bangladeshi of dubious means. At the same time, she felt the peculiar sting of Naeem choosing a girl like Sara when he would not have chosen a girl like her. She would never have been deemed suitable for him or his family. As much as she loved Sara and appreciated her uniqueness, she felt that very uniqueness was attracting Naeem in the most warped way possible. He would view Sara as a novelty and Sara's naiveté and desire to belong would ensure that he did not have to work very hard for the privilege. Abida was enraged on Sara's behalf, but she was angrier for herself, for being placed among these boys who were so prone to picking girls based on who had the fairest complexion and who could best massage their fragile egos.

'I know you care about me,' Sara said, 'but Naeem does too. I'll be careful, okay? Just don't write him off yet.' The protective curl of her tongue over his name sickened Abida.

'I don't give two hoots about him. But you have to be careful.'

'I *said* I'd be careful. We haven't done anything wrong. You heard the other girls, Naeem's practically a saint.' Sara was sharp now, her voice shaking. Inside, the crescendo of violins signalled the closing credits of the soapie, the sizzle of the pan as the cabbage hit the oil.

'If you say so. Is this what your nice little Muslim girl act has all been about? Now I get it,' Abida said. She could not resist the poke, knowing she was being spiteful. Perfect, insipid Naeem. He and Wahid would ascend to the presidency together. She imagined Sara as the first lady of the MSA, waving at Abida from their cavalcade as the crowd cheered her and Naeem onwards.

'I'm sorry I didn't tell you before. That was terrible of me,' Sara said, her anger seeming to dissolve. Abida knew then that she was doing that thing she was so good at, wounding someone else to conceal the extent of her own wounds. She would have to begin again. She reached for Sara's hand and closed her own around it.

'Ignore me. I'm just being a bitch as usual. I should be the one saying sorry, not you. Tell me whatever you feel like.'

Sara began to speak, telling Abida how kind Naeem was, how silly, how she had already met his cousin and that he would soon be meeting her parents. It seemed to Abida like Sara was assembling a case that they were taking this business very seriously and that they should be taken seriously in return. She told Abida she was afraid and excited and uncertain, all at once. She had never felt this way before. Sara paused, giggled. Abida attempted to smile but she could not giggle along with Sara. She did not do giggles, and especially not at news of this nature.

'I know it all sounds so stupid and juvenile. I can barely stand to listen to myself talk about it.'

'And I can barely stand to listen to it.' Abida laughed. The friction was now depleting, another argument circumnavigated yet unresolved.

'But really, I just worry about you, that's all. If Mr Perfect does anything to hurt you –'

'He's been nothing but respectful, I promise. I know what you think of a lot of the MSA guys, but he's the real deal. He's a good person.'

Abida stood up. She could think of nothing more to add. The conversation had been shocking to her but her mind was now searching for the signs of what had been happening. She had wanted so badly to believe that she and Sara saw the world in the same way that she had wilfully disregarded any evidence that they did not. She was alone in her convictions once again, as she always had been. She turned to look across Ahlam's fence. The neighbour's children were bouncing around on a trampoline, their heads bobbing in and out of sight, their mother in a black hijab, puffing on a cigarette as she looked on impassively.

Sara remained on the swing and looked out at the children. Abida wondered if she was contemplating the children she planned to have with Naeem, which languages they would speak in the home. One of the older MSA girls was Indonesian and had married a white convert, and everyone had raved about the cuteness of mixed-race babies, but Abida noticed that this seemed to apply mainly when one half of the mix was white.

When Sara spoke, she did not seem to have noticed the children at all.

'I know you're annoyed over this whole election thing. I haven't been paying much attention to it, and I'm sorry for that too. But, honestly, Naeem has barely mentioned it. He doesn't care about these nominations one bit. Wahid just wants his name on the paper because he thinks it'll make his application stronger.'

'I know he probably doesn't care but having his name on the paper will make a difference. Wahid's not dumb,' Abida replied.

'Maybe. But you can still win this. I'll do a supporting speech at the nomination meeting, okay? I know my voice doesn't count for anything, but I want to do it.'

'Don't say that. You are the best friend I've ever had. I'll be praying for you. And for Naeem too.' Abida made this concession to the boy Sara loved. She wanted to maintain at least the veneer of being a supportive friend.

Sara stood up and the two of them hugged, hard, and walked back inside. The other girls had migrated to the lounge room, where Ahlam's mother had served up petit fours and bitter black coffees, the assembled jars lined up along the floor.

When Abida arrived home, Ammu was combing Tawfiq's hair for head lice, the sharp chemical tang of the shampoo causing Abida's eyes to water. She went and sat in the backyard, where the children were less likely to congregate and disturb her. Although there were some who romanticised the lost era of children playing outdoors, their yard was bare except for a triangular patch of brown grass and a washing line on which someone's sheet or school shirt was hung. Perhaps those who had more picturesque grounds to enjoy could be justified in urging their children outdoors, but Abida thought her siblings demonstrated good sense by avoiding it. She had only come out here, book and laptop in hand, because her absorption in the immediate tasks would render her surroundings irrelevant.

She didn't want to think about Sara and Naeem right now. She had to focus on tightening her MSA nomination speech. For inspiration, she was reading a book on the anti-colonial resistance in the Algerian War of Independence against the French, chronicling the long list of crimes committed by the French against the local population: the Battle of Sidi-Ferruch, the fashionable Parisians watching the spectacle from pleasure boats as Algeria was invaded, the les enfumades of Algerian tribes who were burned in their caves by Marshal Thomas Robert Bugeaud. She had thought this would inspire some more material for her speech, but all she could think was, *If this really is a war, you started it. You started it all.*

She could never say any of this, of course. They were all wary of government surveillance, knowing as they did that an MSA boy had been taken in for questioning two years ago by the intelligence services, his eventual finding of innocence counting for little after he had been expelled from the university. An engagement had been broken off several years ago between an MSA boy and his fiancée because her family had been warned he was being watched by the intelligence services, his anti-Western rhetoric conspicuous on his social media accounts. This same boy now drove a bus, despite his first-class degree, his career prospects ruined. These were the battles which galvanised Abida, the causes she longed to champion.

Inside, Tawfiq was shrieking; the shampoo was burning his scalp. She heard Ammu's soothing tones, the lilt of a song about the moon kissing their forehead, which she sung them all in Bangla when they were distressed. Abida closed her eyes, knowing she ought to go and help, that her grandiose ambitions of social justice counted for nothing if she did not go to the assistance of her own mother. She wished she could be a man, crusading in public, selfish at home, a dutiful wife in the wings.

'Ammu, let me try, I can do it faster.' Inside, she prised the comb from her mother's wet fingers, cursing Sara and Naeem's future children with heads full of crawling, stubborn lice as she did.

18

Naeem

Despite his best efforts, Naeem had not been able to devise a birthday surprise that adequately conveyed the depth of his feelings for Sara. Was it even possible to box and ribbon the scope of one person's feelings for another? Gifts could only ever represent an apology of sorts, *Sorry I couldn't show you what I really feel, but here's a box of chocolates*, or at best, a reassurance that the recipient was being listened to, *Here's tickets to that play you mentioned over breakfast last weekend*. But Naeem could not recall Sara mentioning anything specific that she wanted to see or do or taste, and so he had planned something he felt she would enjoy: a road trip to one of the small towns on the south coast past Sydney, where they would have a packed lunch on the beach. He waited until his parents and Tasnia had departed the house to drive to the supermarket, where he purchased crackers, cheese and drinks, as well as the ingredients for a flourless chocolate cake he had researched. Naeem had never attempted to bake anything before, associating baked goods with white people in chef's hats and aprons.

He had not told Sara what activity they would be doing, but had asked her to wait at her house, which was en route to their destination. The exertion of cracking the eggs, measuring the almond meal and melting the chocolate, then watching it rise in the oven and icing it, made Naeem sweat. He did not have time to take another shower and hoped the spray of Paco Rabanne, courtesy of Professor Kazi's extensive cologne collection, would mask it well enough. He drove to Sara's house, ensuring to take care around the corners to prevent the cake from toppling over in the boot.

The suburb Sara lived in appeared like his own. There were the same steep driveways, the same leafy canopies of trees, but here the houses were mainly single storey and the front lawns varied from manicured to neglected, weeds springing unchecked to the height of windows. The noise of an engine overhead reminded him that they were underneath the flight path from the airport nearby, which Naeem went to several times a year to welcome extended family home from overseas or to go overseas himself, to Bangladesh or Thailand or Malaysia for family holidays.

When he reached Sara's house, he had planned on phoning her and awaiting her appearance, but some impulse drove Naeem to knock on the door. The house had a solid brick exterior and was long and narrow with a recently mown front lawn, and no flowers or hedges to greet guests.

'Oh, it's you! I wasn't expecting you just yet,' Sara said, her hair wrapped in a towel as she beckoned him in.

'Happy birthday, my love,' he said, wrapping his arms around her, inhaling her soapy scent, droplets from her hair leaving a trail of moisture on his shirt.

'Thanks, Naeemy. Just give me a minute to get dressed.' She delighted in devising new nicknames for him, whether a play on his name or a double entendre. He responded to whatever name he was called by; his mother had taught him that was the correct way to behave.

While Sara disappeared into an adjoining room, Naeem sat in the main living room. The room was not unclean, but there were letters and old newspapers flung across the low coffee table, and the couches would have benefited from a wipe with a soft cloth. Two overgrown pot plants sat on the benchtops, which his parents would think unwise; plants were to be kept outdoors. A family photo hung on the wall, taken when Sara was in high school, her hair longer and lighter and tied in a ponytail. Sara's mother had blonde streaks in her hair, her father a ruddy complexion and a limp moustache. Naeem realised that he would be meeting these people in just a few days, and he averted his eyes and tried not to touch or move anything.

'Am I allowed to ask where we're going? I'm not sure if I should wear a dress or pants,' she said, holding both up in front of him.

Once he had assured her that either would do, Sara exited the room once again. A door slammed behind her. She occupied space in this home and made noise; he was a ghost in his, skimming the pristine surfaces but never sinking in. Naeem tried to imagine how his parents would react to this room. They would not comment on or even critique its appearance, but he would read in the stiffness of his mother's posture that she would not think Sara capable of running a home efficiently given her parents' example. His parents believed the behaviours of children could be directly traced to the quality of the parenting they had received. In this way, they derived a level of satisfaction from their own offspring he thought in poor taste. Naeem grinned, wondering what mental acrobatics they would perform to maintain their level of self-satisfaction if they were to discover what their son was now doing.

Sara emerged in the dress, a wide-brimmed hat in hand. The hat reminded him of Kate Winslet's character in the movie *Titanic*, which he had watched six times. This was a fact Naeem had not shared with Sara, and he promptly did so as they walked to his car. It was incredible to him that they had not yet exhausted their supply of inconsequential facts to share with each other, that the picture he had constructed of Sara required such continual readjusting. He had not previously taken enough interest in anyone, family or friend, to perceive them as anything but fixed in the essence of what they were. In his thirst to know Sara, it occurred to him that anyone, even his own parents, could be simultaneously known and unknown, familiar and strange. This realisation frightened him, and he sped up as they began to leave the city behind. He rolled down the window and Sara joked that she loved the feel of the wind in her hijab. He stuck his tongue out at her for being so lame, and she stuck her tongue out at him in return.

The town Naeem had looked up online was Gerringong, which was said to be the most beautiful on the southern coast, and when they arrived on its outskirts, he was thrilled with his choice. Its rolling green hills led seamlessly into the lush coastline, a long stretch of deserted beach he thought far prettier than Bondi or Coogee. He could not recall the last time he had been to a beach in Sydney; the sight of so much bare flesh embarrassed him. His family had built their own pool to ensure that they did not have to compete with the masses for a spot on the sand.

Naeem sent Sara down the hill with the picnic blanket to select a spot while he unloaded the food. He noted with relief that an Indian family had parked adjacent to his car; he had been apprehensive about bringing Sara to a small town, worried people would stare at them both and ruin the day he had envisioned. Sara had descended the hill too quickly and he watched her as she steadied herself, spreading the rug out and straightening its corners. He carried the basket with the cake and snacks, struggling a little with its weight, which Sara noticed. She started to stand to assist before he waved her back down, her dress billowing out across the blanket.

'It's so lovely here,' she said.

'I wanted to make it special for you. It's not every day you say goodbye to your teenage years.' Slowly, Naeem reached into the basket and extracted the cake, which he had attempted to ice with the number twenty on its surface. He knew it was hackneyed, but he hoped Sara would appreciate the sentiment. He cleared his throat and spoke once again.

'These past few months with you have been the most unexpected and amazing of my life. You're beautiful inside and out, Sara, and I love you now and always.' He reached into his pocket.

'I couldn't get you an engagement ring of course, not yet, but I wanted to get you something small to give you an indication of how I feel.'

It took Naeem longer to find what he was looking for than he had anticipated, and for a moment he panicked, thinking he had dropped it in the car or on the slope. But he found it, the thin silver necklace with both of their initials as charms. He crouched down behind Sara, pulling the clasp to fasten it around her neck, listening to the rise and fall of her breath as the ocean lapped ahead of them.

'It's so lovely. I can't believe you went to all this trouble for me.' Sara seemed overcome, her hand to her throat, fingering the charms. He took the charms from her hand and placed them gently into the folds of her dress, placing his hand on her chest where they were now obscured.

'I got you a necklace so you could wear it under your hijab, and no one would see. But the real trouble was this cake, so let's hope it's edible.'

'Let's take a photo of us right now,' Sara said. They had not taken a photo together yet, the act seeming to incriminate them and solidify what they had done. But he leaned in and put his arm around her as Sara held up her phone, the brim of her hat obscuring his left eye as it was taken. She sent the photo to him as he cut her a slice of cake, which she deemed delicious. Naeem could not ascertain if she was being wholly truthful, but he liked the way she devoured it with her fingers and asked for seconds as though she were.

They spent the following hours lying on the blanket, alternating between talking and long periods of easy silence. They spoke about the trip to South Africa Sara would be taking after the semester ended, and how her relatives there would react to the news of her engagement. They spoke of the MSA nomination meeting and agreed that it would be harmless if Wahid nominated Naeem as his deputy. Sara then removed her shoes and walked to the water's edge, pulling the edge of her dress up by several centimetres. A wave crashed higher than she expected, and it got wet anyway. She came back and sat next to Naeem, asking him what he thought of the name Dilara, which she had heard one of the girls in the MSA mention from one of the Turkish soap operas they all watched. It was a game they played occasionally, attempting to think of baby names they both liked, and which would not prove obstructive later in Australian life. They both liked the name Yahya for a boy but agreed its distortion in English was awful. Sara liked the name Nadia for a girl, which Naeem did not care for, but he did not say so, only that he preferred the name Ayah, denoting both a verse of the Quran and a sign of Allah.

The time for dhuhr prayer arrived, signalled by the prayer app on his phone.

'Should we just pray here on the grass? I can use my app to find the direction to pray in,' she said.

Naeem had last prayed several weeks ago, but he could not tell Sara that. Since they had come together he had struggled to stand before Allah. He knew this was foolish and counter-intuitive; Allah continually instructed the believers to never lose hope in His forgiveness, but he was simply too ashamed. He smiled and nodded at Sara. He had to continue to be the person she thought he was, the person who was not sinking under the weight of his sins. He allowed her to move the food off the blanket so that they could pray on its surface, and she moved expectantly into position. He did not want her to follow him; he was not fit to lead prayer, but there was no means by which to prevaricate. He began and immediately it was like a belated homecoming, his hands clasped against his chest as he whispered the words. The sun on his back was warming. He was into the second last set, his knees on the ground, when Naeem heard a voice close to his ear. It required all his willpower to continue praying and not heed the voice, but he could not mistake the words, even as he proceeded into the fourth and final set, turning his head to the right to greet the angel on his right shoulder, then repeating the action on his left.

The voice was now a face, crouched down and too close to his. It was not a face that distinguished itself in any way, being of medium age and neither large nor small, neat stubble dotting the pink cheeks.

'I said, you and your terrorist slut of a girlfriend aren't welcome here.'

The man did not sound venomous so much as utterly assured of what he was saying. His stance obscured Sara from Naeem's direct line of sight, but he could hear her sharp intake of breath from behind him. The man stood up, looking at them and shaking his head, before walking up the path and out of sight.

Naeem could not think, he could not see. He gathered the blanket into a heap and shoved the food into the basket, wildly grasping about for Sara's hand and steering them up the hill.

He unlocked the car and piled their things into the back seat, starting up the engine and trying to reverse while the gear was still in park. He needed to get out and onto the road.

'Naeem, let me drive, you're shaking,' she said, leaning over and turning the engine off.

'They're coming for us, Sara. They hate us, and they're going to get us all, every last one of us. We're not safe here. We're not safe anywhere,' he babbled, unable to stop himself from saying more, telling her of the nightmares, the constant fear, the knowledge that he was hated by people who did not know him and who would do harm to him and his family simply because they were what they were.

Sara was silent for several moments, the only sound being the cries of delight from two little girls who were rolling down the hill, their clothing a blur of rainbow and denim. She held his hand and turned it over in hers, stroking the palm with her fingernails in a motion that tickled.

'I know you're upset, but do you really think that we're all going to be killed just because of that one idiot down there? There are over a billion Muslims in the world, they can't just obliterate us all off the face of the planet.' There was the hint of a smile in her voice. He pulled his hand away from hers.

'Maybe they won't come for you, Sara Andrews.' He extended the syllables of her last name, feeling the rage course through him, long suppressed and transmuted into even, polite tones. 'You'll be just fine.' She was one of them even as she prayed alongside him. She had dismissed his fears as laughable, highlighting the gulf between those who belonged and those who did not. *Do not be angry, do not be angry, do not be angry,* the Prophet Muhammad had warned thrice, but Naeem was too frightened to restrain himself.

'I know you're upset,' she said again. 'But please don't let our beautiful day together be ruined because of someone's stupidity.'

Sara did not seem to comprehend what he was saying. This was not an isolated incident, nor could it be dismissed as one of those things people in small towns did because they were ignorant and did not know any better. This could happen anywhere. If anything, Naeem preferred crude insults like this to the more insidious racism of men in suits who studied Islam and Muslims from their think tanks, or the apathetic masses, who cared only that their lives would remain undisturbed. Indifference and hate, it would lead them to the same end.

'Sara, I can't meet your parents now.' Naeem had not been aware that he would say this until the words had flitted out of his mouth, but once they were said, he knew them to be true. He could not sit with Soraya and Amin and instil in them any form of confidence that he would care for their daughter, that he would nurture and love her for all their days when he was convinced, on some visceral level, that their days were numbered. He was afraid of what was to come and afraid of his own deficiencies in facing them. He was afraid of commitment, afraid to be alone, afraid to be noticed, afraid to be forgotten, afraid of it all.

'All right then. If that's what you want.' There was something terrible about the resignation with which Sara spoke, her utter lack of surprise or fury. He wondered if she had really believed he would attend, or if she had been preparing herself for him to pull out all along. Naeem could not decide which was worse: disappointing

Sara when her hopes had been raised, or the possibility that she had not been disappointed at all.

He rested his head against the wheel, hearing the door on the passenger side open. He panicked, thinking she would run and he would have to chase after her, but she walked around to the driver's side, her movements laboured, like an injured person. He heard her sob and then quickly press it in, apparently unwilling to share her grief with him. 'Thanks for today. I'll drive us home now,' she said.

He craved her anger, deserved it, but it seemed she knew this and would not gratify him.

19

Sara

Sara told her mother that Naeem had fallen ill, but the lie was both unconvincingly told and unconvincingly received. Soraya had been kind in not questioning her any further, saying only that it was a shame and that they would have to meet some other time. Sara was unsure if she had been attempting to shield Naeem from her mother's scrutiny or shielding herself from the humiliation that the boy she loved had bailed on her. Whatever the reason, she had been grateful that Soraya had not challenged her story, and that her father had not been informed of the planned meeting, let alone its revisions.

The birthday dinner had been pleasant, the curries buttery but too sweet, presumably moderated to appeal to the mixed clientele of tourists and locals at Darling Harbour. Soraya and Amin had presented her with a new geometric wristwatch in a style Sara admired, but once they were back home she had shoved it out of sight. It reminded her too much of the other piece of jewellery she had received for her birthday, which had been flung about when they had arrived at her home after the beach and, in their confusion and frenzy, entered her bedroom and closed the door behind them. The violence of what they had acted out had caused the charms Naeem had bought to dig into her skin and almost snap off the chain, which had twisted and wound around her hijab like bindweed. It was the unburdening of two mild-mannered people, exerting all the force they withheld from others onto each other. She wondered then if she had believed Naeem's rantings; the desperation they had both embodied in her room had certainly seemed to suggest so.

For the first time, Sara had been aware of the total senselessness of what they were doing. The sound of their heaving and panting was noisy in the empty house and the sight of their bodies disgusted her. She had pointed to the door and he had taken his things and left without any words being exchanged. Once she was alone, Sara had sprawled on the floor, the ticking of Soraya's grandfather clock in the hallway echoing through the house. An ant had crawled onto the bare skin of her belly, and she watched it crawl up past her breasts and then use her arm as a springboard to jump onto the floor and crawl in the direction of the kitchen.

The sun had been high in the sky when she had finally pulled herself up and into the shower, where she had used a clenched fist to drive the shampoo into her scalp and the shower gel into her thighs. It had not hurt as much as she had hoped, and she had contemplated reaching for an implement which would. But Amin had arrived home from work and Sara had submitted to his scratchy birthday kiss on the cheek. By the time Soraya had arrived, bearing Sara's favourite Lebanese charcoal chicken, garlic sauce and a tub of pistachio ice cream, she had been able to replicate some of the normality they exuded.

Naeem had not contacted her that night, nor the following day, even after she had returned from the scheduled birthday dinner with her parents. They were ordinarily in such constant contact that Sara wondered if her phone was malfunctioning, until she received an influx of messages from Abida regarding Ahlam's upcoming girls-only katb kitab party. Sara ignored the messages, just as she ignored Soraya's message asking if she could come in to the beauty parlour that morning and fill in for the receptionist. She lay in bed instead, watching YouTube clips explaining the introductory principles of the Fourier transform, but she couldn't concentrate. Amin was out at a plumbing job and she was alone. She felt the lack of other children in the house, a sting which she had not experienced for several years, after she had grown to understand that the pain of the miscarriages was not hers to assume. She instinctively reached for her belly, the place where Soraya had loved and lost, again and again.

Sara had always known of this, of the years of loss her parents had endured. One of her earliest memories was of her mother screaming in the night. Sara had not run into the room, trusting that the low, firm tones of Amin would comfort Soraya. It was a part of their history which did not need to involve her, just like their use of Afrikaans when speaking with each other but never with her. But the absence of Naeem had propelled her thoughts in the direction of other absences: the older sister who she imagined telling her that she ought to dump the bastard, advice she would noisily dispute and prickle at. She thought of a younger sister who could befriend Naeem's sister; an older brother who would beat Naeem up for messing his sister around. She thought of how she was an oddity in every space she occupied, recalled Abida's flicker of surprise when they had first met at school and Sara had asked her if she knew where there was a place they could pray.

There was nothing preventing Sara from going to the cemetery. Her car had a full tank of petrol and she did not have anything pressing to keep her at home. Her parents did not need her; nobody did. She could not dismiss the uncomfortable possibility that part of the reason she liked being with Naeem was because he seemed to need her. With him she was a core component of a unit rather than an addendum to it. It had been an unforeseen delight and she was not prepared to be without it.

The graves did not appear to be arranged in chronological sequence. There were sections where identical shiny black gravestones were crammed in together, and other sections where weeds acted as arbiters between tiny mounds rising from the ground. Sara traversed aisle after aisle, initially seeking the children's section before allowing herself to wander and read the inscriptions. She walked past a woman with heavy brown eyeshadow who had brought her three young children to a grave with an imposing charcoal gravestone, and an elderly man with a cane in hand, who sat alone at a grave and recited from a pocket-sized Quran. *Every soul shall taste death*. The verse chilled her. All believers were instructed to undertake regular reflection on their mortality, but Sara knew that death was a certainty and didn't feel the need to confront it. So many Muslims she knew delighted in discussing the gory torments of the grave, of the punishments that would begin at this stage for those who had reaped them, but she could not relate the luridness of those descriptions to the quiet mounds of earth in front of her. She uttered a silent prayer for these people, for the good they had tried to do and the mistakes they had made. In prayer, people stood in formation, side-by-side, toe-to-toe, and here too they were aligned in neat rows.

She did not want to linger in the private spaces of others, even if those others were far below her. She walked by the children's section, noting how small and tightly packed together the mounds were. One grave was decorated with multicoloured love heart stickers, another had a toy giraffe alongside it. It comforted her to think of all the children united, even in death. A bird hovered overhead, and Sara started, thinking of horror movies she had watched where vultures preyed upon the dead. She was a stranger to the grief of her parents, and she knew that she had benefited from being the sole recipient of their time and affection. She had no business among the grieving.

She was unsure now what she wanted with Naeem. In her mind, their relationship was tainted, but it might not always remain so. Did it matter if they had come together, and were to remain together, for reasons other than unselfish love? Were there people whose relationships were sustained wholly by unselfish love and that alone? Sara did not think so. The love that her parents possessed for each other was mingled with familiarity, possibly boredom and resignation. The love she had seen Abida's parents display, mainly through one occupying the children so that the other could have a moment's rest, was rooted in their ability to accept, to cope and seek contentment within the small parameters of their lives.

She dialled Naeem's number. While she waited, she looked at the photo she had saved of them in a hidden folder. In it their heads were pressed together, hers tilted at a perpendicular angle to his. He had blinked at the moment of capture, but this lent his countenance a serenity, as though he had closed his eyes in peaceful rumination. The phone continued to ring; Naeem had not installed voicemail. She hung up, wondering if this was yet another indication of his complacence, that he tacitly believed whoever was calling would take the time to call back, but at this moment she saw that he was returning her call.

'Sara, are you there?'

'I'm at the cemetery,' she said. She knew this piece of information, offered without explanation, would unsettle him, and she was gratified by the immediacy of his response.

'What are you doing there? Don't worry, I'll come to you now, okay? Just stay there.' Sara heard the jangle of keys, the closing of a book. She turned to the graves once again, willing herself to feel. But the tiny mounds of earth did not lend themselves to her purposes, remaining still and silent and dotted with blades of grass. Muslims believed children died sinless and departed this world unblemished by its cruelties, straight into the safekeeping of their Lord. But Sara would not be so fortunate; she knew she would go to Him with the weight of her sins, everything she had yet to atone for.

After some time, Sara saw Naeem walking across the rows of graves towards her. The haste with which he had departed his house was evident in his trackpants, the limp dampness of his hair against his face. He was squinting as he walked, a water bottle clasped in his hand. When he reached her, Naeem enfolded her in his arms.

'What the hell are you doing here? Here, have a drink, it's hot,' he said, uncapping the bottle and tipping it into her mouth. Sara had once imagined Naeem in a white coat striding through hospital corridors, a stethoscope coiled around his neck, but those images had merely transposed his face onto the earnest, handsome doctors she had seen in the hospital dramas her mother enjoyed. The curtness of his manner now was more akin to that of real doctors, and she wondered if he had learned about bedside manner from his father.

She gestured towards the graves in front of them. When Naeem had asked why her parents had not had any other children, she had hemmed and hawed around it, hoping he would interrogate her for an answer. But Naeem had not pressed her. He hadn't been interested enough to find out.

'Do you want to talk about it?' Naeem asked. Sara did not want his gentle voice right now, his tentative feathery dusting of her arm with his fingertips.

To confuse him, she kept her voice deliberately light and cheery. 'Since we're always being told to think about death on the daily, we should make this one of our regular haunts. Pun definitely intended.'

The low rumble he emitted suggested that Naeem was growing impatient with her manipulations.

'I've always been alone,' she continued. 'My parents could never have another child. They tried and tried and there was only me.'

'We're all born alone and we all die alone,' he said. 'Look around you, no one gets to take anyone with them. Your parents were lucky because in you they got the best gift, which they could keep for a little while.'

Sara began to cry, her head bowed. The tears were warm and salty in her mouth. She crouched to the ground and placed her hands beneath her. The earth was dry and seemed to exert pressure against her hand, as though spring-loaded. Naeem bent down across from her, a gravestone between them. He lowered his eyes to the ground and raised his hands, whispering and nodding his head as he did. She had witnessed this rocking motion in those who recited the Quran, their bodies coursing with the words. But Naeem had not read aloud in her presence, withholding from her what he shared with audiences of hundreds.

When he was done, he wiped his face with both hands, extending his right hand across the grave to hold hers. They sat like that for several minutes and Sara closed her eyes, listening to people traipsing their way through the graves.

'I want to stop what we've been doing,' Naeem said. 'This isn't what I want for you, or for me. It's going to destroy us, not just in the here and now but if we keep going, we will be witnesses against each other when judgement is pronounced, and the thought of that is enough to keep me from touching you again until it's permissible.' He did not release her hand but in its grip she felt the firmness of the resolution.

'I want to stop, too,' she said. Sara stated the words definitively to match his, but she wasn't sure she meant them. She did not really want to stop, but she felt that if they did not, they would grow to hate each other. They had acted against their own beliefs, and each distrusted the other for being a party to it. If they continued she would only resent him, and he would blame himself, and they would continue until the bond they shared fragmented and collapsed.

'So we're agreed. Let's stop.' Naeem smiled a little. He released her hand but continued to keep his eyes on hers. She knew he was trying to convey that he loved her still, that he would continue to love her and be with her regardless.

Sara smiled back at him, and found herself laughing at the ludicrousness of sitting in the cemetery with a boy she loved but couldn't touch. As they got up, shaking some of the residual dirt from their clothing, Sara could not help but think it was the kind of thing that only Muslims would do, or understand.

20

Abida

'I have an important question for you: Calvin Klein Euphoria, or YSL Black Opium?'

Sara held up two perfume bottles in front of the mirror and gave each a sniff. They had pooled their meagre makeup and perfume supplies, supplemented by Soraya's extensive collection. Abida reached for the bottles, spraying each onto an outstretched wrist.

'Honestly, they both smell like someone on *Real Housewives*,' she said. She moved closer to Sara's mirror and inspected her own reflection. She had found a calf-length stretchy polyester dress at one of the ten-dollar shops near the train station in a shade of orangey red she did not detest. The theme for Ahlam's engagement party was 'Red Hot' and Abida had done her best to adhere to it. One of the things people did not realise about being poor was that choosing clothes was not a question of what you liked or preferred as opposed to picking between one item made of transparent material that sat well around the waist, or another with passable stitching but which offered no support whatsoever around the breasts. There were no good options, only lesser evils.

'What's this going to be like, anyway? I've never been to a katb kitab party before, and Ahlam's description didn't really give much away,' Sara said.

'Me neither. I think only Arabs do it like this, with dancing and hijabs coming off when the men leave. Bengali stuff is a bit different. You might even find that out yourself soon.'

She winked at Sara, but Sara did not smile, and Abida regretted the offhand reference to Sara's relationship with Naeem. They could only be casual about a topic once it had been dissected, the grit and mess thoroughly sifted through until only the clarity of their stances remained. But Sara had been noticeably silent about Naeem since her revelation. Into this void, this reticence so unusual in their years of friendship, Abida had begun to project a number of theories, each more unlikely than the last. Naeem was a sex addict, a Christian Grey-esque figure with a secret stash of whips and handcuffs. Naeem was going to quit his medical degree and train as a shaykh in Yemen, and Sara was going to join him and become an Islamic scholar too. They were going to get married in five years, or five months, or not at all. She could not get a feel for the contours of their relationship whatsoever, and this was upsetting. She began again.

'So how are things going with Naeem, anyway?'

'They're going good. As good as they can be,' Sara said.

'What do you mean?' She watched as Sara twisted strands of hair around the hot tongs, removing one section from the wand and then reaching for the next. When Sara arrived at the section of hair at the back of her head, where it was hardest to reach, Abida sprung up and took the tongs from her. It was only when Abida had released the last section of her hair that Sara spoke.

'It's complicated. I don't know how else to say it. He's so kind to me, but I sometimes get the sense that he holds all the cards and I hold none, and no matter what I do, nothing changes that,' Sara said finally.

'That's because he's a man, Sara. They always hold the cards.'

'It's more than that though.' Sara tilted her head forward until the ringlets tipped over her face, obscuring it from view. Abida placed both hands on Sara's shoulders and spoke quickly.

'You haven't done anything with him, have you? Please tell me you haven't –'

'Of course not.' Sara shook her head, her curls brushing Abida's face. 'You don't get it.' Sara got up from her chair and began placing her wallet and keys in her bag and reaching for her hijab. Abida felt the dismissal in these gestures and began to assemble her things too. She had only wanted to caution Sara, knowing that the consequences for what a man did and what a woman did were entirely different in the eyes of others. She had read *Anna Karenina* at school; she thought she knew the drill. But it seemed she had blundered once again. She knew nothing about the intricacies of relationships, and Sara was unwilling to share them with her.

They drove to the community hall Ahlam had chosen in silence, with only Taylor Swift to bridge the space Abida felt between them.

She supposed Sara was still thinking of Naeem and she longed to click her fingers and have him disappear from Sara's mind.

If only it were that easy, she would have attempted it. When they arrived at the hall, Ahlam was not there. Her two older sisters – bossy, affable women with three children apiece – delegated tasks, directing them to pin confetti, blow up balloons and sweep the floors, which had been deemed too dirty. The venue consisted of a rectangular room with a schoolroom feel and bare whitewashed walls. Abida was puzzled as to how it would accommodate a hundred guests. When they attempted to push the tables out into an even formation, there was very little standing room except for the empty space at the front which would serve as a dance floor. But the confetti, red helium balloons and candy buffet lent the room a kind of festive cheer which excited Abida. Even Sara disappearing to the bathroom for an extended period of time could not dampen her mood.

By five-thirty Ahlam's sisters had departed to get ready and Abida was left alone with Mariam and Lina, who were in the kitchen inspecting the gigantic aluminium trays of mansaf, fattoush and kibbeh that had been delivered by the caterer. Abida decided to go to the bathroom and put her dress on underneath her abaya. She did not see Sara there; she wondered where she had gone. Abida had shaved her legs for the occasion for the first time in several months, using Maroof's razor and shaving gel in the bathtub. The toilet cubicles were so small that she had to lean against the lid of the toilet seat as she removed her hijab, skirt and top and wiggled the dress over her head, sniffing her armpits as she did so. She caught a whiff of sweat mingled with the artificial floral notes of deodorant, so she went to the sink and scrubbed and splashed at her armpits with her fingers. Abida studied her reflection as she pulled the abaya and hijab back on. Her hair was straight and glossy, and she was not altogether displeased with the fit of the dress around her chest and its flare around her hips and down past her knees.

When she emerged, Ahlam had arrived and was seated in the sectioned-off alcove where they had been storing their handbags. Her hair was scraped back and collected into a series of looped balls around the nape of her neck, tapering off into curls which descended into her cleavage in orderly ringlets. The silvery dress she wore, chosen to offset everyone's red, was encrusted with jewels on the bodice, her head held high and her eyes lined and powdered with soft silver shadow. Abida felt oddly wary of approaching her. Ahlam was a semi-married woman now; she and Ziad would have held hands last night, kissed and possibly more. Abida could name all the territories of the Ottoman Empire at its zenith and all the individual clashes of the Indian Rebellion of 1857, sparked by the rumoured usage of cartridges greased with beef and pork, but she could not claim any experiential knowledge of kissing. She felt the barrier between those who had been kissed and those who had not, the visceral changes it was likely to engender.

Sara finally reappeared, and when Abida asked where she had gone, Sara said she had gone to take a phone call. Abida had no time to question this as Mariam and Lina appeared from the kitchen, their hijabs still secured. They cooed over Ahlam's dress and hair and she slipped into their circle, which expanded to include Ahlam's sisters, one of whom had changed from her hijab and maxi dress into a fitted red and black dress with a slit revealing most of her muscular left thigh. Abida marvelled at the fluidity with which they appeared to change in and out of their clothing, the arms which had just been waxed, still pink from the wrenching of hair from root, but smooth.

Ziad would be arriving soon and they all put their abayas back on and swathed their hijabs around their heads, only Ahlam remaining in her party dress. Abida and Najah, the sister with the red and black dress underneath her abaya, were dispatched to the front doorway to greet people, direct them to the bathrooms and seize the gifts and cash-stuffed envelopes from their arms. There were some girls Abida recognised from the MSA, but many were unknown, arriving in abayas with their hijabs tied loosely over their heads, blow-dried fringes just visible underneath. They ignored Ziad and Ahlam's father and brothers, who stood in the corner furthest away from the entrance, but Ahlam's mother, resplendent in a maroon chiffon ensemble, greeted the guests she knew with aplomb. She had now successfully married all her daughters off, and the night was as much hers as Ahlam's.

There were now enough people present for Ahlam to make her entrance with appropriate fanfare. A female DJ stood at a table at the back of the room, playing a song in Arabic at a volume Abida thought people would object to, but no one seemed to mind, even the woman with a tiny swaddled baby in the crook of her arm. As the family walked in, each person's entrance was announced by the DJ over the scratchy microphone. The women inside ululated, the volume of the song increasing by several decibels. Abida remained outside, greeting the latecomers and ushering them to their seats. She watched as Ziad, looking both proud and uncomfortable to be amid the room full of women, stood with his arm curled around Ahlam as photos were snapped. The two of them performed a brief twirl about the room to a different Arabic tune, this one sung by a male singer with a mournful, chocolatey voice and featuring a rousing chorus with synthesised piano. As the dance concluded and the photos continued, she heard whispers from the girls at the table in front of her, urging the men to leave. After approximately half an hour, even Ziad's smile became noticeably forced, and the men departed, Ahlam's father tickling his wife's hand with his moustache and exiting.

Once the men had left, the women began unpinning and unbuttoning. They disappeared into the bathroom in twos and threes, and when Abida saw them reappear, they became unrecognisable blurs of red and spiky stiletto heels and curtains of straightened hair. When a girl appeared who she knew from the MSA, they complimented each other's faces and hair, but the act was perfunctory, repeated many times with each girl encountered. Something had to be admired loudly in each person's appearance, whether a handbag or a shock of bleached hair. Abida thought the scene tedious and affected, walking away towards the entrance and gesturing for Sara to join her.

She grabbed Sara's arm and led her back to the bathroom, where three girls stood taking selfies in the mirror, their hijabs and pins strewn all over the sink. They shuffled over to make more room, allowing Sara and Abida to press themselves against the wall and yank their outerwear off. Sara's dress was modest compared to the fitted, backless, strapless ensembles of the girls at the mirror, but it revealed more of her legs than Abida could recall seeing. Even in school Sara had preferred to wear pants, donning the school skirt with thick stockings in winter, and when they visited each other's homes, they wore pyjamas or loose trousers.

Sara did not appear to want to leave the bathroom, but the sound of someone peeing in one of the cubicles soon drove them out into the main hall. The music had been turned down as the food was being served, and they joined Lina and Mariam, who were some of the few girls who had not taken off their hijabs. When Sara asked them why, Mariam said that it was because people took so many photos at these parties and it was difficult to track whose photos you ended up in and where they would store them. Sara had laughed then and patted her hair, saying that she would have spared herself the effort of a blow-dry and a leg wax if she had known that was an option. Ahlam had joined them then and stated that she was commencing a series of laser treatments to rid herself of all her bodily hair, which led to the girls teasing her about whether she and Ziad had managed to have any alone time last night. Ahlam raised her eyebrows and winked but said nothing further.

Ahlam returned to greeting her other guests, leaving the four girls to find seats. They devoured their rice and salads off plastic plates, half-shouting to be heard over the background music. Abida was content to listen and people-watch as Ahlam's niece jived with a little boy dressed in a full tuxedo and a red tie. Sara was chewing her food and leaning in to listen to something Mariam said, her hair falling in front of her face from the spot behind her ears she had kept it tucked behind. She wore heavy silver earrings that stretched her lobes and her brow was shiny from the crush in the room, but the effect of her maroon wrap dress and pointy black shoes was one of sophistication and simplicity. Abida was proud to be Sara's closest friend here, proud of the unassuming, quiet confidence with which Sara carried herself and addressed and responded to others. Once the music resumed its deafening volume and pitch, rendering all conversation impossible, Abida indicated that they should make their way to the dance floor. Sara hesitated for a moment, but followed her, taking care to avoid the pram parked across their table.

Ahlam stood in the middle of a circle of girls and they took a place on its edge, watching as she shook her hips and rotated them, bending to the ground as she did. The girls cheered and clapped their hands, and Abida felt her hands move too and a grin spread across her face. There was something wild and joyous about being surrounded by people and music and lights, with no speech to pollute the ambience. Abida thought that this might explain some of the appeal of clubbing, but when people spoke about clubbing, they rarely mentioned dancing. Several girls now joined Ahlam in shaking their hips in a rhythmic manner Abida knew she could not imitate. One of the girls who had kept her hijab on was the best dancer, her skilful hip-rolling causing the crowd to clap and whistle. Ahlam's mother also received lengthy claps for her dancing, holding her daughter's hand as they stepped around the circle together.

Abida did not understand any of the Arabic lyrics and began to tire of the insistent drumming beats. She was relieved when the

DJ began to play songs in English, even if she was unfamiliar with them too. A song came on about taking shots, which everyone seemed to know the lyrics to, mimicking drinking shots with their hands in a coordinated motion Abida thought amusing for a room of teetotallers. She supposed this behaviour would puzzle the white people at university, that they would find the concept of women removing their hijabs and dancing titillating, and this thought irritated Abida so much that she withdrew from the dance floor and walked back to her seat.

She had placed her hijab inside Sara's bag, and she reached for it now, thinking of the long bus and train journey home in the dark. Sara would drive her home if she asked, but she did not wish to ask. She would slip away soon, leave the others to their revelry. Now that Abida was away from the dance floor all that uninhibited shaking and writhing of limbs seemed ridiculous. It only made sense when you were doing it yourself. When other people danced and you were looking from the outside in, it was ugly, incomprehensible. There was nothing titillating about it. She saw Ahlam's lips move to the latest song, something with Spanish lyrics no one understood, saw the clean white skin under her arms as she raised them over her head.

She could not locate her hijab. Abida felt the outline of Sara's phone and pulled it out from where it was weighing down the rest of the bag's contents, placing it on the table next to a plastic cup of Coke. The phone buzzed. Abida glanced over at it, finally locating the fabric of her hijab and extracting the pins so that she could take them to the bathroom and depart. Sara's phone buzzed again, the screen lighting up. She picked it up now, intending to place it back in the bag, reading the words on the screen in passing as she did. But once read, the words could not be viewed in a cursory manner. Abida felt the throb of the music in her temples, the disturbance of what she had read coursing through her and above the noise. She shoved the phone back into the bag, grabbed her things and walked towards the exit. She turned her head once more towards the circle of girls, a blur of swaying arms and bent knees as the strobe lights flashed across them. She pushed the door open, taking care as the floor was wet with someone's spilled drink. She would not betray the extent of her horror by slipping; if she fell to the floor, Abida feared she would remain down there, unable to pick herself up again.

She slipped her abaya over her head and wrapped her hijab across her forehead and shoulders, striding out past where two girls from the party with balayaged blonde hair were smoking. Abida was unsure of where to go, knowing only that she could not return and encounter Sara. The two smoking girls stared at Abida with undisguised curiosity as she walked past them and out onto the road, picking up pace as she crossed to the other side. Her heels were noisy against the pavement, the stillness of the late evening frightening to a woman alone in unfamiliar streets. This was not the city centre or the lively suburbs near it; people did not stroll through these suburban streets, not at night. But even these thoughts, the dimness of the street lights and the distance she had to travel, could not silence her mind from replaying the message on Sara's phone.

Sara had not been so careless as to save the number under its correct name, but there could be no doubt as to the identity of the sender. As Abida walked beneath a low bridge, the sound of a train in the distance guiding her towards the station, she thought of it again and what she would do now that she knew.

Miss the feel of you.

21

Naeem

'What do you think of this line, bro? "The MSA needs strong leadership in these testing times, and I'm the best person to provide it." Too arrogant?'

'Maybe. I dunno,' Naeem said.

'Well, what do you think I should say instead?'

Wahid shuffled along the floor as a boy with a neat ponytail and sideburns reached for a Quran from the shelf. The boy picked it up, kissed it, and perched on the window seat with it on his lap.

'I don't know. How about something about your vision for the MSA?'

Naeem could not think of anything further to contribute, having never considered his own motivation for his involvement in the MSA. It was the place he had gravitated towards, a continuation of the education he had received. He supposed he could have been subsumed into the wider masses at university and abandoned any kind of group affiliation, but that would have required active distancing, something he saw no reason to do. He had instead allowed himself to sink into his Muslimness, the easiest and most natural identity to wear. But this quest of Wahid's was different. This was about power and Naeem wished he had told Wahid some time ago that he wanted no part in it.

'I have no vision for the MSA.' Wahid tugged at the fingers of his left hand with the right, cracking several in succession.

'That's not true,' Naeem said. 'You have so much conviction, more than anyone –'

'It's easy to have conviction. All you need to do is not listen to what anyone else says. It's much more difficult to be like you or Mustafa, people who everyone actually likes because you consider their point of view.'

'Not everyone likes me,' Naeem said, aware that he was not being helpful, aware that there were no templates for this kind of emotional outpouring among boys. He did not touch Wahid now but leaned forward in what he hoped could be construed as a sympathetic gesture.

'They do,' Wahid said. 'You're a hafidh, you're studying medicine and, despite it all, you don't have a big head. This is why I need you as my deputy.'

Naeem thought of the message he had sent Sara several nights ago, the pictures they had exchanged following it. They had not broken their vow; they hadn't touched each other, but that was a point of semantics only. He had stayed up all night praying to Allah to rid him of this weakness of character, that he had really meant it this time. He thought of the elastic band of his relationship with Him, stretching and stretching. The Quran said that the handhold of faith would never break, but he imagined that Allah must be growing weary of his cycle of transgression and atonement.

Wahid continued to speak, saying now that his father had started to drink with more regularity again, that his sister was intent on marrying the Catholic boyfriend she had been seeing for years. Wahid had to be strong for his mother, demonstrate to his younger siblings that there was another way to be. This was why he needed to be harsh at times, because softness was the way things slipped, and once things slipped, they could not be recouped. Naeem wondered why he was being told all of this, what it was about him that prompted people to justify their stances. He had performed his role too well and there seemed no easy way now to exit the stage. He fantasised momentarily about showing Wahid the pictures he had sent Sara, just to shut him up.

'So why not say all this in your speech? Forget the spiel about testing times. Telling people your story is what will win it for you.'

Wahid shook his head. 'Nah, people aren't interested in that. They just want to know I'll do a good job, not all this personal stuff. I'll think of something and send it to you, okay? As long as you're on board I'm good.'

Wahid jumped up from the floor and slapped Naeem on the back. Now that he was standing, Wahid seemed solid and sure of himself again, the glint of his silver chain appearing beneath his shirt. It was all angles, this business of how a person appeared to another. Naeem waved Wahid off, thinking of how he could never decide whether Sara was pretty by conventional standards or not, whether her nose was pert or just protruded.

He looked at his phone. Sara had asked him to come meet her at the library lawn, where they held their MSA barbeques. He began to walk and noticed a small crowd had formed at the spot she had specified. Some people were holding cardboard signs, some were holding Palestinian flags and wearing keffiyehs around their necks. A girl with wispy blonde hair was holding a microphone. He wondered why Sara had asked him to come to this place. There were frequent protests on campus. People held signs and yelled, they did sit-ins and lie-ins and marched up and down the walkways in formation. He had never thought about attending one. They seemed futile except as a way to release pent-up rage and to feel less guilty that you were doing fine while others were not. He stood at the back of the crowd, noting that Sara was standing in the middle of it with Abida.

He waited for Sara to turn around and, after a minute or two, she did, whispering to Abida before walking towards him. Abida raised her hand in a wave in his direction but did not move, instead turning to a boy to her left who was wearing a Socialist Alliance t-shirt and speaking to him.

'Hey, did you just get here? They're about to start in a minute, I think,' Sara said. She was smiling, happy to see him.

'What are we doing here, exactly? Who are these people?'

'It's the Students for Palestine group. Oh, look, there's Mustafa,' Sara said, and they both waved at Mustafa, who was standing on the other side of the crowd and talking to one of the organisers.

'Yeah, but why are we here?' He had not intended to phrase the question so bluntly, but the sight of Mustafa had unnerved him, and he shifted his weight to his other leg to give the impression that he had just stopped by and was about to leave.

'Why wouldn't we be here? Don't we care about our ummah, about justice?'

'Of course. But I don't think me standing here chanting a few slogans is going to help anyone. As if anyone in Palestine actually knows or cares that a bunch of random uni students in Sydney are doing this.'

Sara started to frown, the smile slowly shrinking from her face. He continued, thinking he had disappointed her again, that he had to say something to prevent her smile from disappearing altogether.

'I'm going to head home. I think my dad is finishing up early and it might be a good time to talk to him about us getting married,' he said.

'I know it won't be easy for you,' Sara said. Naeem could not tell if she was expressing sympathy or merely stating a fact. He had somehow managed to communicate to her that his parents required handling, that speaking without forethought would not result in a favourable outcome.

'It won't, but it's well overdue by now. We said we'd get engaged after the semester ends and that's only a month away. We need to get things moving.' Naeem knew he ought to convey this with more grace, to reassure her that it was good news he would be sharing with his parents, but he could not bring himself to do so. As unreasonable as it was, some part of him resented Sara for the ease with which she had conveyed the news to her mother, and her inability to truly comprehend his difficulty in conveying the news to his. She could sympathise with him and offer him support, but she did not know what it was to fear your parents as intensely as you loved them.

When Naeem thought of how he would tell his parents about Sara, he could envisage telling Professor Kazi, not because he thought his father would be more receptive to the idea, but because the sheer noise of his mother's reaction would render any form of discussion impossible. But at least Meherin's reaction could be anticipated and prepared for. She would exclaim, request to see a photo of Sara, then instruct him to forget the whole thing. But he could not predict what Professor Kazi would say or do, and this frightened him. More so than Meherin, Professor Kazi had mastered the art of blending in, of saying only what the situation required. He supposed this was part of what made his father such a feted psychiatrist, and even he was not immune from the urge to confess and have his father listen to the tale in its entirety. In his imagined scenario, Naeem behaved as he thought a real patient would, meek and rambling, and Professor Kazi behaved as he would with a patient, supportive and impersonal and volunteering no moral pronouncements or judgements.

As he drove home, Naeem thought about Sara's parents and the impression he had formed of them. Despite the complexity of his feelings towards his own, Naeem did not wish to trade his for hers whatsoever. He felt that there was something neglectful about the way they dealt with her, the way she was free to come and go and eat whatever and whenever she chose. His mother would be hurt if he did not eat the food she cooked, but Sara's parents did not seem to care whether she ate instant noodles or hot chips or other makeshift meals. He had thought Sara's mother would put a stop to what they were doing and insist upon him coming to the house and properly declaring his intentions. When the time came for Tasnia to marry, he knew his parents would be far more protective and hawkish than Sara's parents appeared to be.

When he arrived outside the house, he saw that Professor Kazi's car was already in the driveway. Naeem had asked Allah for a sign, and it had been placed before him. He could not flee. He was a coward, but he was not faithless. If he did not speak to Professor Kazi now, Naeem would be failing in his duty to seize the opportunities He had granted.

Professor Kazi was in the kitchen, peering into the open fridge. He turned around and Naeem saw a lanyard around his neck, indicating that Professor Kazi had perhaps been attending or speaking at a conference as he so often did. They all had similar titles, The Twelfth Symposium on Personality Disorders, or The Annual International Conference on Substance Addiction. Once or twice a year, Professor Kazi would travel to Lucerne or Quebec City or Osaka for one of these conferences, and would return and go straight back to work, sometimes on the very same day he landed. Their display cabinet was filled with objects from these places, touristy trinkets most likely bought in the duty free shop at the airport, and he and Tasnia would be given new pens and notepads from the conference packs his father received.

Professor Kazi uncapped a bottle of orange juice and poured it into a cup. Naeem knew his father had noticed him standing there, but the son was required to greet the father first.

'Salam, Baba,' he said, sitting on one of the stools at the breakfast bar.

Professor Kazi returned the greeting with a salam but did not say anything else. He took a sip from his cup, holding it to his lips.

'Dad, can I talk to you about something?' He felt he was required to request his father's permission to start talking.

'Of course you can. What is it?' Professor Kazi drained his cup and swirled the lingering pulp around the base, before raising it to his lips again, his moustache tickling its edges. Naeem noted the presence of Professor Kazi's briefcase on the countertop, which indicated that he had only arrived home minutes before Naeem had, but Professor Kazi's belt had already been removed, his shirt unbuttoned. These things Professor Kazi removed immediately upon entering his home, along with his shoes and socks. Inside things, outside things. This was how his father categorised the world.

Naeem could not form the words. His father's moustache was wet with juice, and he did not seem to care. He thought of something to say other than what he had to say, his mind flitting from one forbidden topic to another.

'Why did you and Katherine split up?'

Professor Kazi's eyes narrowed behind his glasses, but when he spoke, his voice was calm, measured.

'Has someone been gossiping to you about her? If they have, tell me now, and I'll deal with it.' Anyone could dole out pills, but only the best doctors could convince their patients that they could *deal with* their problems, and this was just what Professor Kazi promised to do.

'No one's been talking to me, Baba. I was just wondering about her, that's all.'

'There's nothing to wonder about. It didn't work out, and I married your mother, and we've been married for over twenty years now.'

'I know that, Baba. I just wanted to know what she was like, how you met her and why it ended.'

Naeem wilted under his father's gaze, knowing that he had been mistaken in approaching the topic in this manner. He had sabotaged the conversation and ensured it had no chance of success. He could not tell his father about Sara, not now. Professor Kazi would associate Sara with his failed marriage, with the woman he had left behind in Boston when he had commenced the life he had crafted for all of them. Katherine would be described as a mistake, not a bad person, but simply an anomaly. Katherine did not fit into his father's life, and Sara did not fit into Naeem's. He was his father's son, cruel in his inflexibility. At this moment he could not even be certain that he wanted to marry Sara. His thoughts and his behaviour were not in alignment, each suggesting a possibility entirely distinct from the other.

'I see,' Professor Kazi said, relaxing and placing his cup down. 'Can I offer you some advice?'

Naeem nodded. He could no longer pierce the formality and distance of his father's manners. Perhaps he never would. His fantasy was now transpiring before him, and Professor Kazi was speaking to him as he would a patient.

'Much of life involves knowing when to hold on, and when to let go. Once the decision has been made to let go, it is of little use to dwell on it. When a thing is gone, it is gone for a reason, and it is our task not to fight against its absence but to discern what that reason might be.'

There was nothing to say in response, and Naeem did not think his father expected one. After a moment, Professor Kazi put down his empty glass and Naeem carried it to the sink, scrubbing it under a jet of hot water as his father watched on.

22

Naeem had still not spoken to his parents. He had not bought a ring, he had not spoken of dates or timelines or invitations. When she had asked him about Sadia's offers to help and when they would be seeing her again, he had said to give him time. He had then asked her how her afternoon chemistry lecture was and whether he could help her with her equations paper, following which they dissected the MSA group chat discussion about the Islamic stance on Afterpay.

She had to speak to Abida about what to do, but she didn't know how to broach the subject. It had been several days since Ahlam's party and although they had briefly met at the protest, when she had asked Abida to come to the cafeteria afterwards, her shout for a bubble tea, Abida had said she had to go meet her partner in a tort law assignment. Just as she felt the bond between her and

Naeem grow increasingly uncertain, so too did she feel the bond between her and Abida loosen. She had presented a version of herself and her relationship to Abida that was untrue. She had never deceived Abida before. She pretended with people in the MSA, she pretended with her parents and even with Naeem. Pretence was the price she paid to maintain their good opinion of her. With Abida she had not had such concerns. The more unfiltered, forthright and downright bitchy she was, the more it seemed to solidify that they were fixtures in their own universe, and everyone else was just orbiting through.

She messaged Abida, once, then twice.

What's happening, you?

Girl, where you at??

Although she saw Abida was online, no response arrived. She could see that Abida was typing on the MSA sub-chat for girls only and waited to see what she said.

Sisters, it's time to take back our power. Help me by handing out my campaign flyers tomorrow at the fortnightly da'wah stall. A vote for me is a vote for us all.

She waited for Abida to respond to her messages, but although Abida was finished typing on the sub-chat, she still did not respond. Sara sent another message.

'A vote for me is a vote for us all?' Although I'm throwing up a little in my mouth as we speak, I'm defs down for some flyer action tomorrow. Kebab before or after?

Still there was no response. She supposed Abida was so consumed in her campaigning that she had not even paused to read other messages. She sent a message to Naeem instead, asking him to meet her at the da'wah stall as well, possibly even for a kebab with Abida before or afterwards. She did not know if he would say yes, but she wanted to challenge him by asking. He had not spent time with Abida before. Abida would ask him probing questions, seeking not to be liked by him but to see if she could possibly deign to like him. Sara smiled as she thought of it, the two people she had chosen to love most in the world sitting and talking, Abida gesticulating with her fingers and arms, Naeem laughing at the fierceness of her assertions.

Abida had still not replied the next day, but Naeem had said he would join her. She was heartened by this display, that he was no longer afraid to be seen with her. But after her tutorial Ravi had asked her to look at his algorithm for their computing assignment, and by the time she had shaken him off and walked across campus to the main walkway, Abida was already handing out flyers, Naeem manning the stall with Ahlam and Wahid. She waved at Abida and went to stand alongside her as she spoke to a girl in activewear about incorporating an acknowledgement of the MSA operating on stolen land into all their events. Abida used every part of her body as she spoke, waggling her head as she said an Acknowledgement of Country was nowhere near enough, that, as the children of immigrants, they had benefited from displacement and genocide and needed to do more. The girl nodded as Abida spoke and Sara found that she was doing the same. She grinned as Abida hugged the girl and turned to Naeem to include him in her joy. Although Sara did not aspire to change the world she could still appreciate the necessity that someone did. Naeem smiled back at her but turned to Wahid almost immediately, and in the speed of the motion she saw that he was still afraid, and this made her sad.

Abida was now looking at her, and she hugged her to avoid her gaze.

'You're doing good,' she said, her face pressed against Abida's shoulder.

'Yeah, it's going okay, I think. This guy over there doesn't even have any flyers, that's how much of a winner he already thinks he is.' Abida pulled back from the hug and rolled her eyes in Wahid's direction, and they both laughed.

'Do you want to hand some more out? Or is it kebab time?'

'Let's break for now, and then we can come do a bit later? Got loads to chat to you about, plus nothing raises my appetite like trying to explain to MSA folks that reading bell hooks is not going to land them in hellfire,' Abida said, reaching for her backpack and sliding the remaining flyers inside it.

'Don't kill me, but I told Naeem he could join us. Is that okay?'

Abida hoisted her bag onto her shoulders and was silent. Sara could not read her silence, the careful arrangement of her features into something resembling blank inquisitiveness. Abida was ordinarily so noisy, so transparent in her likes and dislikes. She wore her opinions like chainmail, resplendent and clanking. Sara loved this about her. But Abida was not saying anything now, and Sara was unsure of what this meant.

'Sorry, I should've mentioned it before. I can tell him not to bother. I just thought you two should start to properly get to know each other.'

'Sure. Tell him to come. Go tell him now,' Abida said.

This was the Abida she recognised. Abida was testing Naeem, seeing if he would speak to Sara in front of the others and depart with her. She walked the few metres to the table, where Ahlam, Wahid and Naeem were listening to an elderly woman with immaculately coiffed white hair. The woman was saying that she had nothing against Islam, that it was no better or worse than any other religion, and all religions were equally misogynist. Sara saw that, although Naeem was nodding and smiling with his mouth closed, he was not really listening. He was waiting for her to appear, and when she did, he silently shuffled away from the table as the woman was still speaking. He did this so well, this discreet extrication. He turned towards her and they walked to join Abida, the gap between their bodies so wide that a whole person could have run right between them.

They did not speak as they walked, Naeem walking slightly ahead of her and Abida. Sara turned back to the table and saw that Ahlam was looking straight at her. Ahlam was not smiling, her pink lips were pursed. She knew then that Ahlam suspected that there was something going on with her and Naeem, that Abida was an addition to their party of two. She continued to walk, her heart thumping as the three of them traversed the lunchtime crowds. She watched the back of Naeem's head, the flatness of his hair as it rested against the nape of his neck. She had sought this meeting and now she did not know what to do or say. Abida was walking faster and faster and she struggled to keep up, eventually allowing Abida to walk ahead, just behind Naeem.

As they reached the cafeteria, the clamour of trays hitting tables and students talking with their friends was overwhelming. Groups of Muslims sat outside the kebab stall. There were bearded boys guffawing, girls in hijabs looking at a video on one person's phone. She did not recognise anyone, but that did not mean that she was unknown to them, or that Abida and Naeem were either. There were no free tables and the smell of hot oil and chicken salt was overwhelming.

'Quick, you two get that table. I'll get our food,' Naeem said. He pointed to a table where two people were standing up and unplugging their laptops.

'I was going to shout –'

'Don't worry about it. Besides, I have to buy this one a meal so she'll be interrogating me on a full stomach,' he said, smiling at Abida before noting down their orders and walking to the counter.

Abida was looking at her phone. Sara leaned forward.

'Before he comes back, what did you want to want to chat to me about?'

'I dunno,' Abida said, still looking at her phone.

'Come on, tell me,' she said.

'Honestly, it's nothing. You'd better tell me what you want me to say to your boyfriend over there,' Abida said.

'He's not my boyfriend.'

'Well, what is he then? You're not engaged, and you're not friends.' Abida sat back in her chair and looked towards the kebab stall, where Naeem was now carrying a tray of food and walking towards them.

Before Sara could respond, Naeem arrived and began distributing their orders. He unwrapped the paper casing of his kebab down the middle before picking it up with both hands.

'Eat, eat,' he said.

Abida's arms were crossed. She was looking around the cafeteria, up at the television screen ahead, across to the sushi stall where the queue was snaking around the corner. Sara pierced the felafel on her plate with her fork and put half of it in her mouth. She wished Abida would make some effort to engage with them. She knew that, Abida thought Naeem insipid, but thinking someone boring and rich did not warrant such a response.

'How's Wahid's campaigning going?' Abida bit into her tabbouleh as she spoke, bits of parsley and burghul falling under the table.

'I don't really know. I'm not very involved in it,' Naeem said evenly.

'You're his nominated deputy. How can you not be involved?'

'How's your campaigning going?' Naeem bit into his roll, separating the paper from the sogginess of the bread. Sara recognised the way he used questions to shift the onus of response. He was not doing it to be obstructive or cruel; it was just how he spoke. He was so sincere in his interest in the people he was speaking to that most would not think to characterise it a deflection. But she knew this way of speaking would not placate Abida as it had so often placated her.

'Enough about that,' Abida said. 'Have you told your parents about Sara yet?'

Sara reached for her water bottle, fumbling with its lid. This was different to the gentle concern Sadia had directed at them both. Abida was addressing Naeem only. She had not raised her voice and she was not even looking at Naeem, but Sara was aware of every sound now: the man at the kebab stall calling out order fifty-six, the shaking of excess raw onion slices into the waste bin.

'Not yet. But I will soon, inshaAllah, and once that's done, Sara and I can get engaged after the semester is over.' Naeem sounded so sure. He was smiling again with his teeth, which were clear of any gristle or sauce. If she had not been placated before, she was now. Naeem was sitting with her and her best friend in the cafeteria, informing them that he was going to tell his parents that he was going to marry her. He was relaxed in the face of Abida's questioning, and he was certain of the future they would have. It would just take more time, and they had time.

'You're very sure of yourself, aren't you?'

Abida had noticed the same calm certainty that she had, but Sara could hear the slight inflection of Abida's voice which indicated that she was angry. Sara was unsure why. Naeem had said that the two of them would discuss everything. He had not mansplained, a crime Abida was forever accusing the boys of. He had answered the question he had been asked and had answered it unequivocally. Abida was being unreasonable in a misguided attempt at protecting Sara, as she had done so many times before. She thought about saying something to diffuse the tension, but before she could form the words, Naeem began to speak.

'If Allah wills it, nothing can stop it from happening. His will is the only certainty we have,' he said.

Abida stood up now, pushing the chair against the table, metal clanging against metal. She smiled but it was not a smile Sara recognised. With a sharp pang she saw the falsity of it and wondered at what it was concealing. She was conscious for the first time that just as she had not been truthful with Abida, so too could Abida dissemble with her.

'You're right. I gotta get going. Don't get up to any funny business when I go, you two, even the walls here have eyes.' Abida squeezed Sara's arm and waved at Naeem before leaving.

'Why did she say that last bit?' Naeem reached for her water bottle but retracted his hand and reached for his own instead.

'She's just being funny. Her idea of humour, you know. She just wants the best for me, that's all,' Sara said. For once she was not focused on Naeem. She was still thinking about Abida, about why she had behaved the way she had.

'I think that went well, though,' Naeem said. 'I thought she'd go much harder at me than she did, actually. She acts like she's your guard dog or something.'

'Hey, don't say that.' She would not permit Naeem to speak about Abida like that. She would talk to Abida, and she would orchestrate more meetings with Naeem, and over time the two of them would begin to understand each other. Or perhaps they would not. The lens with which they viewed the world had produced entirely different fields of vision, overlapping only in the space she occupied. Sara felt the loneliness of it then, that she could not compel the love of these two people, even though she loved them both.

She looked up at Naeem as he arranged their empty plates and containers in the centre of the tray.

'Sorry, Sara. I'll try harder next time, I promise,' he said.

They sat still and silent for a moment, before Naeem was approached by one of the bearded boys for a handshake and Sara rose, thinking she would get herself another felafel because she had not paid attention to the eating of the first one at all.

23

Abida

Abida settled herself on the couch with an open pack of Pringles that she had found in the cupboard. Her parents had gone to the mosque and taken the children with them, and Maroof was out somewhere too. There was a stain on the backrest which looked like either daal or coffee. Whatever it was, it didn't bother her, being long-dried and crusty. She switched on the television, flicking away from the Islamic channel reruns of Dr Zakir Naik refuting a Bible verse to the mainstream channels. To her disappointment, there was not much of interest on, just an animated children's film and one of the recent Bond films. Abida had been to the cinema with Connie and some of her other friends to watch one of the Bond films in high school, an outing neither Abbu nor Ammu had sanctioned. Her act of rebellion had been wasted: the popcorn was overpriced, Connie had spent most of the movie outside arguing with her boyfriend on the phone and the character of Bond had seemed rather awful, a bland roué with very little to recommend him other than some nifty gadgets. She had not been to the cinema since, and she had no desire to.

She left the television on the channel with the children's film, which appeared to be about a group of shifty Mafioso sharks. A rattle from the back door caused her to get up, check that it was bolted and switch all the lights on. There had been a robbery two streets behind them the previous month, and the robbers had punched and kicked the occupant of the house, an elderly woman, prior to making off with the money she had kept in her bedside drawer. Abida turned the volume on the television up, the sharks now dancing around and singing in their underwater lair, thinking again of her election speech. She began to recite potential opening lines, raising her voice above the shark song, raising her voice so that she would not again think of Naeem and Sara and the things they had done with each other.

She had sat with the two of them and allowed them to play their parts, driven by a morbid curiosity more than anything else. She observed Sara's happiness in Naeem's company, his watchfulness of her. She had attempted to not allow the images of them to burst through her mind, but when Naeem had invoked Allah's name she could bear it no longer. He was a hypocrite who cloaked his lust and ego in a veneer of righteousness, secure in the privileges he had done nothing to earn. Worse still, he had smiled at her as though they were friends, when they both knew that he would not have spoken to her at all had it not been for Sara. She could not permit herself to think of Sara's lies, the way that she had condescended to her when Abida had been right about her relationship with Naeem from the outset.

The front door jiggled and shook. The turn of a key in the door indicated that she had been saved from intruders on this occasion, and Abida put the Pringles back in the cupboard and turned down the volume of the television.

'Oh, it's just you,' she said, seeing Maroof. He had long ceased accompanying their parents on visits to other Bangladeshi families, saying he would next accompany them when they had a nice girl to show him, as though he were inspecting a car.

Maroof did not respond with a sharp retort or a snort as expected, sinking into the couch next to her.

'Maggie dumped me,' he said simply.

Abida's first impulse was to make a snide remark, that it had taken Maggie long enough to do it. But the angle at which Maroof's chin met his chest told her that to do so would be cruel and vengeful. Abida could be cruel and vengeful, but only when she did not recognise the cruelty of what she was doing until after it was already done.

'What happened?' The softness of her voice startled Maroof into raising his head, although he did not look at her, staring at the television, where a shark was now chasing a fat, inept goldfish.

'She just told me it was over between us. She said she still wants to be friends. As if I'd want to be friends with her after that.' Maroof uttered the last statement with such vehemence that a globule of spit landed on Abida's nose, which she dabbed at delicately so that he would not notice.

'Did she give you any reason why?'

'She just said she didn't see any future for us and that there was no point continuing to see each other. What an absolute bitch,' he said, sounding more like himself.

'Girls aren't bitches because they break up with you. Besides, she's right. You knew there wasn't a future for you two anyway. You weren't exactly planning on telling Abbu and Ammu about her, were you?'

Once it had been said, she worried Maroof would snap at her, perhaps even strike out. He had smacked her once when they were very young, and the vague memory Abida possessed of this incident included the somewhat more concrete memory of her father smacking Maroof, both occurrences never having been repeated since.

When he responded, Maroof sounded almost nonchalant, reaching for the remote.

'I guess you're right. She was a hottie though, right? Do you think Mum and Dad will find someone as hot for me or will I have to go hunting myself?'

'I'm not going to dignify that with a response,' Abida said tartly. She hated men, hated their inconstancy. Their propensity for violence guaranteed their dominance, their fists and penises wielded as weapons, and when they were not violent, they were pathetic.

Maroof laughed. Maggie had been correct in her assessment of their future; Maroof would have dumped her in six months or a year, once he had tired of the play at rebellion and gotten on with his real life.

'Do you want to get a kebab or something?' Maroof spoke affably, the tightness of his jaw the sole indication of the sadness he had carried when he had entered the house. Abida could not determine if this was because he did not want to appear sad in her presence, or if it was because his pride had been bruised and not his heart. Whatever it was, she did not want any part of it. She shook her head and he shrugged and walked back out, the revving of his car against the road rattling around before it faded off into the stillness of the night.

The next day Abida woke up, her mind turning over line after line from her speech. She fished out one of Ammu's old red lipsticks, rolling it over her lips until they were covered in it. When she entered the meeting room, she clenched her teeth together. She was here to win. But underneath the table, her fingers shook, the back of her knees wet with sweat.

'Assalamu alaykum, all,' Mustafa began. 'Thank you for coming to the nomination quorum for MSA president. This will be my last official act as president. The post of president is one which comes with a large amount of responsibility, guiding this MSA to constantly strive for greater. As most of you know, according to our constitution, elections commence with a statement of intent from candidates. We will then ask for statements from members, following which the voting will open and remain open for ten days. Remember that the president gets to choose their deputy, so Ziad will not be the default deputy unless chosen by the new president. Any questions?'

Mustafa was dressed in a sleek grey suit, his beard shaved from its former length. He had probably made these concessions for his new job, but it lent the proceedings an added air of formality. Across the table, Wahid had his hands in his lap, his biceps visible even as he sat slumped in his chair. Naeem was gazing down at the floor. Abida couldn't see his expression, but his posture betrayed no sign of nervousness. She loathed him then, longed to grab him by his shirt and force him to lift his head and face everyone, the truth of what he was apparent to all.

'What happens if there's a tie?' Fitri's voice exuded casual disinterest.

'The outgoing president has the deciding vote. That means me, I'm afraid.' Mustafa chuckled, then rearranged his face into an appropriately serious configuration. They were children, Abida thought, children playing at activism and righteous outrage through their social media profiles. But this did not dim the knowledge that she would have to beat the boys across the table if she were to retain any semblance of dignity. Dissipating now was her desire to do good, to affect change; there was only me versus him; win, lose. She wondered if this was what all politics came down to in the end, nothing more than a desire to decimate the other person and grind their face into the dirt.

'Okay, if that's all, we'll start with the candidate speeches. We've had two candidates express interest, so we'll start with the person whose nomination was submitted first, Wahid Faridi.'

Wahid stood up from his chair, cleared his throat with a whack to the chest. Abida was gratified to see his fingers curl and uncurl as he did, breaking the appearance of cool he maintained.

'Assalamu alaykum, guys. I'm honoured to be standing before you today and to be considered for the leadership of this group. We're in testing times, now more than ever. We're vilified on the streets and told we don't belong here. The kuffar want us to break and leave this deen. Many people have already left, and the one way to protect ourselves from the same fate is to stick together. We need to help each other to stay on the straight path, and I'm committed to doing that as president. I'm not saying I can do this all on my own. I'll need your help to do it, and I'll have the help of brother Naeem too, who as we all know is our resident Quran expert and future doctor and all-round brilliant guy, mashaAllah. It's people like this who will carry our ummah into the future, and people like all of you around the room. Thank you.'

Wahid sat back down, grinning now that it was done. There were a few scattered claps, murmurs of assent. Abida felt Sara reach for her hand under the table, whisper a fervent good luck, but she did not acknowledge the gesture. She noted the movement of Mustafa's lips, the sweep of his hand towards her.

'Abida?' Mustafa repeated her name, and Abida rose from her chair. Wahid had stood in the same spot as he had been seated, but Abida walked instead towards the front of the room. She stood at the centre of the table, in the empty space which demarcated boys from girls. This was her place.

'Bismillah. In the name of Allah, the Most Gracious, the Most Merciful.'

In her hand Abida clasped a few sentences she had composed some time ago, back when Mustafa had first announced that the MSA would be seeking a new president. She had written of broadening their focus, had listed the Muslim population of China, statistics on First Nations dispossession and the count of Australian women killed by their partners this year. But now the words seemed grandiose, inflated in their estimation of what she could and could not do.

Abida scrunched up the piece of paper. She was aware of the silence in the room, which seemed to stretch and thicken before her. She saw the acknowledged couple, Ahlam and Ziad, exchange a glance across the table; the unacknowledged couple mirroring each other's stances with their heads bowed. In these gestures Abida read the essential futility of what she was attempting. She had once deemed this MSA the prime opportunity to make her mark, but what would linger of this motley student group and their ambitions once they exited these walls? She would complete her degree in two years and the MSA and its lofty pledges would mean nothing at all, while the others would depart university with graduate jobs and a partner by their side, their lives defined by the vagaries of suburbia and interest rates and annual leave balances. Nobody in here cared about remedying the world's injustices as she did, only the performance of it.

'There are people in this room. In this very room. They're sitting around this table right now. Let me tell you about these people and their shit.'

She heard someone hiss, the commonplace swearword sounding sordid in this setting. Abida continued, looking straight ahead at the blank wall and not at Mustafa, whose expression of bemusement she observed peripherally, or Naeem, whose head was now raised, alert. The motion reminded her of a dog, its ears perked at the suggestion and scent of a threat. He was a dog, this boy, the very embodiment of the injustices she so hated, and he had corrupted the one relationship she had believed in.

'You know who you are, I'm sure. You've been doing things you shouldn't be while sitting here putting on this big show of piety. We know what that's called – hypocrisy, right? Does anyone want to own up to what they've been doing?'

The room was silent. Abida felt a tug at her arm, her eyes swimming with tears. She was determined to continue. Now that she had commenced with this spectacle, she had to finish. She saw Sara staring at her, the raw hurt and confusion apparent in her eyes. Sara had known immediately what she was talking about, and it was now too late to retract anything she had said. She wanted to go to Sara and remove her from these people who would harm her. She would explain everything to Sara and she would understand, as she always did. But the person holding her arm was escorting her out of the room with some force, out into the corridor and away from the hum of voices.

She had assumed it would be Sara rescuing her, her best friend, her would-be nemesis. But when Abida finally looked up she saw that it was Ahlam, who placed her hand on Abida's forehead as though she were ill. She supposed she was. What had transpired inside already seemed distant, a vista from some other time.

'Abida, what the hell are you doing? Have you lost your mind?'

'I told you. There are things you all should know. You heard me.'

'I heard you, but I don't want to know,' Ahlam said.

'You don't understand. I need to tell –'

'Listen. Just listen for a second,' Ahlam interrupted. 'I have no idea who you were talking about and I hope I never find out. Whatever you think someone's done, if they haven't made it known, it's not because they're hypocrites, it's because they're probably ashamed. Let them have their shame in peace. We all make mistakes, and we have to try to find a way to live with them and hope that when the final day comes, Allah will forgive us for what we did.'

There was something in Ahlam's tone, something amidst the speech she had made, something that compelled Abida to ask what she knew she ought not to.

'Did you and Ziad do anything you shouldn't have? Is that why you're saying all of this?'

Ahlam did not flinch. She placed both hands on Abida's shoulders, steadying her, steadying them both.

'No, we didn't. But would I have if we'd ever been allowed to be alone together? Maybe. I hope not, but it's not impossible. I can't say. But that's how I know – it's easy to say you wouldn't do something if you've never had the opportunity to.'

She had thought Ahlam ridiculous for so long, had presumed she had the measure of her and everyone else in the MSA. But Ahlam was now peering at her with concern and an astute half-smile Abida had not expected. Abida inhaled, then exhaled. Her body throbbed as though she had just been tackled to the ground.

She wondered what they were saying inside, what Naeem and Sara were planning to do. She realised she did not especially care. It was not her business; she cared only that she could somehow repair her friendship with Sara. Naeem and Sara had committed their mistakes and she had made hers, and they would all have to find some way of reconciling themselves to the foreignness of this new world.

'Let's get you inside, and you can finish your speech. Don't worry, I'm sure Mustafa has smoothed things over. He's good at that.'

Ahlam pulled Abida up until they were standing, placing her arm around her and letting go when they reached the doorway to the musallah. Abida walked back inside, a hush now falling over the room.

'Sorry, everyone. Ignore me. I'm ready to start now.'

Abida stood in the centre again, stretching her arms out in front of her and muttering a silent plea, heaven-bound, for grace. She did not await anyone's permission to commence; she spoke and spoke and spoke, the words seeming to flow out of her without end.

24

Naeem

The votes for MSA president were now open. Wahid had taken Naeem aside after the meeting and said that he was not sure how Abida had found out about that one time – just that one time – and Naeem had interrupted him, stating that he didn't want to know. It had taken every inch of his self-control to stop himself from running from the room as Abida had spoken; he had felt the fear course through him like an electric shock.

His final classes for the semester were held and he was now on a study break before his first exam. He remained at home for the first two days, studying in his bedroom. He did not want to see anyone from the MSA or engage with them about what had happened at the meeting. When Sara sent him messages asking what to do about Abida, he was vague and non-committal. He did not understand Abida's motivations and he did not want to. Now that he knew no one in the MSA was aware of who and what she had been referring to, she no longer held any interest for him. If Sara forgave Abida, he supposed he would have to tolerate her. It was a matter for them. His main preoccupation now was what to do about Sara.

He could have spoken to his mother any time now. Each day Meherin came to his room to see how his studies were going, asking to see his notes and diagrams, picking up his textbooks and reading aloud from a page at random. She spoke about the new suitor she had arranged for Sadia and the difficulties she was having with scheduling connecting flights for the conference Professor Kazi was attending in Johannesburg shortly. He thought about telling her that the girl he loved was also going to South Africa soon, that he wanted to marry her when she returned. But he had not, and Meherin departed the room, leaving the door open behind her.

He counted down the days until his first exam. Fourteen, thirteen. He was certain that if he did not do something before then, his relationship with Sara would end. The date he had pronounced in the throes of love now hung over his head like a guillotine, ready to descend. Already they had come so close to spectacular ruin, but it was not an explosion he now feared but a sluggish, aimless drifting. He had not yet repented for his sins. He had chipped away at Sara's trust in him, and he did not know if it could be regained.

Sara had not given him any ultimatums, but Naeem was certain that she would leave very soon if he did not act. It was not that Sara seemed eager to get married, unlike some of the other MSA girls. It was simply that he knew Sara to be a person of efficiency and good sense, and he could not envision her lingering in a relationship without an aim. Her feelings would not override her reason, and he would lose her. Naeem would not meet a girl like her again; he would get married in half-a-dozen years to an attractive doctor or lawyer who would be content to live with his parents until they had a child of their own and possibly even afterwards.

Sara had not once asked him if he had spoken to his parents. Naeem knew it was something she thought of constantly, and yet when she did ask, five days after the MSA meeting as he walked her to her car, he did not have an answer prepared for her.

'I'm so fucking stupid, aren't I?' Sara folded her arms in front of her, the soft cotton of her shirt bunching up around her elbows.

The anger with which she spoke caught him by surprise, as did the use of expletives.

'I've been waiting and waiting,' she continued, 'not wanting to badger you about anything, not wanting to upset you, never pushing, always waiting like a good little girl, and I am tired of it.' The dramatic emphasis with which she spoke would have been amusing if it had not been so clearly true.

'I'm tired too, Sara. This hasn't exactly been easy for me either.' The knowledge that she was tired of him rendered Naeem bullish, aggressive. He was tired, but not of her, never of her. He was tired only of the awareness of his own flaws which she exposed, and tired of the way in which they could love and laugh and care for each other without altering the essential wrongness of what they were doing.

'Easy is exactly what it's been for you. In your entire life, all you've ever had to do is hold out your hand and whatever you wanted would come to you. You're weak, and you're a coward, and you're never going to be anything except what everyone expects you to be,' she spat, looking at him squarely.

Naeem realised that she had known of his weakness all along, and where she had previously felt the urge to cradle him and nurture was now raw contempt.

Sara held his gaze for a moment longer before opening the door of her car. Without thinking, Naeem reached out and placed his fingers in the space where the door met the interior, and so too did Sara, unthinkingly, close it. He reacted fast enough to remove all but his index finger, which remained wedged.

Sara yanked open the door and fell on him. There was no other word for it; he had to cling on to the door with his other hand in order to keep them both upstanding. Once she realised he was having difficulty remaining upright, she placed her arm around his and led him to the back seat. The pulsations of his index finger indicated that there would be bruising, but Sara was gripping it so tightly and kissing it so that Naeem could not see if it was bleeding. Her tears dripped onto his fingers and it was then that he knew he was bleeding, because the saltiness stung so much that he jerked his hand and she was forced to release it.

'Here, take this,' she said, reaching over to the glove box and pulling out a wet wipe. She pressed a wipe to his hand and the other to her face, sinking back into the seat next to him, her head lolling about his chest.

'I didn't know you kept wet wipes in your car,' he said weakly. The coolness of the wipe against his finger soothed him, but not as much as the realisation that they were touching again after all this time. Naeem wondered if their recent disagreements could be attributed to this simple fact, that they had not touched each other in so long. What would validation from his parents or hers achieve? They required no such validation inside their own space. But the thought disappeared as soon as it came, leaving only the guilt that he had formed it to begin with. They had violated His commands and it had not bound them together except with the same shame they now carried inside their separate bodies.

'I'm still pissed off at you, by the way. Don't think you're off the hook, buddy,' Sara said, removing the wipe from her face and throwing it to the floor. She elbowed him, hard, but the way she turned his finger over to look at both sides was deliberate and tender.

The nail of his index finger had emitted a few paltry droplets of blood, but it was now starting to turn blue. Naeem was not squeamish, and neither was Sara, and she did not fuss, wrapping it up again in the wipe in an amateurish tourniquet he admired. Sara could have been a far better doctor than him. Naeem struggled with the more practical elements of his course, his hands not as deft as some of the other students, and he had once palpated on the wrong side of a patient's body for their heart, a mistake the supervising doctor had missed when her attention was drawn to her pager. The patient, a man with curly whorls of hair on his chest, had sniggered and Naeem had driven home and sat in the driveway for almost an hour, his palms clenched and coated in sweat.

He started to speak, to attempt to put words to all he was feeling, but Sara began first.

'You know I'm going away soon,' she said.

'I know you are, silly. But you're coming back, right?'

He attempted a laugh, but it was weak and she did not join in. 'I'm coming back, yes.'

They were silent again. He knew he ought to say something now to assure her that their future was guaranteed. But he was no longer sure it was, if he had ever been. More than ever, he was reminded of the temporality of his life and his relationship with Sara. *The life of this world is nothing but a brief passing enjoyment.* But he loved her still. He was certain he did.

'I know we've lost our way a bit recently. But we love each other, and that's all that matters. You love me, right?'

Sara nodded. He continued. 'You love me, but you have to understand me too –'

'I do understand. You know I do. I understand you and I love you, and that's why I know we can't continue like this. Didn't you see what happened at the meeting? Love on its own isn't enough to keep us together. Something is going to give.'

He waited for her to pronounce words of finality, to definitively put an end to what they had begun, but Sara did not. They sat in silence, nestled together like animals in search of heat, in search of shelter, all the fingers of her hand closed in around his one finger.

25

Sara

In the days since the meeting Abida had sent her nineteen messages, and two voice recordings. Sara had not listened to the voice recordings and had only scanned the messages. Abida was so sorry, Abida understood if Sara was angry at her and would do anything to make it up to her, if Sara would just pick up the phone. Abida was giving her permission to be angry and she took it, raving to Naeem about how Abida was no kind of friend and no kind of Muslim, exposing people's sins and lording it over them. But she could not maintain her rage, knowing that the configuration of her and Naeem on the inside and Abida on the outer perimeter was all wrong. Still, she clung to the illusion of it, agreeing to visit Naeem at his home the day after they had fought and made up in her car.

When Naeem opened the door of his house and removed the shoes from her feet, Sara felt the utter futility of what they were doing once again. They had resolved nothing and nothing was now certain about what they would do next. She thought of the Sara and Naeem who existed in a parallel dimension, the one in which they were getting engaged in just a few weeks when the semester ended. That Sara was aflutter with anticipation, selecting rings, ordering cakes and floral decorations. That Sara was applying makeup in her bedroom with Abida, dancing around to Taylor Swift and listening to her friend dissect the social hierarchy of Naeem's family and friends. But she spoke to Naeem now, not about what could or should have been, but about the immediate: Naeem urging her to at least reply to Abida's constant stream of messages, the upcoming multi-station practical exam Naeem feared he would fail, the movie selection on the flight to South Africa Sara would take once she had completed her final exams. They walked up the staircase and entered his bedroom, where Naeem sprang onto his bed, where he slipped and caused it to reverberate.

'Easy, tiger. I think I've finally figured out why your mum called you Rocket!'

It was a clumsy joke; by mutual consent, they were not to speak of their parents anymore. Naeem passed over it smoothly, laughing and beckoning her to lay beside him. It was a reconstruction of their early days, when they had been so uninhibited. She could not lose herself in this, but she could memorise the way it felt, the way he looked at her and the way she looked at him.

When it was done, she turned onto her side, facing Naeem as he lay on his back. His face in repose was immeasurably beautiful, the roundness of his cheeks dipping into a firm chin. His eyes were clear and bright, attesting to the purity of spirit which had so enthralled her from across the table at MSA meetings and other events. She had not been wrong in her initial estimation of him, and that was what rendered it so very difficult to give him up. She could not give him up, not yet. There were still remaining diversions to be explored, means of prolonging and dodging around what would come.

'Will you read me some Quran? Please?'

Naeem turned to face her and nodded. Sara did not need to say anything further. They both knew that he was gifting her something to remember him by. He rose from the bed and brought his gold-embossed Quran to her, sitting against the wall with his back curved inwards.

'Is there any verse you want me to read?'

'Surprise me.' Sara closed her eyes and stretched out on his bed. She knew its dimensions so well that she could stop and tuck her feet in at the precise point where it ended. She knew all the different sheet–duvet combinations he possessed, and she recognised the scent of the washing powder his mother favoured, a combination of freesia and jasmine Sara thought sickly sweet.

Naeem began and the rich melody of his voice forced her eyes open in sheer surprise. His voice assumed a commanding tone and the rocking motion he performed as he recited frightened her, until he switched to a silky undertone and grasped her hand in his.

Let there be no compulsion in religion: Truth stands out clear from Error: whoever rejects evil and believes in Allah hath grasped the most trustworthy handhold that never breaks.

Naeem read the translation for her benefit, and Sara turned onto her stomach and buried her face in his pillow to stifle the tears.

She did not want to know what it meant; she did not want to hear what he was imparting to her. He was telling her that they would each continue without the other, that the handhold that they had seized in each other would inevitably break, whether by their own doing now or the doing of death or disease later in life, but that the handhold they had chosen in Allah never would. He was reinforcing that they had been brought together by His will and His will was that they should marry, or part. Marry, or part. They would not marry, and so they would have to part, but neither could compel the parting.

'Sara? Are you okay?' She heard Naeem close the book and place it on his bedside table. He did not attempt to turn her over, running his hands through her hair and down her back. It was the sort of touch Sara's mother might use, with her firm, cool hands, which reassured and plucked and pressed her clients.

'I'm going downstairs to get you something to eat. Just wait here, okay?' He patted the back of her neck. The touch was imperceptible, heard more than felt, but it kept Sara rooted in place. She heard the door close and the softness of his footsteps on the staircase before they disappeared. She had learned that Naeem accomplished most tasks in this soft way. She thought of the unguarded glance he had given her across the lawn at the MSA barbeque, long before they had been lovers, and the way she had returned it in the same manner, without shame or fear of reprisals.

She allowed herself to fantasise about the possibility of her and Naeem being other people. They could be together then, together without thinking of whether there would be a future, savouring the days and the outings and the trips interstate and overseas.

But Sara did not wish to be such a person, and she did not wish for Naeem to be such a person, even if it allowed them to retain each other for a year or two. She could not live with turning him away from Allah any more than she could turn away herself. She rolled over and touched her fingertips to the smoothness of the wall, her hair splayed across the pillow.

Downstairs, Sara heard the front door swing open. She could hear Naeem in the kitchen, the microwave humming. Panic and terror held her in position.

'Whose shoes are these?' She heard a trilling female voice call out, the pretty cadence of it filling her ears. A woman, with the easy confidence of someone entering their own home.

Naeem had not answered, and the question was stated once, then again, its volume and pitch increasing with each repetition.

'It's a girl, Ammu. She's upstairs.' Naeem's voice sounded unfamiliar, and Sara realised why: he was afraid, more afraid than she had ever heard him, even when compared to how he had behaved that day at the beach. Then, Sara had been able to use her body to contain and shield him, but there was no such recourse available to them now.

'You brought a girl into the house? You brought a girl into our house?' This was followed by a scream, and a dull thump which could have been a slap or perhaps something falling to the ground in a distracted motion. Sara imagined the woman entering her house, clasping a jacket or an umbrella in her hand, thinking of a shower and dinner as she went to put her shoes away. She had styled this house, crafted her children to sit upright in its varnished chairs and utter their pleases and thank yous, and now her son had brought a stranger inside without her permission.

The screaming stopped, then continued without pause. It was terrible to hear, a mother's anguish at being so deceived by the child she had raised with such care, the son she had thought devoid of the ugliness in other people's children. Sara could understand this woman's fury, but she could not escape it; the only viable exit was to go down the staircase and out the front door. She was trapped inside this house. The screaming ceased, and when the woman spoke again, it was clipped and precise.

'Bring her down here now, please.'

Sara had thought Naeem would protest and tell his mother that she was being ridiculous and hysterical, that she had no right to demand such a thing, but he did not. Instead, she heard his footsteps on the staircase and his hand turning the doorknob, and then he was standing before her. He did not speak, but instead began shoving her things inside her bag with a ferocity she had never imagined he could possess. Sara did not object as Naeem crumpled her hijab and put it in the bag alongside her phone and car keys. She could not speak to him or look at him, just follow him down the staircase, bare-headed and barefoot, where the woman stood waiting.

'Give us a moment, won't you?' She gestured towards the garden, indicating that Naeem should leave.

In the minutes since Naeem had gone upstairs, the woman had composed herself. Although her words had been phrased, if not delivered, as a question, Naeem complied, closing the door behind him so limply that it remained ajar by several centimetres. The woman moved and shut it in one neat flick of the wrist, before proceeding towards the front part of the house. She did not turn around to see if Sara was walking behind her, but Sara followed her anyway. They turned into the guest room and sat on sofas facing each other, reminding Sara for a moment of the very first time she had come to this house.

'Make yourself comfortable,' the woman said, sitting with her legs crossed. She seemed far too young to be the mother of an adult son and was one of the most beautiful women Sara had seen, her face carved with such skill by Al-Musawwir, The Fashioner. Only the slight dampness of her sleeve and the hard gleam in her honey-brown eyes hinted that she was the same woman whose screaming had so chilled Sara. The long eyelashes were the same as her son's, as were the long fingers, but these fingers and wrists were glazed with jewellery: a gold band and a tiny, brilliant diamond ring on the left hand, a thin gold bracelet on the right. This woman wore her wealth tastefully, just as her son did. These people seemed to know how to be wealthy in a way that did not offend, but suggested the existence of further riches.

'Mrs Kazi, please –'

'Call me Meherin, please. I didn't catch your name, dear? Your full name.'

It did not occur to Sara to lie, or to walk out of the room. Naeem had left her alone with this woman, whose force of will had Sara affixed to her seat, her eyes downcast. She felt she owed Naeem's mother a debt for her gross misappropriation of her house, and by extension, her son. This was a mere preview of the judgement she and Naeem were to receive on the day after which there would be no more days, and she could not contemplate fleeing from this woman any more than she could contemplate fleeing from the judgement to come.

'It's Sara Andrews,' Sara said. She would not address Naeem's mother as Meherin, but neither could she call her Aunty as she did with the mothers of friends. Sara wondered what she would have called this woman if she was her daughter-in-law, whether they would have cooked in the marble kitchen together for the men of the house.

'Sara, you're a nice girl I'm sure, but my son has been very foolish.'

'I'm sorry, I didn't mean to –'

Again, Naeem's mother cut across her, her English faintly accented with something that was not Australian, but which was nevertheless faultless in its execution.

'There's nothing to apologise for, dear. It's my son who's been in the wrong. I don't like the idea of him disgracing himself and leading on poor girls like yourself. I will talk to him myself, don't you worry. My children sometimes tell me I can be dramatic, but I will deal with this all discreetly. There's no need for his father or anyone else to know at this stage, unless there are any further complications,' she continued, sweeping over the last word in a manner that left little doubt as to her meaning.

Sara realised then that she was not wearing her hijab and that Naeem's mother had taken her for a white girl, and that, because of this, she would not exact punishment. She was not going to punish

Naeem for a relationship that would not threaten his eventual marriage prospects, and she was certainly not going to punish Sara for something she assumed a girl like her would see no shame in. The horror, the utter grotesqueness of it was devastating, but Sara could not bring herself to correct the error. It was better this way, sparing them all any further embarrassment and grief. There was no future for her and Naeem. They had been aware of this for some time, and his mother had ensured they would not prevaricate any longer.

'Naeem? Can you please come walk Sara to her car?' Naeem's mother stood up and extended her hand, the slender fingers oddly comforting against hers. Sara respected this woman, even if she could not like her. They were women and women understood the fallibility of boys. Naeem appeared at the door as if he had been waiting there all along, and Sara felt her legs moving and her feet slipping into the offending shoes, which had been placed next to the front door. She turned her head back to the couches, the gleaming floors, the ripple of the swimming pool behind the garden. She would not see the inside of this house again, and she wanted to etch its expanse onto her memory where she could access it, keep it safe in the months and years to come. One day, she might tell her daughter about all of this, not as warning but as fable, a boy and a girl and the things they had done in the big house with the brocade curtains.

'You take care now, dear,' Meherin said, shutting the door behind them and withdrawing back into her house.

Once Sara was out in the bright sunshine, she longed to run down the driveway and away from this place. She felt strangely grateful to Naeem's mother for what she had done. But she could not run, matching her steps to Naeem's instead, which were heavy and shuffling.

'Sara, I'm so sorry. I'm so, so sorry.' Naeem's voice was choked, but his head was bowed, and he did not make any attempt to touch her. His mother could still be watching them from one of the house's many windows and they both knew the time when they could hold each other and forget was gone.

'There's nothing to apologise for.' Sara echoed his mother's words. She supposed he ought to apologise but at this point the semantics of apology were immaterial. She loved him still, but it was time to go. She saw now that she would have to drive away from this house and leave Naeem, and that she could do so because, for all his goodness, she was ultimately tougher and stronger and more durable than he was. He would have permitted them to totter on, had it not been for the strength of his mother, a strength that Sara would now have to assume for herself.

'I love you so much. It's all my fault for being such a fucked-up coward. You don't have to leave.' Naeem was sobbing now, thick white mucus from his nose dripping all over his face and down his sweater. Sara did not wish to be cruel, but she would not linger to offer any more of herself to him. There had been too many offerings, too many opportunities for withdrawal she had refused to take.

'I love you too, but I do have to go.' Sara got in the car and closed the door, and before Naeem could say anything further, she turned the keys in the ignition and drove away, the image of him standing on the footpath with his hands to his face flashing briefly in her rear-view mirror before disappearing. She sped up. She had to go somewhere else and put her hijab back on. Absurd really, to have removed what Allah commanded for a mere boy. She would not be making that mistake again.

26

Abida

Sara had phoned her, sobbing so noisily into the phone Abida had been forced to hold it several centimetres away from her face. Sara's speech was incomprehensible and garbled, but Abida did not need to know the details of who had said what and who had responded in which fashion. Naeem had behaved as she had been certain he would from the outset, abandoning Sara in favour of his pleasant, dull life. Abida was surprised at how little solace she drew from her foresight. Even through the grief she felt for Sara, she was so overjoyed that Sara was speaking to her again, that she had forgiven Abida for her outburst.

Abida proposed that they go out somewhere for a greasy meal, and Sara had acceded, despite their looming exams. She had volunteered to drive to Abida's house, arriving so promptly that Abida had not yet dressed. Sara came in and sat down with Ammu, and the good manners and total lack of conceit she displayed in watching a video Farah was showing her made Abida think of the daughter-in-law Naeem's parents could have acquired. Sara aimed to please her audience; she would have donned an elaborate red sari and bejewelled veil for her wedding, allowed Naeem's parents to choose the caterer and the venue and the bulk of the guest list. She would have attempted to learn Bangla and emulate the way Naeem's mother served her guests, noting her own errors before anyone else would. A Bangladeshi girl would bring her own notions of how things should be done, of how she had seen her own mother entertain and cook certain dishes, but Sara would have provided a blank template upon which Naeem's parents could construct the expectations of what a Bangladeshi daughter-in-law would or would not do. They could have done far worse.

As soon as Abida entered the room, Sara rose and kissed Ammu on both cheeks, hugging Farah and whispering something in her ear which sent her into peals of giggles. Sara was good with children because she did not use that peculiar babyish tone of voice so many adults did, as if children could not understand them if they spoke in their ordinary voice. Abida kissed her mother, and together they turned and walked towards Sara's car.

Inside the car, the pretence of cheer that had propped Sara up in the house seemed to desert her, and the hand not holding the wheel was shaking. Abida was afraid to speak. She did not know what to say of a relationship which had so offended her sensibilities, but had evidently meant a great deal to her oldest and dearest friend. She was a stranger to heartbreak and was curious as to what it might entail, but her immediate priority was to listen, to assuage Sara's pain. Maroof had recovered from his heartbreak with obscene haste, requesting their parents set about finding suitable girls for him to meet in the coming weeks and months. Abida hoped he was repressing his feelings. The reality, that he did not in fact possess feelings potent enough to warrant suppressing, was far too grim.

'We can talk about it, or we can just go eat. It's up to you,' Abida said. She was aware of her own shortcomings in handling the feelings of others. It required an intuitive knowledge of when to be silent and when to speak, the capacity to withhold opinions and pronouncements that could affront. It also required the ability to quieten one's own inner monologue, a task Abida found difficult. But she would attempt anything for Sara now. They had passed through the greatest moment of crisis, and the fact that Sara was trusting her with her anguish meant more than any other gesture she could have made.

Sara did not reply. Abida marvelled at how ordinary she looked. Her hijab was pinned, her clothing was ironed, and she had the raw pink remnants of a pimple on her chin. She wondered if other people's bodies conspired against them in such underhand ways, wondered if Naeem had adored Sara's imperfections. She would not ask, would not allude to anything of that nature again.

The kebab shop Sara had chosen was the one Maroof frequented, which was well-known for its snack packs. Sara ordered an entire one for herself, but Abida could not stomach the concoction with its piles of meat and hot chips and cocktail of sauces, so she ordered a small hot chips instead. The crowd was mixed, girls with ripped jeans and wedge heels on the arms of their muscled boyfriends mingling with families in tracksuits and hijabs. The friendly banter between the kebab servers and their customers precluded any conversation, but when they sat outside Sara began to speak without prompting.

'I'm so stupid. I knew all along that it was going to end and I kept going and going, and he knew it was going to end and he let me keep going, just because he could.' Sara scraped her plastic fork against the surface of her styrofoam container, leaving three even lines down its centre.

'He's boring and he's a loser, Sara. I honestly have no idea what you saw in him.'

'He's not a loser, I am. He's a good person in a world with very few good people in it, and I'm never going to meet someone like him again.' The resignation Sara spoke with was terrible. How could they have come to this, at the age of twenty, to believe their best was already behind them? Few of Abida's non-Muslim friends would speak about themselves in such a manner; they were absorbed in their jobs and parties and travels, deriving meaning from the heartbreaks and the slights, wallowing in the rebounds and the casual, undefined flings. Her Muslim friends could be just as blithe, but she and Sara were sitting here, thinking of the world and all its tribulations.

'You know what? Fuck it. Fuck it, and fuck that fucking idiot, Sara. It's all fucked. Let's just enjoy our fucking meal.'

Sara stared at her across the table. Her expression was almost angry, her fork paused mid-air. The laughter seemed to pour out of her in a great big spurt, causing tears to run down her face and her hand to clutch her belly. Abida chuckled, uncertain of how she ought to respond. She stuffed a chip into her mouth, opening Sara's container to dip another into her garlic sauce.

'It's just – I've never heard you swear, not like that.' Sara was snorting, her nostrils flaring as the spasms in her belly appeared to recede.

'And you won't again, not any time soon. And if you tell anyone, you're deader than the animals who were sacrificed to bring us this beautiful meal, so let's enjoy ourselves, okay?'

They chewed on and on, opening the cans of Coke Abida brought them from the fridge and guzzling them down until they were empty, and she rose to get them two more. The gristly bits of doner meat disappeared into Sara's mouth, leaving a greasy sheen on her lips and chin. They communicated in half-grunts and nods, and when they were done, they scooped the lot into the bin and walked to the car in silence.

'I still love him, Abida. I can't say I don't,' Sara said, as though the question had been posed and she had been compelled to answer.

'People don't just fall out of love just like that. I might not know a whole about love, but I do know that.'

'Do you think you'll ever fall in love?'

Abida considered the question. She had experienced crushes on various teen heartthrobs, but the boys she encountered did not hold much appeal for her. She was yet to meet a boy-man who could be soft without being weak, and who could be strong without also being callous or aggressive. She did not think such a man existed, not in the present age. Sara would have to learn what Abida had learned some time ago: love was a crutch used by the feeble, and once removed, the world could be understood for the pile of shit that it was.

'I don't know, Sara. I don't think so. I just don't see the point of it.'

Sara shook her head, looking more grieved than she had when they had been sitting at the shop.

'Well, you've always been smarter than me, but I guess everyone's entitled to get it wrong on their first go, right? I'll have to try harder next time.' This play at being facetious did not suit Sara and, although Abida knew it was feigned, she wanted desperately to put a stop to it. Not every difficulty could be snipped into a tidy anecdote, a cautionary tale to be told to one's self and others. The relentless, tedious struggles of her parents through war and poverty had taught her that much. She wanted Sara to stop torturing herself, to understand that only those with sufficient courage to open their heart could withstand the rupturing of it. But she knew she could not fast-forward Sara's healing. It was too soon for that.

'Just because it ended doesn't make it wrong,' she said, squeezing Sara's hand.

'It was wrong, in so many ways. I was so angry at you when I should have been angry at him. You already know, so I might as well tell you everything now.'

'You were right to be angry at me, and you certainly don't owe me any explanations,' Abida said. She was still curious regarding the details of how it had all begun, of how far they had gone and what it had been like, but she did not think she could bear the weight of what Sara would divulge. Some things were best left unsaid; to speak of them would be to irrevocably tear at their capacity to understand each other. Abida was beginning to understand her own limitations better, and although she was learning all the time, she did not think she was yet capable of accepting that Naeem and Sara had spent all their time in the back seat of their cars or that Sara had had an abortion or anything else. Those secrets would remain theirs to whisper to Allah in the night.

Sara nodded, her thoughts now elsewhere.

When they arrived back at her house, Abida squeezed Sara's hand again and waved her off. It was evident that Sara was still very much with Naeem in a place where Abida could not reach her. It was this retreat that Abida had resented, this sense of things guarded and set aside that had so galled her.

Abida knew then that she would have to withdraw from consideration for the MSA presidency. Her wide sweeps of judgement would be her undoing; she still had too much to grow into, too many mistakes to make. She would fight, she would always fight, but in doing so she would always strive to acknowledge the truth. In this instance, the truth was apparent: she had sought dominance, had been jealous that her best friend had kept secrets from her and had been chosen by a boy who would not have chosen her. She had not wanted to share Sara with anyone, especially not with a boy like Naeem who had likely never had to share a single thing in his life.

Although it was past midnight, she sent Wahid a message and asked if they could speak soon. He replied immediately, saying that he was free tomorrow afternoon if Abida wanted to catch up at university. Abida confirmed with a thumbs up and tried to lull herself into sleep, but her sleep was fitful and interrupted by the glow of Farah's phone in the dark. She pulled the blanket over her head and willed her eyes shut, wishing, not for the first time, that she had a room of her own.

The vote was due to close today. Abida had no reason to go to university now that her classes had ended, but she got dressed and travelled there anyway, venturing directly to the musallah. She had asked Sara to come too but she hadn't yet heard back from her.

After praying dhuhr, Abida felt a tap on her shoulder. She turned and hugged Sara. Sara's face was pale inside her hoodie, but she was not crying. Abida hugged her again.

'Let's go study in the library together? I just have to talk to Wahid about something first.'

'Sure, just let me pray dhuhr first.'

Sara raised her hands and began to pray. Abida's phone buzzed. Wahid was waiting for her; she had to go speak to him. She stood up and watched as Sara pressed her head to the floor, lingering there for many seconds.

Wahid was waiting outside the entrance, his hair now shorn in a buzz cut which revealed the irregularities of his head, the peculiar roundness of its shape. She noticed he was smiling and although she didn't smile in return, she felt the corners of her mouth relax from its former tightness.

'Assalamu alaykum, sis. Everything okay with you?'

'Alhamdulillah. How about you?'

Wahid seemed pleased at being asked, pausing before answering.

'All good, alhamdulillah. Busy studying for final exams so I'll be glad when it's all over. What did you want to talk to me about?'

'Firstly, I wanted to say that I was completely out of line at the meeting and I'm sorry. I'm not going to go into the details, but a few things were boiling over and I just lost control.'

'You don't need to apologise to me of all people,' Wahid said, his mouth twisting.

'I know. But that's not why I wanted to speak to you today. I'm going to pull out of the vote. You'll have no opposition so that means you'll be the new president.'

'You can't do that. You really shouldn't. You were right in what you said, even if it did come out in a weird way. There is a lot of shit going on behind the scenes here, but you're above all of that. You actually care about things, and you're a whole lot more intelligent than I am, that's for sure.'

The swearword again, this time coming from someone else's mouth. For someone who thought crying the most irritating reflex action of the human body, Abida felt close to it again. She opened and closed her mouth, thinking of how openness invited openness in turn, how there was something to be said for the rapport to be built from losing all your inhibitions and embarrassing yourself in front of others.

'Thanks,' she said, finally.

'Don't thank me. Now don't say another word to anyone about this pulling out stuff. Just see what happens, and in the end it's all with Allah.'

He placed his hand over his heart and said salams before entering the boys' side of the musallah. As he stood at the door, he turned around and nodded at her. He was still smiling and in spite of herself Abida found herself smiling too.

She had not noticed but Sara was now standing behind her. Sara was wearing the same smile as Wahid and Abida was comforted by this until she realised that Sara was mimicking Wahid, not smiling of her own accord.

'What was that all about?' Sara continued to smile even though her eyes were sad and red-rimmed.

'What was what all about –'

'Oh, don't play dumb with me. I saw the way Wahid was smiling at you. Now that I think about it, he's always seemed to have a bit of a thing with you, all that combative energy, that tension brimming over –'

'You aren't seriously trying to suggest what I think you are, girl. But it's okay. I know you're not yourself at the moment, so I'll let it slide,' she said. She laughed, although she was conscious that the volume of her laughter was higher than usual. Sara's brain was addled by heartbreak. She began to walk, and to her relief Sara said nothing further about it. Wahid's smile flashed before her eyes before she walked faster to erase it.

As they exited the corridor they saw Mustafa walking in the opposite direction. Abida was unsure whether Sara could handle conversation and hoped Mustafa would pass them with a wave, but the purposefulness of his stride suggested otherwise.

'Assalamu alaykum, sisters. How are you both?'

'Doing good, alhamdulillah. Getting some last study in before exams start,' she said, hoping he would not address Sara directly. Sara's eyes were already brimming with tears. In Mustafa's face Abida guessed Sara was reminded of Naeem, and the MSA, and

Abida watched as she crouched down on the floor and reached for something in her backpack.

'Well, I won't keep you too long. I only wanted to tell you that although the votes are just about to close, there can be no doubt about what the final result will be. I'm thrilled for you, Abida. You're a shining star of this MSA. But this is all off the record, of course. You'll be hearing from me very soon officially, inshaAllah,' he said, waving as he walked on.

Sara was still on the floor, but she stood up now. In her hand were two tissues she had retrieved from her backpack. For a moment they were silent. Abida heard Sara sniffle and before she could say anything about the tears now flowing down Sara's face, Sara handed her a tissue.

'Thought you might need one of these, miss MSA president,' Sara said.

It was only now that Abida had realised that she too was crying. The two of them were alone in the centre of the courtyard, the soft grass under them, the sky open and clear above them. She had done it, she had done it! She was the new MSA president. The realisation was overwhelming, and she would need time to process it. She pressed the tissue to her face, dabbing at her cheek, her eyes trained to the sky as she and Sara cried together.

27

Naeem

When Sara had driven away, Naeem had hoped and hoped she would return. He had stood on the street and dialled her number again and again. But she had not responded, and eventually he got into his car and drove aimlessly for hours until he stopped somewhere up on the northern beaches. He entered a mosque near Dee Why, begging Allah for release from the yoke of his own failings. He would start praying all of his prayers again, he would ask for repentance and not be governed by fear. If the ummah was destined to be incarcerated or killed, he would die along with them. Not only had he sinned with his body, but he had been grossly unjust to Sara, and he would reap injustice in this life and the next. *Surely Allah does not do any injustice to men, but men are unjust to themselves.*

He had returned home late into the night and found an assembled plate of food had been left on the counter for him, as though his mother had anticipated that he would be out late. If Meherin had sworn at Sara or abused her, Naeem would have been justified in blaming her, but he knew with heavy certainty that his mother was not to blame. He could not hold her accountable for the way he had abandoned Sara to her charge, the way he had been relieved when he had been sent outside and away from them. He had longed to sink into the pool and travel even further away from them, as deep under as he was able to go. His mother, and the girl he loved, not adversaries, but conspirators against him.

The melodramatic sway of his thoughts distracted him even from Sara, from what she must be feeling or thinking. He could think only of his own wretchedness. Over the next few days, Naeem turned off all the notifications from the MSA group chat, attempting instead to study for the six exams he was due to sit. Sadia had messaged him and said the meeting with the suitor, a doctor, had gone well and that there was talk of a second meeting with both families present. He had ignored her message, just as he ignored his mother, and beyond the civilities necessitated by daily life, his mother ignored him too. He knew she would speak to him soon, but it seemed that she was content to allow him to study without disturbances, now that she deemed the immediate threat to be extinguished.

The written examinations were inoffensive enough. Regurgitate, scribble, scrawl. But it was in the practical examinations that he unravelled. In each of the five stations, he had blundered, interpreting an ECG incorrectly, failing to ask about a patient's family history of diabetes in the history-taking exercise, and in the neurological examination component he had forgotten to test wrist flexion and extension. The examiners had provided no feedback, stating that he would be notified of his results in the coming month. When he exited that brightly lit room, Naeem realised that he had not spoken to Sara in almost a fortnight. In all this time, he had not allowed himself to picture her face or her voice. His capacity to shut out external noise had served him well throughout his studies and his memorisation of the Quran, and it had now served him well in silencing thoughts of her. But it could only offer a temporary reprieve, and when the pain did strike him, approximately ninety minutes after his exam was over, the awareness of his loss was so terrible that for the first time in Naeem's twenty years, he had contemplated the option of bringing about his meeting with his Lord, who was both Al Muhyi, the Giver of Life, and Al Mumit, the Bringer of Death.

The idea of ending his own existence had been appealing but fleeting. He knew he did not possess the singularity of purpose to take his own life, nor the conviction that the judgement that awaited him would be in any way kinder than his present challenges.

He would have to contact Sara, but he could not think of what to say to her. All the words he conjured seemed inadequate. The magnitude of what had happened was far beyond what could be distilled into a text message. But words on a screen were his only option. They were back to where they had begun, with typed words and nothing else to bolster their contact. After several hours of deliberation, he decided eventually to message and simply ask how she was.

There was no response from her, and his mother was calling him downstairs for dinner. Professor Kazi was departing in three days for the conference in Johannesburg and their dinners lately had been jumbles of takeaway grilled chicken and leftovers. Naeem smelled the fried rice before he saw it, the tang of Thai basil and fried egg filling his nostrils.

'We haven't had a proper meal in weeks. Would it kill Ammu to actually cook us something?' Tasnia stage-whispered to Naeem. 'Najwa could cook for us, but instead she's stuck mopping the floors all the time.'

Professor Kazi was on his laptop and speaking to Meherin about changing his hotel booking from a single room to a double as Meherin ladled rice onto their plates. But when Naeem sat down, squeezing his lemon wedge onto his rice, his mother broke off their conversation and addressed him.

'Kabir's parents came from Perth yesterday to meet Sadia and Chachi and Chacha. It's all looking very good, and we really think we might have a match this time.'

Naeem continued to chew his rice until it turned to sludge in his mouth. He slurped and cleared his throat before answering.

'Did they have to pay his girlfriend to disappear before he could meet Sadia?'

Naeem wanted his insolence to be noted and dealt with as a pretext to begin an argument. But his mother's response indicated that she understood what he was doing and that she was not inclined to indulge him.

'Sadia wasn't very happy about taking off her hijab when they met, but I told her that it was okay, that they just wanted to see what she looked like without it once. And look how nicely it's turned out for everybody.'

Professor Kazi had left the table and taken his plate to the kitchen. Tasnia nudged Naeem under the table and rolled her eyes, bored by their mother's talk of marriage and her part in it. Meherin did not wait for Naeem to reply, dishing Tasnia more rice before joining Professor Kazi in the kitchen. There were deep shadows under her eyes; she had been working long hours to try to finalise Professor Kazi's trip and reschedule appointments at the practice for when he would return.

'I can't wait until Dad goes. Mum's always more relaxed when he's gone,' Tasnia said.

'Don't be stupid,' he snapped. 'It's because Dad's going that Mum's so stressed out.'

'Geez, you're just as bad as them, bhaiya.' Tasnia abandoned the pretence of their unspoken alliance against their parents, pushing her chair hard against the floor and running upstairs, leaving her plate still full of rice and sauce. Naeem sat alone at the table, the murmur of his parents' voices from the kitchen low and indecipherable. He pressed his forehead against the cheap plastic tablecloth they used when there were no guests about, swooshing his feet back and forth against the floor.

'Sorry, bhaiya, I'll put it away,' Tasnia said, the thinness of her voice hovering about Naeem's ear. Naeem could feel the soft brush of her fingers against his plate as both plates were stacked and removed, but it was a long while before he could get up and move his legs well enough to reach his bedroom. He had not opened any windows in several days and he inhaled, hoping to catch a trace of

Sara, but all he could detect was his own unwashed smell. He could not recall when he had last showered. He had been performing wudu, but that did not require washing his armpits or his groin, and a quick sniff confirmed that these were the two parts of his body producing the odour.

In the shower, Naeem turned the temperature up as high as he could stand, the heat reddening his skin and scalding his scalp as he dug his fingers into his hair and combed it with them. Sara had said his hair was silky, but Naeem knew it was just oily. Her gaze had rendered him beautiful. Naeem did not think anyone would marry him for his personal charm; he did not possess much of it. He would be married for his title, his family and his background, and if he was fortunate, his marriage would be uneventful and easy.

His body tingled and burned. In giving up Sara, he would not be touched now until he was married. He could do otherwise, of course: go on dating apps, or select another girl from the MSA who would stray. He could find himself a girlfriend at hospital or at university, tell her that he loved her and always would. But what he had done with Sara did not alter the essential fact that he did not believe in physical intimacy outside of marriage, and that to continue along the path he had forged would be a far more deliberate sin than that which he had done with Sara. He did not want anyone else to touch him. Perhaps if he and Sara had not touched, they would still be together now.

His phone remained silent and uncooperative. When it finally rang Naeem answered it on the first ring, his voice hushed.

'Salam, Naeem. Finally! I was starting to think you were ignoring me.'

Sadia sounded cheerful, brisk, jarring against his ears.

'I've just been busy studying for my exams, that's all. How are you?'

'I'm good, alhamdulillah. Did your mum tell you the news? She said she did, but I wanted to check with you?'

'What news?' He was repulsed by the upward inflection with which she spoke.

'We met with Kabir's parents and everyone seemed to get along well. We're meeting tomorrow, inshaAllah, and if everything continues to go well, we're going to go ahead with an engagement,' Sadia said, more definite this time.

'Did you really take your hijab off when you met that first time?'

Sadia laughed, unbothered by the crassness of his approach.

'I thought it was a bit silly that they asked, but I did it and it was fine. They're a really nice family.'

Her persistent pleasantness, the hopefulness with which she imparted her news disarmed Naeem. He directed his rage inwards once again, at his own conduct.

'I'm really happy for you, apu. When do I get to meet him?'

'Soon, inshaAllah. You've seemed a bit down recently, Naeem. Are things okay with you and Sara?'

There would be little use in imparting the news to Sadia, or anyone else. The omissions Naeem would have to make would render real confidences impossible. The truth of his relationship with Sara could not be spoken to his family and friends, and he could not bear to sanitise what he and Sara had shared, to sell it as a tale of epic thwarted love. People would certainly buy it, but Naeem's conscience would not permit him to capitalise on their good opinions. There was nothing to be done but wear his failings and wear them in silence.

'Everything's fine. I'll talk to you soon, inshaAllah. Hope it all goes well tomorrow,' he said.

'Thanks. I really think this could be the one,' she said, and the wobble of her voice conveyed the weight of this to Naeem. He could not begrudge her, even if he disapproved of the way in which she had discarded parts of herself with such ease in the process of obtaining a husband.

'I'll make dua for you both,' he said, hanging up.

Shaykh Hassan had once said that people misunderstood fate, that it did not entail awaiting things to come your way. You were always required to strive. But in doing so, you were required to accept whatever outcome arose, no matter how painful or unwanted. The Prophet Muhammad had once been asked by someone if they should tie their camel to secure it, or leave it untied and trust in Allah, and the answer had been conclusively given, that one's camel must be tied. But Naeem could not seem to apply this story to his own situation. In practical terms, how did a person elucidate the boundaries of fate and choice, of knowing when to yield or continue to generate a thrust? To believe was to submit but not be submerged and inert. Did trusting in Allah mean forsaking Sara or pushing for her to return to him? There were only general principles; he would have to deduce the rest for himself.

Of one thing Naeem was certain: if he did nothing, nothing would eventuate. He could not guarantee that Sara would be receptive to any efforts, but if he did not try, he would be sure to lose her. He dialled her number, but it went straight to voicemail and he hung up before the beep could prompt him to speak. After several minutes had passed, he dialled it again, this time encountering her impersonal voicemail message, *You've reached Sara Andrews. Please leave me a message and I will get back to you as soon as I can.*

'Sara, I need to know how you are. Please send me a message or call me back, okay? I love you.'

Naeem waited ten minutes, then forced himself to wait another ten. His phone's placid immobility taunted him. He wanted it to dance, to squirm around as he was. He contemplated driving to Sara's house, but the image of her father chasing him away and cursing him in Afrikaans was too frightening to contemplate. He would not be one of those men who intimidated women into their company and their bedrooms, into accepting their public proposals of marriage. Instead, Naeem switched off his lamp and lay on his bed, thinking of the lonely camel tied up in the desert and wondering if it would have been better to simply cut it loose.

28

Sara

There was something about the unambiguity of airports which appealed to Sara. Stop, go. Load the bag on the carousel sideways, not face down. No liquids above one hundred millilitres, all in clear plastic casing. She did not even object to being stopped for random selection; the bearded man was gentle with her things and spoke in a lilting accent that reminded her of Naeem's mother. She smiled as he wished her a good onward journey, inshaAllah.

When they had travelled to South Africa before, they had flown via Dubai or Singapore, but this time they had opted for a direct service to Johannesburg, a fifteen-hour flight. Sara wondered if she would be on the same flight as Naeem's father, but she remembered he had flown out four days ago. She had imagined conversations they would have had about South Africa, composed scripts of the discussions they would have had regarding the crime rate and the nouveau riche over tea and gulab jamun.

In the departures lounge, she reached for her phone without thinking before remonstrating her hand, tucking it under her outstretched legs. She had switched her phone off two days ago, when Naeem's messages and calls had required some sort of final response. She had messaged Abida to tell her she would be uncontactable while she was overseas, and Abida, no doubt cognisant of the reason, had approved and urged Sara to enjoy her trip.

Abida had been preoccupied with coping with the congratulatory messages and online posts about her ascent to the MSA's presidency. Nevertheless, she had been solicitous in the days before Sara's departure, visiting her with flowers, as though she were bereaved, and sending her daily messages with enthusiastic prompts and reminders to study and focus on her exams, such as, *the ummah needs more female engineers. You go, girl!* Sara had not known how to respond but she appreciated the sentiment.

She could have forgiven Naeem. Had he contacted her after the incident at his house, she would have met him, held him in her arms. But he had not. He had remained silent for many days, and when he had completed his exams, he had barraged her with calls and messages, pleading for a response. But he had not spoken of his mother or of their future together, and she knew that she could not respond to him.

The first three or four hours of the flight passed without incident. It was when her body began to relax into sleep that the panic began to set in. The darkness of the cabin, its complete absence of sound, seemed designed to recreate the atmosphere of Naeem's bedroom. She could not block the images from her mind. She gripped the arm rest and turned over, pulling the thin aeroplane-issued blanket over her head and stretching her legs out under the seat in front, willing the torment to subside, invoking Him to ease her pain. *Please, Allah, please. Please free me from the shackles of my sins. Please, my Lord.*

The clarity of the images and her body's instinctive response to them was devastating. Sara got up and paced the aisles, the strip of lighting along the floor guiding her towards the toilet. Inside, she pressed herself against the door, the smell of fresh urine overpowering her nostrils until she became accustomed to it and it no longer registered as a smell at all. She did not know how long she passed time in this manner: her body cupped against the toilet door, her forehead pressed into it with such force that Sara felt a circular dent where it had been when she eventually pulled herself away.

The briskness of the landing at Johannesburg and the blur of suitcases being hoisted down and children being comforted by harried parents jolted Sara back into the present. The connecting flight to Cape Town was conducted by one of the local carriers on a tiny aeroplane with smiley attendants and plenty of legroom, but the turbulence was as awful, if not worse than she had remembered from their last trip. She could think of nothing except the yearning for solid ground; the man in front of her vomited into a paper bag and a baby howled from somewhere towards the back of the aeroplane. Sara placed her head on her legs in the brace position as the aeroplane fumbled its way onto the tarmac, the city of Cape Town dark and quiet beneath them, the rocky crag of Table Mountain framing the city skyline.

In Cape Town, they were met by Aunty Ayesha and her husband, Uncle Tahir. Sara inhaled the warm air and realised that, for all their hours of flying, they were still in the Southern Hemisphere. She had always known that Australia was isolated in its geography, but she had not realised its isolation was so complete. She wondered if her parents had thought so too when they had travelled from their homes across the ocean for the very first time, their suitcases loaded with photo albums of people who would soon be dead.

Still woozy, Sara stumbled into her bed in Aunty Ayesha's guest bedroom, raucous laughter from the other room pounding through her body before she fell fast asleep, fully clothed.

Her dreams of Naeem were so lucid that Sara woke up fumbling for his face on the spare pillow. She could not comprehend that she was in Africa, that she had gone to sleep and woken up on this continent. It was still early and she had Aunty Ayesha's back-yard, and its view of Table Mountain, all to herself. There was something familiar about this place, not so much a homecoming as an easing into her own body, an unravelling of the stiffness she carried herself with in Australia, where she would always have to explain who she was and where she came from.

The grass was still dewy, but Sara breathed in the fresh air. She did not want to think of Naeem here, but he accompanied her as she walked to the perimeter of the yard, the mountain surveying them both as they did a slow lap in its shadow.

The hiss of a kettle from the kitchen reminded Sara that she ought to shower and don fresh clothing. By the time she was done,

Naeem had slowed his pursuit of her and she was able to stand in the kitchen with Aunty Ayesha and help her assemble breakfast. Her aunt shared Soraya's aversion to cooking and had purchased an assortment of traditional goodies: koeksisters bathed in sugar syrup and coconut flakes, slices of pink polony dotted with chilli and peppercorns, and fresh crusty bread. Within a few minutes, Soraya emerged, bleary-eyed, followed by Amin, still in his striped pyjamas. Once the coffee had been drunk, they set out on the necessary tasks: visiting Amin's great-aunt, who served them tea in chipped cups and stale Romany Creams; visiting Amin's three brothers, who did not seem to much care for their presence but also served them tea; and visiting Soraya and Amin's parents at the cemetery. The cemetery was Sara's favourite of the three stops, being set against the base of Table Mountain, where the ground was sloped and mossy. She located Sara Andrews's grave first, whispering a prayer for the woman she had not known, and a prayer for the women she did, like her mother and Abida. She even prayed for Naeem's mother and Naeem's grandmothers, at least one of whom she knew to be still living. She wanted to ask him what had happened to the other, but the time in which they had discussed their families and the intricacies of their ancestries into the early hours had long passed.

The second day passed in the same way. Together with Soraya's sisters and their families, they drove to Hout Bay, and its raw beauty momentarily distracted Sara from her sorrow. This was the land of her mother and father, the earth which had swallowed the bodies of the servants and prisoners and rebels she was descended from.

But once they were out of the car, she was irritated by her cousin Faiza's giggly antics with her hipster boyfriend, irritated by Soraya constantly taking photos, irritated by being surrounded by so many people who were not Naeem and who did not know who he was or what he had meant to her.

Soraya did not appear to notice the scowl Sara wore, laughing and joking with Aunty Ayesha as they ordered snoek and hot chips by the water. She watched Soraya as she ate her vinegar-soaked chips, thinking how happy she looked and how she had not seen her mother so happy in many months. She had been so consumed in Naeem that she had not thought of the anxieties her mother had faced in the slow winter months at the beauty parlour, watching her daughter shrink away from her and into the arms of an unknown boy.

Sara got up and threw a chip onto the rocks below, then another. Faiza clambered onto the sand below, clutching the hand of her boyfriend, whose name was Kasim and who Sara knew to be an engineer of some sort. She watched as the two of them walked along the water as a gaggle of children wrestled for control of a single worn fishing rod, the oldest of the bunch finally relaxing his grip so that a boy with a missing front tooth and bright blue eyes could hold it. Here, no one was interested in her. No one looked at her or asked her where she was from, except when they heard her Australian accent. Her looks and her name were of little notice. In the Cape, so many carried the blood of various nations and tribes, occupying the in-between space Sara had presumed to own. Here, she was the plain girl she had always been.

Soraya came up behind her and placed her hand on Sara's shoulder, her grip solid and damp from the baby wipes she carried and used on her fingers after eating.

'Did you eat enough? I can get you something else if you like.' Her mother's voice was low, so as not to attract the attention of Aunty Ayesha, who had a habit of interrupting conversations with her own amusing, but not always welcome interjections.

'No, I'm fine,' she said. They stared out at the ocean. Hout Bay was on the Atlantic seaboard, while Muizenberg Beach, just a few kilometres away, fed into the waters of the Indian Ocean.

'I know you're not having much fun right now.' In the wind, Soraya's hair brushed against the side of Sara's face, and the touch reminded her of the way Naeem's hair had tickled her lips and nose. She bowed her head and said nothing, waiting for the image to diminish.

'We'll go somewhere else, just me, you and Dad, okay?'

Soraya patted Sara's shoulder and walked back over to the group. She had not asked Sara what had happened when she had found her crying over her notes back in Sydney but had hugged her and tied her tousled hair up to better see her face, and when she had, she had hugged her again. Her mother had longed for a child for so many years, but when one had come, she had not tried to control or enforce or impose. She had permitted Sara to be independent and breakable, trusting that she was sturdy enough to put herself back together.

The next day was a Monday, and Aunty Ayesha and Uncle Tahir went to work, leaving Aunty Ayesha's car for them to use. They kept the doors and windows locked, but Sara studied the dry scrub of the landscape as they drove inland, the sight of a lone wild ostrich in an empty field causing her to clap her hands in delight. She had forgotten how Cape Town was random and brilliant and frightening all at once. Sydney demanded attention, its beauty insistent and organised, but Cape Town was beautiful just because it was.

When they got out of the car, they appeared to be at the foot of a deserted and disused fort with a bent sign marked Macassar. The landscape was not the spectacular jagged coastline or the grassy rise of the mountain, but dry and red and hilly, as though they had entered a different country altogether. Sara began the steep ascent to the fort, her feet catching against the rough, overgrown grass, until she reached the top. There, she could see the town below, the small dome of the mosque blending seamlessly into the crevice of the hill. She continued walking until she reached a small enclosed room where a gravestone stood, covered in a green shroud. The plaque above read, *Here lies Shaykh Yusuf of Macassar, who was exiled to the Cape of Good Hope in 1693 on the* Voetboeg *vessel for his resistance against the Dutch in Indonesia. Shaykh Yusuf is considered to be the founder of the Muslim community in South Africa and it is after him that this area, Macassar, is named.*

Soraya and Amin had now reached her, and were surprised to find her kneeling, her hands raised in prayer. Soraya led Amin to the undercover seating area overlooking the valley below, leaving Sara to her prayers. Sara thought of Shaykh Yusuf, his long journey to the other side of the world on a tall ship, the final glance he would have given his homeland as he was led off into an exile from which he would never return. She wondered briefly whether she was descended from him but it didn't really matter. She was from this place where empires had fought and crumbled and the people continued to resist, where her grandparents had raised her mother and father, where she was Muslim down to her very bones.

'I can't believe we've never been here before,' she said, sitting on the grass near her parents and looking out to where two sheep grazed next to the mosque.

'This is where I brought your mother on our first proper date,' Amin said, looking at Soraya from the corner of his eye.

'And you're lucky there was a second. What kind of a place is this to bring the girl you wanted to marry?' Soraya asked.

Their laughter seemed to echo down to the empty scrub below, and Sara joined in as she realised, with a swell of joy, that she had not once thought of Naeem since they had arrived in Macassar. She, too, would remember this place.

29

Abida

The MSA election had been a landslide. On the MSA group chat Wahid had conceded with grace, and when he had sent her an individual message to congratulate her, she had sent him a thumbs up accompanied by a smiley face. When the verdict was pronounced, the on-campus *Erudite* magazine had dispatched a reporter to cover it as Abida Hoque was only the third woman to be elected president of the MSA. In the interview, she had said that she was grateful for the opportunity, that she was proud to be Muslim and proud of the MSA. When the reporter had asked her why she decided to wear the hijab, she smiled and said that she did it because Allah told her to, and had smiled even more widely at the look of confusion this caused.

The semester had concluded and Abida had passed her exams with distinction, thanks to her furious perusal of

Connie's notes from the previous semester. She would turn her attention to MSA matters closer to the commencement of the new academic semester, but that was some months away. Sara had taken her broken heart and departed for South Africa, and Ahlam was preoccupied with outings to Brighton-Le-Sands Beach with Ziad and posting photos of them online, waffle cones in hand. Abida had now been successful in an interview at one of the state government departments. The role was unexciting, an administrative officer in a small financial reporting team, but it promised a decent salary and flexible working hours. She needed to earn some money; it was school holidays and her siblings were clamouring for outings to theme parks and the movies.

Abida could not process what had happened to her, the magnitude and scope of the things she had learned. She was certain only of Allah, of her knowledge that the climate was changing and that slavery and conquests and colonialism could not just be forgotten and that the rich would always say that anyone could make it with a little bit of hard work. She was her mother and father's daughter and Sara's best friend, and the rest was all background chatter. She could think things and change her mind when she read and examined the issue further, and that was just fine. She thought others would do well not to appear so certain of their opinions, but she supposed that, underneath their bravado, they were probably just as confused as she was.

The morning commute to work was unpleasant, crammed in between fragrant bodies in the morning and staler bodies in the afternoon. But Abida derived a quiet sense of gratification from the routine. She had once detested the thought of being just another face in the crowd, another tap of the rail pass through the automated machine, but she saw that to be a face in the crowd was a privilege. She would enjoy it; a time would come when she would have to speak again, remind herself and others of the truths they did not wish to face.

30

Naeem

Sadia wore a shimmery head covering which was not quite a hijab, long strands of her henna-stained hair poking out from underneath. Naeem had not seen her hair in many years and would have been embarrassed at the sight of it now, had he not been in a room with one hundred others, including his parents, Sadia's and many others he did not know. He felt the eyes of the mothers on him as he sat with Tasnia, and it amused him to think of their reaction had they known of the things he had been doing with a girl who was not any of their daughters.

The engagement had been organised in haste to accommodate Kabir's parents, who would be going to Bangladesh, Canada and the US for a six-month stint once they left Sydney. They appeared disgruntled at everything, labelling the food too spicy, the floral arrangements too scant and Sadia's veil too thin and unadorned. Naeem had expected the much-lauded Kabir to be as chagrined and difficult to please, but he smiled throughout the evening in a manner which told Naeem that the request to see Sadia without her hijab had most likely originated elsewhere. He was not handsome, his eyebrows being bushy and voluminous and his chin jutting under a few strands of beard, but Naeem hoped he would prove as agreeable a partner to Sadia as he appeared tonight.

His mother had still not spoken and Naeem was beginning to think she would not. He was relieved that they would not have to confront the ugliness of what had happened, but perversely, he rather wished she would speak to him so that he would know that it had all been real. Sara was gone, and with each day that passed, the grip she had exercised over him lessened. He did not welcome its absence; he wanted to be absorbed by her, to be able to maintain the illusion that she had gone on holiday and would be coming back to him with tales of what she had done there. Professor Kazi had sent them a handful of photos from the safari trip that he and some other doctors from the conference had taken at a discounted price as part of their conference package. The bushland and elephants had looked like a stage backdrop, and the bucket hat and camouflaged vehicle Professor Kazi had posed in furthered this impression. Naeem had checked Sara's profile to see if she had posted any photos of South Africa but was informed that her profile was no longer available to view, indicating that she had blocked him.

He wanted her to return to his side, and yet he did not see any way to bring it about. Naeem was ashamed to think of the dozens of unanswered calls and messages he had sent her; the undisguised desperation he had conveyed to Sara. He could not attempt to contact her again following such a display, and now that the semester was over, he would not have any incidental opportunities to see her. He went to Kmart and printed out the sole photo he possessed of the two of them, from their disastrous day at the beach, folding it up and storing it in his wallet where it would be close to his body. He did not want to forget Sara. He could not forget her; she had overwhelmed his reserve and rendered him full of her. He tried to tell himself that worldly attachments were fleeting, and although he recognised this to be true, he had to repeat the verse as he lay in bed at night before sleep would come. *Wealth and children are an adornment of the life of this world, and the ever-abiding, the good works, are better with your Lord in reward.*

Several days into the semester break Naeem received an email. His final results were now available for collection at the university. A spate of cheating scandals had led to increased security procedures around examinations, and students were now required to collect their results in person. Naeem was glad for the diversion. Since it was semester break, he found a parking spot with ease and walked to the medical faculty building, thinking of how he and Sara had once met behind the anatomy laboratory and he had held her pinkie finger in his hand before they had departed for their respective classes.

A receptionist with choppy grey hair inspected his student card and rummaged for his papers. Naeem thanked her, too profusely, and clutched the papers in his hand as he walked across the main lawn. Here, he had stood with Sara after they had pinned posters for Islamic Awareness Week, her mouth set in a grim bow.

Naeem was so absorbed in calling the precise configuration of Sara's lips to mind that he did not immediately realise that Ridwan was standing in front of him until he had been hugged and released.

'What are you doing at uni, bro?'

'I'm just collecting my exam results. How about you?' He had not seen Ridwan in some months, and he could not recall the last time he had seen his friend in casual clothing. He looked far younger without his suit, and less assured.

'I missed one of my exams because of the flu, and lucky me, I have the supplementary exam in fifteen minutes.' Ridwan groaned.

'That's a real bummer, bro.' Like Naeem, Ridwan seemed distracted, looking at his phone.

'I'd better get to the exam room before they shut me out. We'll catch up soon, okay?'

'Sure thing. Good luck, bro,' Naeem said, watching him walk across the lawn, before he turned around and looked at Naeem, grinning.

'Which one was it? Did you forget the girl, or are you going to marry her?'

Naeem shrugged and waved until Ridwan turned back around and walked off into the distance, breaking into a jog as he reached the staircase and disappeared around the corner.

The piece of paper bearing his results remained clutched in his hand, forgotten. Naeem stood still, unclenched his fist and held it up for inspection, scanning the list of numbers. They were all passable, if not up to his usual standard, but the very last number in the row was forty-six, a fail. The typed text stated that he would be required to reattempt the practical examination in eleven days time, and that if he did not pass on the second attempt, further options would then be discussed with the dean.

Naeem read the bland message again, then stashed the paper away in his bag. He felt no fear and no remorse; the worst had already transpired. He would pass his exam on his second attempt, and he would continue with the degree. With the passing of each year, he would become less and less acquainted with the person he had been with Sara, the bitterness of that thought slowly turning to glee as he reached for his phone to inform his mother of his results. It was time to speak of all that they had been avoiding.

Epilogue

A hlam and Ziad had remained devoted to each other following their katb kitab, and the day of their wedding had now arrived. Ziad had scraped together the funds to host a large, ostentatious wedding with all the trimmings and secure a rented flat for them in the western suburbs. They had both finished university; they could afford such adult necessities now. Sara had been invited, along with four hundred others, to one of the nicer reception centres in Lidcombe. Although she had arrived early, too early for a wedding she knew would run hours behind schedule, the parking lot was full, requiring her to park on one of its uppermost levels. She examined her reflection in the mirror, reapplying a layer of mascara before stepping out, her block heels noisy against the gravel. The men would be seated in a hall adjacent to the women, but she had not bothered to style her hair underneath her hijab, resolving to keep it on. As she waited for the elevator to arrive, she felt the presence of someone by her side.

'Salam, Sara,' Naeem said. His hair was slicked back in the same manner, suit jacket in hand, but he appeared diminished, their eyes meeting at an even height, until Sara remembered that she was in five-centimetre heels and he was not.

'Salam, Naeem. How are you?'

'I'm good, alhamdulillah, and yourself?'

'Alhamdulillah, I'm well.'

These were the rituals to be observed, rituals they had once discarded in favour of drawing closer to one another, but in this moment, Sara appreciated their utility far more than she had previously. They allowed them to say something, when there was so much they could not say.

The elevator pinged, indicating that it was time for them to enter its confines and descend. They got in together, a pantomime of what had come before: eyes lowered, their backs pressed against either side of the elevator to create the impression of distance.

'I haven't seen you around in a long time,' Naeem said.

'I was on exchange in Jakarta for six months. I only got back a fortnight ago.' Sara was surprised at the readiness with which she volunteered this information.

It had been implausible to her at the time they had parted that their lives would not overlap once again, that she would not yield to the urge to speak with him. But they had not, and she had not. She had thought of him, of course, thought of him each day in the months and years after they had ended what they had so clumsily begun, but she had long since ceased to feel haunted by his image and the image of what they had done together. She trusted that Naeem would tell no one what they had shared, and although they had never discussed it, she trusted that he felt the same of her. His betrayals of her had been private. Where others were concerned, she still believed that they would protect each other.

'Jakarta! That must have been so amazing.'

The polite interest was familiar, but the frank loquaciousness with which he expressed it was new, as was the scent of some woody aftershave which filled the elevator. The boy Naeem tapped his foot and smoothed his hair, which did not require smoothing, but his outward appearance was that of a man into his twenties, the scion of a reputable family and an almost-doctor. This was a man people would respect, hold out their arms for him to draw blood from.

'It really was. I sometimes wish I could have stayed there and not come back at all,' she said, thinking of the frenzy of the markets and the blur of millions of lights in the distant fog.

The elevator pinged again, indicating that they should exit. Naeem held open the door, allowing her to walk ahead. Sara wondered if anyone would see them walking towards the venue together and whisper behind their hands about it, but she had been absent for so long that such concerns seemed immaterial, even laughable. The world was so vast, and they were so small, silly, tiny beings who took themselves far too seriously. She would no doubt relearn to immerse herself in trivialities, but Sara still felt estranged from it all for now.

Naeem straightened and looked at her through those eyelashes she had so loved. There was something expectant in his gaze which made Sara uncomfortable, and she could not hold it.

'Are you seeing anyone at the moment?' Naeem's tone was deliberate and neutral. He had certainly improved in his capacity for pretence, but Sara felt they knew each other too well for it to succeed.

She did not feel he was entitled to an answer to the question, but she provided it anyway. She did not wish to be coy, not with Naeem.

'No, definitely not. I haven't at all, not since I was with you.'

They had arrived at the entrance to the function centre, where two men in their fifties stood, smoking rolled cigars and conversing in Arabic. Sara could hear Arabic music from inside, loud and warbling, and her stomach rumbled in anticipation of the mezze.

'Neither have I,' Naeem admitted, looking at her again with that expectant gaze. Sara realised that they were not beyond it yet, that she could regress into the life she had once occupied with him. He was still attractive to her, now with the additional potency of revisiting a familiar place and running fingers over its edges to see what, if anything, was altered.

Two girls Sara recognised from Ahlam's party passed them, but they appeared not to recognise her, continuing up the stairs and into the hall.

'I should go inside now,' Sara said.

'Maybe we could catch up sometime? I'd love to hear all about your time in Indonesia.' There was a note of pleading in Naeem's voice, but Sara ignored it and began to turn her head towards the hall, where she was now longing to be.

'Maybe,' she said. She would think about Naeem later, or likely not at all.

'Oh, here you are, Abida,' she said, waving. Abida had arrived, luminous in a purple sari, her eyes brushed with purple eyeshadow. They hugged and linked arms, admiring each other's outfits. Only after a few seconds did Abida nod slightly as she looked at Naeem. Her manner was not rude, nor was it friendly. It was the kind of look one colleague might give another in the corridor as they hurried to their respective ends of the office. Abida was clerking at a top-tier law firm now; it was a look she was accustomed to giving. The look reorientated Sara. She straightened, smoothed the billow of her dress.

'Well, we'd better get inside,' she said, turning to Abida. Abida smiled and turned to face the entrance, stepping forward.

Sara nodded to Naeem, and he placed his hand over his heart in farewell as she turned around and began her ascent.

Acknowledgements

First and foremost, I begin in the name of Allah, the Most Gracious, the Most Merciful – anything good in this is from You and all my shortcomings are my own.

Thank you to Westwords for the Westwords–Ultimo Prize and the wonderful opportunities I've had since, especially the Varuna residency. I really appreciate it.

Thank you so much to Ultimo Press for being fantastic throughout this whole process. Special thanks to Brigid Mullane for believing in my work from the outset and being so supportive, engaged and lovely to work with, and to Alisa Ahmed for all your fantastic and hard work on this, as well as the whole team at Ultimo.

Thank you to my parents for plying me with books, stories and love and for being the best parents in the world. There is no thank you that will ever be sufficient for everything you've done and continue to do for me, but I am very grateful to be your daughter.

Thank you to the rest of my big, funny, intelligent family as well (GG represent) and to Ovi's parents for all your kindness.

Thank you to my friends who so generously shared their thoughts on the book and all things related to it, especially Sana and Abdul Hadi, Annarose, Sara and Mostafa. Special shout-out to Sana for all the love and voice notes. You are a gem. Thank you to Nadine for being my very first, trusted reader all those years ago. Thank you to my other wonderful friends for all the great conversations and shared experiences over the years – you know who you are, but special mentions go to Noor, Nada, Tasnim, Miran, Oishee, Hannah and Thulasha.

Lastly, a very big thank you to Ovi. Thank you for the adventures to Royal Leamington Spa where this all began and for everything before and since. I love doing life with you.

Zeynab Gamieldien is the inaugural winner of the 2022 Westwords–Ultimo Prize. Her work has been shortlisted for the Rachel Funari Prize for Fiction and featured in publications such as the *Sydney Morning Herald*'s Daily Life section and the *Australian Muslim Times*. *The Scope of Permissibility* is her first novel.